Murder Every Monday

Murder Every Monday

Pamela Branch

Introduction by Tom & Enid Schantz

Felony & Mayhem Press • New York

All the characters and events portrayed in this work are fictitious.

MURDER EVERY MONDAY

A Felony & Mayhem mystery

PRINTING HISTORY
First UK edition (Robert Hale): 1954
First US edition (Rue Morgue): 2006

Felony & Mayhem edition: 2024

Biographical note included with the kind permission
of the Estate of Tom Schantz

ISBN: 978-1-63194-327-0 (paperback)
978-1-63194-328-7 (ebook)

Manufactured in the United States of America

Cataloging-in-Publication information for this book
is available from the Library of Congress.

For Christianna Brand

═══ CLASSIC MAYHEM ═══

Devoted to the best traditional mysteries of the 20th century, both Golden Age charmers, written before about 1960, and those from the Silver Age, which shine just as brightly and have much in common with their older cousins. If you love twisty puzzles, witty characterizations, and the art of the civilized crime novel, pull up a chair!

FELONYANDMAYHEM.COM

More Classic Mayhem

L.R. WRIGHT
The Suspect
Sleep While I Sing
A Chill Rain in January
Fall from Grace
Prized Possessions
A Touch of Panic
Mother Love
Strangers Among Us
Acts of Murder

PAMELA BRANCH
The Wooden Overcoat
Murder Every Monday
and coming soon...
Lion in the Cellar
Murder's Little Sister

JUANITA SHERIDAN
The Chinese Chop
and coming soon...
The Kahuna Killer
The Mamo Murders
The Waikiki Widow

EVELYN E. SMITH
Miss Melville Regrets
and coming soon...
Miss Melville Returns
Miss Melville's Revenge
Miss Melville Rides a Tiger

Cast of Characters

CLIFFORD FLUSH
President and founder of the Asterisk Club for wrongfully acquitted murderers, he was once known as the Balliol Butcher.

COLONEL QUINCEY
Treasurer of the Asterisk Club and an expert hunter.

MRS. BARRATT
Nee Naomi Wottling, she's a self-made widow twice over.

THE CREAKER
Still referred to as such, though the wooden limb that gave him the name has long since been replaced. He is not allowed to talk shop.

MISS DINA PARRISH
Secretary of the club and its newest member. Despite being paid a handsome salary, she generally wears very few clothes.

PAGET
The butler, who worked at Dankry Manor in its glory days. His smile can strike terror in all but the strongest hearts.

BARKER
The chef, who reports to Paget.

MRS. CHLOE CARLISLE
A romance writer who plans to murder her husband.

CYRIL   *Her handsome younger companion, whom she intends to marry. He turns out to be the most promising student in the current class.*

BILL THURLOW   *Another student, commissioned by his father to right a wrong so terrible the entire Asterisk Club wants to be allowed to do the deed.*

JOE "SLOTS" MANELLI   *A gangster from Chicago who wants to brush up on his skills.*

BLACKIE RODDEN   *His bodyguard.*

AL   *His chauffeur.*

ANTONIO GROSSI, AKA PETER KALDER   *Another gangster, Slots's archrival. We never learn his bodyguard's name.*

HOBSON   *The Creaker's protege, who worships at his feet. He exists on a regimen of meat, eggs, and vigorous running.*

MR. WHITE   *An estate agent.*

ARMITAGE   *Clifford Flush's nemesis, whom he nearly murdered because of his overly cautious bidding at bridge.*

Murder Every Monday

Introduction

Pamela Branch: "The funniest lady"

With major revisions to the introduction to *The Wooden Overcoat*

Pamela Branch was "the funniest lady you ever knew," according to fellow mystery writer Christianna Brand. Brand was referring not only to her books but to Branch herself, who delighted Brand by sending her countless "postcards with smears of pretense blood on them, purporting to be from her various characters," or "a dreadful squashed box of chocolates with very obvious pinholes into which poison had clearly been injected." That wicked sense of humor permeated Branch's four mysteries as well, leading contemporary reviewers to describe her first book, *The Wooden Overcoat*, as a "delightfully ghoulish souffle" (*The Spectator*) where "even the bodies manage to be ghoulishly diverting" (*The Sunday Times*) graced with "the gayest prose" and a "gloriously gruesome" touch (*The Queen*). *The Spectator* welcomed her second book, *Lion in the Cellar*, as a "charnel-house frolic." Nancy Spain, to whom Branch was favorably compared, called it a "master-piece," a blend of "the Marx Brothers, Crazy Gang and the Little Intimate Reviews." *The Times Literary Supplement* strayed from the mystery field to compare her third book, *Murder Every Monday*, to satirist Evelyn Waugh. Her fourth and final book,

1

Murder's Little Sister, was published in 1958 and was the only title to see publication in the United States. American mystery writer Carolyn Hart listed it among her five favorite mysteries of all time. It was reissued in 1988 in England as part of Pandora's Classic Women Crime Writers series after twenty-five years of being out of print. In spite of these extravagant reviews, Branch is rarely mentioned in any of the standard reference books devoted to the mystery genre, perhaps because her career was cut short by cancer at the age of forty-seven.

Nor does anyone have any idea what happened to her fifth book. In 1962, her paperback publisher reported that she had begun the book in the Scottish Highlands and was finishing it in Ghana, West Africa. She would not die for another five years, so either her illness prevented her from finishing the book or she encountered a major writer's block. Or it just might have been that she made a good marriage at last and no longer needed to publish to make ends meet. No one knows for sure because she appears to have left no estate behind. Since she died so long ago, even the literary agency which holds her copyrights doesn't know what happened. Why she isn't better known among the historians of mystery fiction is perhaps even stranger. She rates an entry in the third edition of *Twentieth Century Crime and Mystery Writers* but is dropped from the fourth edition, retitled *The St. James Guide to Crime and Mystery Writers.* Critic Gillian Rodgerson summed up Branch's writing by saying: "The humor in Branch's books lies in the situations, the outrageous characters and in the dialog which almost makes sense but not quite. This is life viewed through a fun-house distorting mirror where the ordinary suddenly becomes bizarre and then ordinary again." Rodgerson admits that the situations, as in *The Wooden Overcoat,* make for "a very silly book but the writing is seamless and witty and the denouement makes it all worthwhile." It's a fair judgment, though Branch's books are no more "silly" than those of P.G. Wodehouse or Sarah Caudwell. Looking back on her career from a vantage point of fifty years and an era in which humor and homicide have truly come into their own, one could argue that Branch rates as perhaps the premier farceur in a now overcrowded field.

In her own time, there were a few contemporary reviewers who were not enthralled with the idea of introducing humor into crime fiction. English critic Sutherland Scott admitted in his 1953 study of the genre, *Blood in Their Ink*, that writers such as Phoebe Atwood Taylor (aka Alice Tilton) and Constance and Gwenyth Little "serve up a sparkling cocktail" but he questioned if the idea of "mixing hectic humor and even more hectic homicide is entirely to be recommended." Taylor and the Littles were American writers who were very popular in Britain. Scott was somewhat alarmed that British writers might follow suit in turning chills to laughs. "It is interesting to note that the most recent addition to the mix-your-murder-with-plenty-of-fun brigade is also a lady, this time a home product. If you can digest this kind of hot-pot, Pamela Branch's *The Wooden Overcoat* and *Lion in the Cellar* should be to your taste. Some digestive systems may tend to rebel." It's an odd judgment, given that Scott called another, somewhat earlier English female farceur, Nancy Spain, one of the genre's emerging talents.

While Scott merely comes off as being more stuffy than perceptive, it has to be admitted that humor is subjective. Yet, other English writers were known to go for a laugh. There's more than a touch of the absurd in many of the books by Edmund Crispin (*The Moving Toyshop*, 1946) or Michael Innes (*Appleby's End*, 1945). Branch's humor, of course, was a bit blacker ("ghoulish" is an adjective that often pops up in her reviews) than either of those two gentlemen. Though a bit more farcical and madcap, Branch may also remind some readers of Richard Hull (1896–1973) who plumbed the darker side of humor in his crime novels, most notably in *The Murder of My Aunt* (1934), a book whose marvelous title can—and should— be read with two vastly different interpretations, or in *My Own Murderer* (1940), wherein a staid Londoner's lifestyle changes when he comes across a murderer in his apartment and decides to hold him captive rather than turn him over to the police.

Anthony Rolls's homicidal clergyman in *The Vicars Experiment* (aka *Clerical Error*, 1932) would be perfectly at home in Branch's world. Her brand of madcap black humor was also present in many of the British film comedies of the 1950s, especially in such Alec Guinness vehicles as *Kind Hearts and Coronets*.

While these British films fared well in the U.S. during this period, American publishers didn't believe that readers on this side of the Atlantic would embrace Branch's odd brand of gallows humor. Of course, one has to remember that the early 1950s were seeing a change in direction among publishers, who were pulling away from the traditional mystery so popular before World War II and replacing it with action thrillers by the likes of Mickey Spillane and John D. MacDonald. The 1970s and 1980s saw a rebirth of the comic traditional mystery. The blackest of these were the early biting satirical novels of English writer Robert Barnard, whose *Death of an Old Goat* (1974) and *Death by Sheer Torture* (1981) remind one of a less frenetic Branch. Even closer in tone to Branch are the recent "subversively funny" (*New York Times*) novels of another English writer, Ruth Dudley Edwards.

She was born Pamela Byatt in 1920 on her parent's isolated tea estate in Ceylon (now Sri Lanka). Her earliest memory is of helping her father persuade an elephant to swallow a homemade aspirin the size of a croquet ball. The elephant did not oblige.

She was educated at various schools along the south coast of England and then went to Paris to study art. She quickly tired of painting the traditional still lifes of "guitars, grapes and Chianti bottles" and returned to England where she studied at the Royal Academy of Dramatic Art for a year, once performing in a modern-dress version of Hamlet wearing a mackintosh and gumboots. This flirtation with an acting career led some researchers to confuse her with the actress Pamela Branch, best known for playing one of the nuns in the Sidney Poitier film *Lilies of the Field*. After she left the RADA, she returned to Ceylon and then moved on to explore nearby India, starting in the north and gradually working her way south. For three years her home base was a houseboat in Kashmir. She trekked across the Himalayas by horse, living out of a tent during the summer months, and went skiing in the winter. She learned to hunt with guns and falcons, once shooting a black bear. During this period she also learned Urdu, with a special emphasis on the racier words in that language, painted several murals, and trained two racehorses.

Or so she claims. Alice Woudhuysen, a close friend who met Pamela in 1950, said Pam never referred to these adventures. "I did think at that time though that Pam and Newton (her first husband) were both inclined to live in a fantasy world and their tales were somewhat embellished to make an amusing story." Pamela met and married Newton Branch following her return to England. The two of them moved to Cyprus where they lived in a twelfth-century Greek monastery poised precariously on the edge of a cliff overlooking the sea. Both tried their hand at writing, Pamela producing *The Wooden Overcoat*, Newton possibly a number of boys' books. During this period, they also lived in a small fisherman's cottage in Ireland where she worked on *Lion in the Cellar*. Back in England, Newton worked as a staff writer for Adprint, a publishing firm, and edited *This Britain*, a collection of essays by various hands written to celebrate the 1951 Festival of Britain. The son of a distinguished judge, Newton qualified as a barrister but never practiced law and lived much of his life in the shadow of his more accomplished father and wife. Writing, according to Alice Woudhuysen, did not come easily to him. "He was not as focused as Pamela, who must actually have worked very hard at her writing but talked very little about it. She may possibly have played down her role as a writer in order not to seem to complete with Newton." Pamela is said to have collaborated with him on film scripts but there is no record that any of them ever were filmed, although Newton was employed by the British Institute of Film Censors. Newton complained about having to sit through innumerable second-rate films but endured it because he and Pamela needed the extra income. The name "N. Branch" appeared on many a movie screen.

Although the two of them gave off the impression of what Alice Woudhuysen described as a "devil-may-care affluence," money was obviously tight. "In 1950 Pam and Newton were living in a gloomy mews flat in Elvaston Place, Kensington. London was still a depressing city after the war, flats were hard to find, rents were high, food was still rationed and life was rather tough and bleak, especially in the winter," Alice Woudhuysen recalled a half century later. "We were always cold as few people had central heating and the smog made even the daytime seem bleak." Branch vividly recreates that period in *Lion in the Cellar*.

The Branches were able to get the flat in Kensington on the cheap because Newton claimed that a previous occupant had gassed himself in the tiny kitchen. Although these flats, carved out of old stables and carriage houses, were apparently much in demand by bohemians, many were far from pleasant places in which to live. "The sitting room was a long, narrow room with no windows, only a skylight which let in a dismal, yellowish glow," according to Alice Woudhuysen. "I think there was a sort of curtained-off alcove for a double bed. There was also a small dining room with rather heavy, dark furniture where Pamela wrote her books."

The Branches drove about London in an old taxicab, often accompanied by a young boxer dog named Culley. Alice Woudhuysen said Culley was very affectionate "but slobbered dreadfully" and was known occasionally to have a glass of beer with his owners at a local pub. Later, the taxicab was replaced by an old tradesman's van in which the Branches installed a mattress for overnight trips. She and Newton continued to travel extensively. Pamela was apparently able to write anywhere. *Murder Every Monday*, her third book, was written in various parts of England, France and the Channel Islands. It was dedicated to Christianna Brand, to whom she had once expressed amazement at having readers write her asking for her castoff clothing. These requests so amused Pamela that she has one of the characters in

Murder Every Monday, a romance novelist, repeat the story.

Her last published book, *Murder's Little Sister* (1958), was written in that mews flat in Kensington. This was a very tense period in her life. By 1954, the strain on the Branches' marriage was beginning to show. Pamela dropped hints to Alice that she was "finding Newton very difficult" to live with. She suggested that he was drinking a great deal at this point and had lost much of his motivation to write. Pamela went from merely helping to possibly actually writing his stuff for him. Friends were not surprised when they parted and eventually divorced a year or so after the release of *Murder's Little Sister*. Newton remarried but the old troubles continued to haunt him and this marriage apparently soon failed as well. He died sometime in the 1970s.

Pamela also remarried, to Wing Commander James Edward StuartLyon, and her final years were apparently lived in relative comfort. With the exception of the rumored fifth novel and a play based on *Murder Every Monday*, written in collaboration with Philip Dale and performed at the Civic Theatre in Chelmsford in October 1964, Branch's career as a professional writer appears to have ended. Ironically, it was during this period that several of her books, originally published by Robert Hale in hardcover, were reissued by Penguin in paperback.

Friends described her as a very glamorous woman. "Beautiful, marvelous Pamela, with eyelashes like bent hairpins," is how Christianna Brand remembered her. Alice Woudhuysen, six years Pamela's junior, was in awe of her. "She seemed incredibly glamorous and sophisticated. She wore a lot of makeup, painting her lips in an astonishing Cupid's Bow above their natural line and she had masses of tawny, blond hair. She was slim and elegant in a casually dressed way and to me she appeared rather dauntingly self-possessed and confident but I soon discovered that she was also very warmhearted, amusing and likable and when she related that she had been voted the most popular girl in her school, I readily believed her."

While the Branches were still together and living in Kensington, Pamela's mother was taken ill and died in great pain. Thoughts of that period were no doubt in Pamela's mind when her own health took a turn for the worse in the mid-1960s. But that marvelous sense of humor which permeated her books didn't desert her.

"No, I can't come tomorrow, darling," she said to Christianna. "We're flying to Geneva." Pamela paused, then added, "My husband wants to buy a watch." That was in 1967. Brand never spoke to her again. Shortly afterwards, Pamela died of cancer. The woman whose books were perfect specimens of gallows humor couldn't resist making a joke in what well may have been her darkest days.

Tom & Enid Schantz
November 2005, revised March 2006
Lyons, Colorado

The editors would like to thank Barry Pike, Alice Woudhuysen, and H. R. Woudhuysen for their invaluable contributions to this introduction.

Chapter One

Clifford Flush had murdered nobody since 1939. For fourteen uneasy years after his acquittal, he had tried to persuade himself that the tiger in him was fully tamed. He assured himself that he had no desire to lay a hand in anger upon anyone in the world except a fellow member of his bridge club named Armitage. In 1953, unable to endure the man's pleasant smile and cautious bidding for another hour, he was overcome by an irresistible impulse and pushed him under a bus in Piccadilly.

Armitage, with his customary resource, flung himself into the road parallel to the pavement. The bus passed over him and he rose unharmed. "Clifford, old boy," he said shortly. "You should not have done that."

Flush, biting his lip, produced a notebook and wrote down the number of the bus. He bought Armitage a new hat and showered him with small courtesies. Indeed so hypnotized did he become by the man's appalling *bonhomie* that he found it difficult to concentrate upon anything else.

Armitage, who knew Flush's history and understood his friend's predicament, tried to avoid him. Finding this impossible, he eventually protested. "Clifford, old boy," he said mildly, "your game has deteriorated. Perhaps you need a change."

Flush met the honest brown eyes and attempted a smile which did not disclose his clenched teeth. "You may be right," he murmured.

For a moment, Armitage stared at him. Then he said, "Perhaps you should leave London for a while. Somewhere right away in the country." He poured himself another glass of port. "Soon," he added with an encouraging smile.

Flush sat looking at his well-manicured hands. "I can't understand it," he said irritably. "I have known you for years."

"It may be the heat," said Armitage.

Flush glared out of the window. The heat haze trembled over the plane trees in the square. "Possibly," he said.

"I'm sure that I did nothing to provoke you."

"No."

"I always imagined that we rubbed along quite well."

"Your bidding sometimes antagonizes me."

"And yours me, old chap. But I wouldn't dream...I really wouldn't, my dear fellow."

"Extraordinary, I grant you."

"Amazing." Armitage hesitated. "Tell me, does hot weather always have such an effect upon you?"

Flush picked a match from the ashtray and broke it in half. He did not answer.

Armitage crossed his legs and stared at the toe of his sober shoe. "Well," he said apologetically. "It's all most unfortunate. I can't tell you how sorry I am, old chap."

"You might have been killed," said Flush accusingly.

Armitage blushed. "A spell in the country," he said. "Nothing like it." He coughed. "Apart from any purely selfish considerations, I really must insist upon it."

"Are you threatening me, Armitage?"

Armitage blew his nose and blinked several times. "Yes," he said unhappily. "Matter of fact, I am, old man."

Flush nodded. He lit a cigar, twirled the match until it burnt down to his fingers, then carefully blew it out. "Pass the port, damn you!" he barked.

Half an hour later, he left the club. Waiting at the mercy of the sun for a taxi, lowering himself onto the hot leather seat, his mood degenerated.

He took his problem home to the residential club of which he was the founder. This was situated in an agreeable Chelsea street overlooking the river. It had been instituted in 1940, six months after Flush's trial had drawn to its surprising conclusion. As a sanctuary for those with similar histories to his own, it had proved an immediate success. It now had not only a large country membership, but affiliations overseas.

Paying off the taxi, passing through the wrought-iron gate into the neat walled garden, Flush paused to look up at the pleasant Georgian house. He realized suddenly that he had become extremely attached to it. He did not want to leave it. Damn Armitage! If only...Flush gnawed his lip and let himself into the dim, cool hall.

The homely scene in the drawing room depressed him still further. Mrs. Barratt sat behind the tea tray. She looked up from her knitting and gave him one of her faint sweet smiles. The Colonel was sitting on the window seat by a vase of wilting roses. He had attached a paper clip to an elastic band and was twanging it absently at his cup. The Creaker lay on the sofa beneath the chandelier eating peppermint creams and reading an old copy of the *News of the World*.

Flush sat down as far as possible from the unnecessary summer fire, admitted his lapse and described its consequences.

"I am surprised at you, Clifford," said Mrs. Barratt. She pursed her lips and poked at her thin white hair with a knitting needle. She wore mauve, still in semi-mourning for her last victim who had been buried thirteen years before.

Colonel Quincey blew up his white mustache. "Gad, sir," he said. "All these years." He used his prepositions with economy and spoke as if there were good food concealed in his mouth.

Flush turned on him. "During the years to which you refer," he said, his fine eyes flashing, "it has not escaped my notice that you too, have been tempted to repeat your former indiscretions. In one instance, may I remind you, you fell."

"Blighter," said the Colonel. "Asked for it, got it."

"To think that *Clifford*," remarked Mrs. Barratt, "should be threatened by a gentleman who does not dare to bid a slam." Her frail shoulders shook.

"Sauce," growled the Creaker. His old wooden leg had been replaced by a new and silent model, but the nickname of its master persisted. "The country, eh?" he said with a rough laugh. And added enigmatically, "Sheep an' that."

Flush rose and opened the window. The set of his shoulders caused Mrs. Barratt to draw a sharp breath. The Colonel and the Creaker followed her eyes. They exchanged brief, uneasy glances.

Flush stood silhouetted against the fading light as erect and apparently unruffled as a general about to give the command for some fearful yet calculated risk.

"You all know," he said into the silence, "that my interests are mainly urban." He paused and looked in a preoccupied manner at the peonies at the bottom of the garden.

The three waited, watching him.

"However," he said heavily.

The Colonel, realizing that some momentous decision was at hand, swayed automatically towards the tray of bottles and fortified himself with a large pink gin.

Flush produced a handkerchief and blew his nose. "I intend," he said, "to put into operation a scheme which I have been considering for some years." He replaced the handkerchief. "It will, I believe, satisfy a long-felt demand. It should prove a valuable addition to the amenities already offered to our members. Moreover," he raised a hand to his lips in order to conceal a wolfish grin, "it will afford us a modicum of vicarious satisfaction."

"*Us?*" asked Mrs. Barratt.

Flush nodded.

Mrs. Barratt, troubled, picked up her knitting and cast off two stitches. "In the *country?*" she said, knowing that her fear of and affection for Flush would force her to follow wherever he led.

The Creaker took hold of his collapsed nose and moved it gently from side to side. "Stuff you 'ear at those country assizes," he muttered. "'S 'orrible."

"I have no choice," said Flush. "Armitage is a man of his word. I do not wish, after all these years of retirement, to be reported to the police as an unsuccessful assassin."

There was a long silence.

"Clifford," said Mrs. Barratt faintly. "What are you going to do?"

Flush stood frowning up at a portrait of a man in a silver helmet. "Are you with me?" he asked. "Can I count upon you?"

"Of course," said Mrs. Barratt.

"Yus," said the Creaker.

"*Tik hai,*" said the Colonel. When in doubt, he frequently lapsed into Hindustani.

"Thank you," said Flush. He picked up a fallen rose from beneath the vase and threw it onto the fire. "I have decided," he said casually, "to become a Homicide Consultant."

"Got to be in the wilds," remarked the Colonel two days later. He glanced at Flush. "Far enough make journey London intolerable." *Game,* he consoled himself. He had had little opportunity to use his Springfield in Chelsea. *Fur, feather!*

"Nowhere near a railway station," said Mrs. Barratt. "Somewhere really inconvenient. We don't want to attract the frivolous."

"'Orrible grub," offered the Creaker the next day. "Real muck."

"Perhaps unlicensed," suggested Mrs. Barratt.

"No, madam," snapped the Colonel. "Going too far."

"It is essential to achieve real discomfort," said Flush. "We want no fellow travelers."

A week later, Flush tossed aside a sheaf of stenciled lists from a dozen estate agents and ran a hand through his hair. He sighed. "It seems hopeless," he said.

"Clifford," said Mrs. Barratt. "Why don't you *tell* them that you want somewhere repulsive?"

"Anything settled, old chap?" asked Armitage the following morning.

"You insist upon this buffoonery?" Flush cracked his knuckles.

"Yes," said Armitage. "Yes, I do."

"Very well." Flush pinched his lower lip between finger and thumb. "I shall resort to advertising. I shall word the announcement in such a way that only the most disreputable agent will reply. I shall make several elementary spelling mistakes and imply that I intend to open a…"

"Good," said Armitage.

Away in the wilds, in the dogged hinterland beyond the Purbeck country, William White, the sole agent who had replied to Flush's advertisement, greeted his client with old-world courtesy. He had lunched liquidly, but he gave no sign of this except that his large red ears were pressed flat against his head.

"Dankry Manor?" he said. "It might suit you, but I very much doubt it." He read the details and named a price. "Absurdly cheap," he said gloomily, "but no bargain. It has a most unfortunate historical background."

Flush lit a cigar. Had he been impelled to kill Mr. White, he thought idly, he would have picked off the great head with a telescopic rifle. He glanced out of the window at the gaunt ruins of the castle.

"Ravaged," said Mr. White, following his client's eyes, "by the punitive expedition of King Sweyn to avenge the massacres of St. Brice's Day." Behind a discarded copy of the day before's *Telegraph*, the top of a bottle of liqueur mead gleamed red from its hiding place in the wastepaper basket. "The sweat of the Romans," he said vaguely. "The tears of Boadicea. The clay dyed crimson with the blood of the Jutes." He licked his lips, put his elbow onto the desk and propped up his left eyebrow with his thumb. "Frankly, sir, I do not think that this property will suit you."

"It is in good repair?"

"The very opposite, sir. It is falling apart. Moreover, it is hideous and reputed to be haunted."

"What of the fishing rights?"

"Oh, there are no fish, sir. The stream is polluted. The house has a horrible reputation. The villagers will not pass it at night without a bulb of garlic. Now really," he pleaded, "you don't want it. Nobody does. Why should they?"

"I intend to found," Flush hesitated, then smiled blandly, "a small country club."

"That would be a grievous error," said Mr. White, tapping his long brown teeth with a pencil. "Not in Dankry Manor, sir. Disastrous."

"Please give me an order to view."

"No," said Mr. White. "Honestly, sir, it is absolutely awful. Come on, sir, have a mead and forget all about it."

Flush strode across to the mullioned window. At one end of the narrow, cobbled street was a fearful statue of Charles Stuart being gored by a stag; at the other, a monument recalling in bronze some forgotten martyr dying in irons and agony. Flush smiled. In his present mood, he found the village irresistible.

"The keys, please," he said, snapping his fingers.

"You will regret it, sir." Mr. White reluctantly pulled open a drawer and took out a massive key with a curling label attached to it. "Honestly, sir," he said earnestly. "I hate to handle this key. You see this stain? That is not rust, sir."

Krunte Abbas dated back to the Durotriges—the Dwellers by
the Water. It had been ravished by the Jutes, the Saxons, the
Angles, and the Danes. It had been occupied by the Romans.
Elfrida had borrowed a knife there before proceeding to Corfe
to stab her stepson. King Sweyn had razed it to the ground;
Stephen had rebuilt it; Maud had torn it down; Henry VIII had
recreated it from the original stone. When the topmasts of the
Spanish Armada had been sighted from the Lizard, a man named
Jeff White had destroyed it by fire while attempting to light the
warning beacon. During the Wars of the Roses, King Charles,
recognizing its strategic position, had resurrected it, only to lose
it to the Roundheads. In the Pilgrim Ho!, the fleeing monarch
had drunk a stoop of ale; so, some thirty years later, had the
invading Duke of Monmouth. In the Staunch Adherent was a
scythe reputed to have been used by Daniel Defoe in the cause
of the Protestant Duke.

Judge Jeffries, William of Orange, George III, the Pilgrim
Fathers, the martyrs of Tolpuddle, had passed along the main
street. Queen Elizabeth I had, of course, slept in all three inns,
several times. In 1916, the crew of H.M.S. *Ultimatum*, suffering
from chicken pox, had been isolated in the remains of the castle
where Maud, in a fit of ill temper, was said to have cut off one of
her braids and tossed it from the tower to the hungry serfs
beneath, crying, "Gorge, curs! May it choke thee!"

Twenty-five years later, a Messerschmitt 101 had fallen
flaming out of the sky and, after raking the village with cannon
and machine gun fire, had crashed onto the Roman earthworks.
The pilot had lurched in the Wassail and demanded a double
whisky in the name of the Führer. One of the first General Grant
tanks to arrive in Britain still remained in the marketplace, sabo-
taged by a drink-crazed crone named Nell White. Half a mile
from William White's office, a wounded American bomber had
jettisoned a full cargo of K rations on the section of the Via
Iceniana which the Romans had built too far to the south...

All these generations had left their mark on the hamlet; or if they had not done so, the omission was speedily rectified by the Antiquity Department. Each cottage bore plaques in remembrance of some scene of brutality or horror. Several had cannon balls embedded in their ancient stone walls.

An aura of violence, bloodshed, and doom hung heavily over the whole valley.

The Manor stood to the west of Krunte Abbas and above it. It was built in an Anglo-Saxon quarry on the slopes of Hanger Hill. It faced north and was denied the early morning sun by the heights of Seven Barrow Down. It was large and rambling, of many periods all warring but none victorious. It had mellowed uneasily and the wisteria vine intended to mask its architectural gaffes had never borne flowers.

The distemper had been conquered by lichen; it had flaked and fluttered down to lie like dandruff under the cedars. The terrace was the battleground of a million ants. The swimming pool was home to scores of flat black beetles which zigzagged on the surface, crash-dived and vanished. The roof leaked. The delicate gray blooms of dry rot flourished in the basement. A crumbling oubliette beneath the back stairs had been partially disguised as a broom cupboard. There was an irregular stain on the floor of a bedroom in the east wing which centuries of treatment had failed to remove.

"You see?" said Mr. White, standing waist-deep in hay on the lawn. "Is it not horrible?"

"It is ideal," said Flush. "*Ideal*."

Armitage delivered his ultimatum late in August.

Early in September, Flush, Mrs. Barratt, and the Creaker left London by train. The Colonel followed three days later in his monstrous old Bugatti with a startling young woman of twenty-four. It had been whispered that she had recently pushed her fiancé over Beachy Head, which Flush considered qualified her for the post of Librarian and Secretary.

As Flush's own steward was serving a short sentence for Loitering with Intent, a mournful old man named Paget was approached at Mr. White's suggestion. He had served the previous tenant of Dankry, a dissolute earl who had met his death in the hunting field, for over thirty years. Flush interviewed him without hope.

"You have, of course," he asked, drawing a small cosh on his blotter, "a blameless record?"

Paget moved his long feet inside his shoes. "Well, sir," he said. "Thirty years ago there was a lot of vicious gossip about this mare…"

"Ah," said Flush, clearly relieved. "You stole it? Doped it? Shot it?"

Paget was puzzled. He realized immediately that his prospective employer would prefer him to have erred. He was for an instant filled with foreboding, yet his desperate need of employment, his deep affection for the hangdog Manor and his austere little room which overlooked the quarry, prompted him to say quickly, "Yes, sir." It was the first lie he had ever told.

Flush nodded, satisfied. "I require one whom I can trust implicitly."

"I do not hobnob, sir." Paget glanced down at his bowler. "The earl, sir, was a terror at times."

It took Flush less than a month to discover that Paget was invaluable. It took Paget nineteen weeks to discover the identity of his new master. While he was delighted to be back in his old home, while the dank stone of the corridors, the faded and peeling wallpapers, the sudden and familiar icy draughts solaced his old heart, he was extremely uneasy.

He did not like the look which Mrs. Barratt had given young Miss Dina when the latter had failed to mail a letter. He was not convinced that it was entirely an accident when Colonel Quincey asphyxiated a chicken by leaving it in the garage and neglecting to turn off the engine of his car. He did not care for the manner in which the oafish cripple refused to allow anybody into the summerhouse. What could this lout be doing behind the locked door? Why did he emerge after some hours of complete silence looking benevolent and rested? And there was the master himself. Why did he stand for so long at the bottom of the orchard, watching the disused, weed-hidden railway line, as if hoping for a train to go by?

As Christmas came and passed, as the snowdrops died for want of air beneath the giant weeds in the garden, new questions reared to which Paget refused answer. Why did the first ill-assorted batch of guests arrive on the same day and depart likewise? Why did they stop talking abruptly when he entered a room? Why did they so contemptibly overtip him? What sort of club was this? What manner of people were attracted by the unattractive house and the dubious reputations of the residents?

In the village, there was much speculation.

"Doo zeem beä zpeizen," said one.

"En beä goostie writëarn," said another.

"Beä a-trainen für winnick jobsen aëft A-irenen Ringle," said a third.

Paget, fearing for the prestige of his employers and indirectly his own, would incline his head obliquely and allow himself a faint smile. This, owing to a facial peculiarity, would disperse the gossips immediately.

Even to himself, Paget refused to admit that he knew. He knew also that Flush knew that he knew, but refused to admit that either. More and more frequently, his thoughts turned to the past years with the earl. Less and less often did he allow himself to dwell on the problems of the present. Hardly ever did he acknowledge that he had already been subtly drawn into the conspiracy. In rare moments of truth, he knew that were he to leave or make any official complaint, he would be found dead almost at once in curious circumstances. Only in his dreams did he admit of the bungling student who would one day, any day now, destroy forever the reputation of his beloved Manor. And not even his subconscious would allow that he was trapped, that there was nothing he could do to prevent disaster, that it was only a matter of time...

Chapter Two

As the summer sun blazed over Krunte Abbas, the twenty-sixth batch of students closed in upon Dankry Manor in various conveyances yet with a single thought in common.

In a first-class carriage on the rocking single-gauge train bound for Poxwell Regis, Chloe Carlisle balanced her typewriter on her knees and scratched her scalp with the point of a pencil. *How many words have I written?* she wondered. Thirty-eight books, an average of one hundred and twenty thousand words a book. She made no attempt at the multiplication. She had never understood figures.

In spite of a definite feeling of guilt about her destination, she was in good vein that day. Her characters were behaving in the lovable manner demanded by the majority of her readers. That morning, irritated by the long wait on the platform at Gulley Low, she had made Lady Diana pregnant. She made a note on her manuscript reminding herself to relieve her heroine of this burden. She sighed, adjusted the typewriter and tapped, "donned her negligee of costly satin."

Cyril raised his head from the faded seat and looked over her shoulder. "She was wearing jodhpurs on 109," he said.

Mrs. Carlisle stiffened. She resented criticism. "Are you inferring that I have forgotten to change her? Do you imagine that with all my experience I would make a fool error of that type?"

Cyril shrugged. He edited every word she wrote. He knew well that Lady Diana had not yet taken off her jodhpurs. He knew equally well that such a sartorial blunder would in no way disenchant Chloe Carlisle's public. Her readers had long been indoctrinated to accept such inadvertent changes as the color of a character's eyes, profession, or even name during the course of a chapter.

Mrs. Carlisle uttered an unfeminine word. She changed the full stop after "costly satin" into a comma and added with a spurt of ill-temper "having torn off her damnfool jodhpurs." Cyril raised his eyebrows. She looked sideways at his petulant profile, his beautiful hands, his long legs. He was twelve years her junior and she intended to commit murder in order to marry him. She rustled her manuscript and said in a conciliatory manner, "Terence has got to go."

Cyril shut his eyes. "Hunting accident?" he said. He was astonished all over again that he had agreed to remove the obstacle which prevented them from regularizing their relationship. Ned Carlisle meant well. *I love her*, he reminded himself. *I love her, I love her. I would love her even if she hadn't a bean.*

Mrs. Carlisle was annoyed. She postponed the hunting accident until the next book, stripped Terence of his pink and his bowler and poured him into an immaculate lounge suit. "I thought a plane crash," she said.

Cyril lit a cigarette without opening his eyes. "Mm-hm." He nodded. "Yes, you're good at them." *Lick on, tongues of flame*, he thought. *Stagger, aircraft. Clutch at your bosom, beautiful stewardess. Between you, you will keep me in the fashion to which I am already accustomed.* He opened his eyes. "Have them run into a flying saucer," he suggested earnestly.

For a second, Mrs. Carlisle considered this. Then she saw Cyril's serious face and lost her temper. "You mustn't be too funny, angel," she said. "I don't want to die laughing." She controlled herself. *I dote upon him,* she told herself. *With his brain and my publishers, we shall write a bestseller which even Ned will read.*

Cyril rose gracefully and looked at himself in the glass which protected a framed picture of Land's End. "We must be nearly there," he said. "How is your conscience? In itself, I mean?"

"A bit queasy," she confessed. She closed the typewriter and wrestled with the lock. "How about yours?"

"Not a murmur. Silent as the grave."

"Was that in the best of taste, dearest?" She crushed her hat over her flaming hair, produced her compact and slapped herself in the face with the powder puff. "Cyril," she said, "I've got remorse. Let's have a sandwich at Poxwell Regis and go straight back." Her handbag fell off the seat, scattering its contents over the grimy floor.

Cyril stood looking down at the small automatic. "No," he said. "The means sometimes justify the end."

"Whose means?"

"Not to be bitchy, dear."

"All right," she said. "Give me a cigarette. Cyril, do you love me *enough?*"

"You know I do," said Cyril, picking up her checkbook.

Joe "Slots" Manelli leaned forward and tapped his chauffeur on the shoulder. "Hey boy," he said. "You didn't see that notice? Hanger Hill, it said, one in four. Now that's dangerous." He worried about his cars. This one was new, a large black Studebaker, and, except for the tires, completely bulletproof.

"I know what I'm doin'," said Al. His voice, as usual, was expressionless.

Manelli leaned back. His swarthy, aging face was not quite repulsive under the snap-brimmed hat. He stroked the ash off his cigar with his little finger and nudged his new bodyguard. "I won't have the Boys on my payroll thinking they are geniuses," he said. "I will never tell you you are smart, I will only be discouraging."

Blackie Rodden, the only Englishman of the trio, was not listening. He had been on maneuvers in the area in 1943 and was recognizing the terrain, associating it with almost forgotten romances in the only honest period of his life. He had, he remembered, greeted each conquest with a totally different personality. He was an expert in disguises. "Cromwell come along 'ere," he remarked. *So did I an' that Patricia*, he thought.

"'Orrible battle, there was. 'Undreds cut to ribbons."

"Yeah?" Manelli yawned. "That's too bad." He bounced forward in his seat. "Slow down, you punk!" he yelled. "You want to kill me?"

Antonio Grossi, alias Pete Kalder, drove the custom-built, super-charged Allard and his bodyguard sat beside him. He slowed down to pass a cart. "Hey you!" he shouted to the yokel on the reins. "Which way to this Dankry Manor?"

The yokel opened his mouth and pointed a finger into it.

"So," said Grossi. "Another mute. Okay, I give up." He stopped the car in the middle of the road, got out and went around to the far side. "Drive," he ordered his bodyguard. "Follow that cart."

He climbed in, leaned his handsome, restless head against the suede upholstery and began to sing. He improvised, to the tune of "Old Man River." "Old Manelli," he sang, "that old Manelli; he don't keep contracts; he shoots his mouth off; on television; that old stool pigeon; he won't be livin' for long."

Bill Thurlow got off the Greenline bus outside the Staunch Adherent and turned round to see whether the flamboyant young beauty was getting off too. She was. He had sat behind her on the bus, unable to take his eyes off the tender brown curve of her cheek and her long pale hair. Somewhere, he was sure that he had seen her before. He had the curious impression that he knew her well. He straightened his tie and marched up to her. "Do you happen to know," he asked, "where I can find a taxi?" He decided that he would offer her a lift.

She smiled. "There isn't one," she said. "Where are you going?"

Bill hesitated, then assured himself that the activities at Dankry must be a closely guarded secret. "The Manor," he said, carefully casual.

"Are you?" she said, clearly surprised. "Well, I suppose you never can tell."

A yokel in a brimless hat shuffled up to Bill, peered into his face, then shuffled on.

"I'm on the staff," said the girl.

Bill stared. *On the staff!* The implication from his contact had been that all the staff had...no, surely it was unthinkable. "You must be Miss Parrish," he said, trying to remember what he had been told about her, whom she had killed.

"Call me Dina," she said.

As she said it, Bill knew where he had seen her before. She was Pearl of the Lucky Left strip cartoon, Pearl of the provocative legs and the constant state of undress.

She laughed. "Yes," she said, apparently reading his thoughts. "I used to pose for all the women's parts." She took his arm and led him across the road and up a narrow side-turning between two eager surfs of cow parsley.

Bill looked down at her. The artist who had drawn the strip had not done her justice, he thought. And remembered that there had been some sort of scandal about him. The strip had stopped abruptly.

Dina slid a hand down the front of her dress and produced a small handkerchief. She blew her nose and slowly replaced the handkerchief. "Poor Sammy," she said, raising her startling eyes to Bill's. "He jumped over a cliff." She clung to Bill's arm. "Jumped," she added sadly.

They walked for some way in silence. As the road climbed, the distant sea flashed momentarily between the humped Barrows. Ahead, beyond a pine copse, rose an uncouth green dome and a suggestion of battlements. Dina led the way through the pines. Rooks hurled themselves from the green branches with mad abandon. Dina turned left through a massive gate partially concealed by an overhanging yew. The graveled drive twisted towards the Manor, permitting a glimpse here and there as if to soften the blow of the sudden sight of the monstrous whole.

"My God," said Bill.

Dina squeezed his arm. "Yes," she agreed.

The front door was opened by Paget. He inclined his sad head and possessed himself of Bill's suitcase without appearing to move. "Will you step this way, sir?" he asked. He hated greeting new students. He knew that they all thought that he was a murderer. Once and once only had he lost his temper. During the course before the last, a certain Mrs. Larsen had approached him. "Paget," she had said. "I'm a ghoul. Do tell me..." Paget, trembling with rage, had told her that he had been responsible for twelve recent cases remarkable for their bestiality. Her eyes had sparkled. "The Cooden killing? And those two hikers? And Madame Groppi?" Paget had bowed.

Bill, unnerved by the man's suicidal expression, stepped past him into the dark hall with reluctance. He jumped as he felt the old hands slide over him with the discreet thoroughness of a tailor.

"I presume, sir," said Paget gently, "that we are not armed?"

Chapter Three

Some time ago, Flush had found it preferable to allow a new batch of students to meet each other casually and, if possible, singly. He therefore made no attempt to introduce them to each other or to the staff. During the first course, before he had appreciated the inadvisability of such a procedure, he had arranged a mass introduction over a glass of sherry. This had proved a spectacular failure. Two students had fainted, one had rushed through the French windows never to return. The staff, after this blunder, did not appear on the first day of a course until dinner time.

At three o'clock, Mrs. Carlisle, who had lunched in her room with Cyril, met Manelli where both had hoped to be alone, in the conservatory where the orchids grew. Both hesitated uncertainly.

"How do you do?" said Mrs. Carlisle loudly. Who was this ugly, well-dressed man? Was he one of the staff? Had he already...or was he only a Potential?

Manelli, who felt nervousness in others much as dogs scent an excess of adrenalin, was immediately reassured. He introduced himself suavely. In an explosion of relief, Mrs. Carlisle admitted her dread of meeting her instructors. After all, she said, no murderer was quite sane. Who knew when they would break out again? Nobody.

Manelli did not comment. He placed his finger in the oozing purple maw of an orchid and the calyx closed around it with a slight click.

Mrs. Carlisle looked at him more closely. His profile was vaguely familiar. "Manelli," she said. "Of course, you're no relation of the notorious 'Slots'?"

Manelli produced a penknife and cut the head off the orchid. "They used to call me that," he said. "Way back."

Mrs. Carlisle swallowed. Photographically, she remembered front-page pictures of three drowned gangsters being dredged out of the East River. All had been sunk to the neck in barrels of cement. On each barrel was painted the word SO. "Slots" Manelli had been questioned and released. There had been a small picture of him smoking a cigar and waving one hand.

Manelli turned, thinking to offer her the orchid with a pleasant smile.

But she had disappeared.

At half past four, Bill was wandering round the grounds, hoping to meet Dina. Crossing the yard under the big stable clock, he was waylaid from the garages by the Colonel.

"Know anything about cars, sir?"

"Not much," said Bill. He looked the old man over carefully. Although he wore dungarees and was smeared about the forehead with grease, the other had an air of sinister authority which immediately suggested staff.

The Colonel went back into the garage. "Recruit?" he shouted above the throb of some high-powered engine.

Bill followed him. "Yes. You're on the staff?"

"Carburetor playing up," said the Colonel. He patted his Bugatti. It stood trembling and shivering beneath his hand. Four chromium exhaust pipes curved back from the strapped bonnet. The Colonel plunged under the dashboard and reappeared holding a yoke-shaped piece of metal stained green and bronze and flecked with soot. "It's the flames," he said proudly.

"I met Miss Parrish this morning," said Bill after a slight pause.

The Colonel detached a length of green wire from the self-starter and nodded. "Nice little filly," he mumbled, picking up a heavy rasp. "Not really eligible here."

Bill's heart rose like a bird. "Really?" he said carefully. He sat down on a pile of coiled-up hose and waited.

The Colonel crawled back under the dashboard. "Shorting," he said curtly.

Cyril, who had noticed Dina from Mrs. Carlisle's bedroom window, was also prowling around the grounds hoping to meet her. He found her in the orchard at five-fifteen. She wore a small piece of material around her bosom and an abbreviated pair of shorts and she was feeding a large black horse.

"Hullo," said Cyril.

She looked him over with approval. "I'm Dina," she said, handing the horse another rotten apple.

"Staff?"

"Yes. Course?"

"Yes. You don't *look* like staff."

She smiled. "You don't look like course," she said. "Would you like to sit down on this root? If you don't mind rather a squash, there's room for both."

At half past six, cocktails were served on the terrace.

Manelli offered Mrs. Carlisle a glass. He saw her nervous smile and said gently, "I never carried poison and I haven't chilled anybody in years."

Cyril and Dina appeared from beneath the cedars. Cyril sprang up the steps and hastened over to Mrs. Carlisle.

"Oh, there you are," she said with an air of surprise. She appraised Dina, cleared her throat and added, "What a pretty girl."

Cyril tore his eyes from Dina. "In an obvious sort of way," he said.

Mrs. Carlisle dropped her cigarette onto the flags and ground it out with her heel. She sniffed. "Staff," she said. "Obviously."

Bill came across and touched Manelli on the arm. "Are you 'Slots'?" he asked bluntly.

Manelli smiled amiably. "They call me Joe these days."

Bill nodded, walked across the terrace and sat down next to Dina. *Slots*, he thought. He had lunched alone with Slots Manelli and lived to tell the tale. He bit his lip. He had a sudden ghastly vision of machine-gun massacres in soundproof garages; of witnesses gagged and bound and branded on the forehead with the word SO; of an entire funeral procession, except the front car in which Manelli sat apparently sorrowing, mown down by the wicked crossfire of forty sawn-off shotguns.

At half past seven, the first gong boomed through the house.

Half an hour later, Flush, immaculate in a dinner jacket, presided over the table in the dark, ill-lit dining room. Mrs. Barratt, in a lavender tea gown, sat at the far end. The Colonel sat between Bill and Dina, facing Cyril, Manelli, and Mrs. Carlisle. The Creaker had as usual dined in his room. His repellent appearance alarmed new students on their first night. Antonio Grossi had not arrived. He had been misdirected by a native of Krunte Abbas and had returned to Wiltshire.

Paget stood out of range of the candlelight, his mournful head hanging. It infuriated him that none of the new arrivals had bothered to change into evening dress. The earl, he remembered proudly, had always worn tails. *Oh, sir*, he thought, looking upwards. *I told you that you should not have gone hunting with that knee, sir.* He glanced around at his present employers. He hated and despised them all. Flush, he admitted, was a passable survival of better days; Mrs. Barratt's pearls were real; the Colonel knew wines, but tested them too frequently and in mixed company; Miss Dina had an engaging smile, but her swimming costumes made him hot with shame. But the Creaker…Paget drew a deep breath through his nose.

The Colonel was telling Manelli an interminable story about how he had bagged his first black bear in the Lydda Valley. Manelli was attempting to counter with the tale of how an acquaintance of his had bagged his first FBI man in Greenwich Village.

"I read your last one," Mrs. Barratt was telling Mrs. Carlisle. "I confess that I became quite attached to Michel. Such a pity that you had to drown him."

Mrs. Carlisle looked thoughtfully at her hostess, disbelieving, as had twelve good men and true, that she had destroyed two husbands.

Mrs. Barratt smiled back at her guest, thinking that with her flaming hair and her ruthless attitude towards Michel, Mrs. Carlisle should make an adequate murderess of the *crime passionnel* type. But bad in the dock and the cruel light of the Old Bailey unless it were a dull day and an entirely masculine jury. Perhaps in the more becoming Assize Courts such as Lewes and Winchester…Mrs. Barratt looked with interest at Cyril, wondering whether she too would ever have been sufficiently bemused by him to regard him as a compulsive motive.

He was talking to Bill Thurlow about Rouault.

Bill was only half listening. He looked past the Colonel at Dina. She wore a challenging white dress and a flower in her hair. The Colonel had said that she had pushed a lesser artist than Rouault over a cliff.

Paget stepped delicately from the shadows and removed the plates.

He felt Mrs. Barratt's eyes upon him and tried to look pleasant.

"Don't do that, Paget," she murmured as he bent over her. "Don't try to smile."

Paget stacked the plates silently on the tray and left the room. He went along the stone passage to the kitchen and laid the tray on the table. Barker, his underling, who had once served four months for shooting a poacher, was taking a soggy rice pudding out of the oven. Juggling the hot dish, he stood looking down at his uncompleted crossword puzzle.

"Small dagger," he said. "Seven, something O."

"Poniard," said Paget absently. He flicked a heavy dumpling off a plate into the sink tidy. *Oh, sir,* he complained silently to his dead employer, *look at me, sir. See me obeying these gladiators. Oh, what have I come to, sir?*

"Animal in three letters," said Barker. He hooked a piece out of the pudding with his finger and ate it.

"Dog," said Paget. "Cat. Pig. Hog. *Ape!*" he shouted suddenly, his arms hanging low. He snatched the tray from Barker and slammed the door behind him.

Al, Manelli's chauffeur, was teaching Blackie Rodden, the new bodyguard, to shoot craps at the far end of the room. He looked up. "What's eatin' him?" he asked.

Barker looked after Paget with an odd gleam in his eye. "Old goat," he said, kicking a chair.

In the dining room, Paget offered the rice pudding to Mrs. Carlisle. Over her head, he met Manelli's eyes. The ex-gangster was examining him with unwinking interest.

"His name is Paget," said Flush. "His ancestors have held similar posts here since the time of the Stuarts."

"Yeah?" Manelli explored a back tooth with his tongue and stared at Paget. "The real thing, eh? Say something historical, Paget."

"Dinosaurs, sir," said Paget tight-lipped. "Ichthyosaurus, giant crabs."

Nobody accepted the pudding. When all had refused a cracked square of processed cheese, the ladies repaired to the drawing room. Dina announced immediately that she was going down to the pool to swim and departed across the terrace at a run.

"So soon after dinner, the silly girl," said Mrs. Barratt. She poured coffee. "She will get cramp and drown herself. Sugar?"

Mrs. Carlisle watched the fragile hands fluttering over the tray. Was it possible that they had ever been steady and decisive enough to grind two electric light bulbs into a fine dust and beat them briskly into a Yorkshire pudding for her first husband?

Paget bent over her, offering liqueurs. She nodded at the brandy. Paget frowned. He considered that it was an unladylike choice. He resisted the impulse to offer her a cigar. Mrs. Carlisle misinterpreted his expression. Thinking that he was smiling at her, she smiled back. He poured the brandy, looked at her and left the room.

"I'm so glad," said Mrs. Barratt cozily, sipping coffee, "that you are a sensible age. We have had so many young hotheads."

"I am thirty-nine," lied Mrs. Carlisle coldly.

"I was only twenty the first time." Mrs. Barratt's faded eyes smiled back across the years. She opened a large locket which hung around her neck. "This was my second husband. I missed him dreadfully at first."

Mrs. Carlisle looked down over the old shoulder. Bert Barratt's heavy face glowered up at her from the filigree frame. It was the same photograph which had been, years ago, reproduced in many Sunday newspapers at the time of Naomi Wottling's trial. She did not know what to say. Did one admire a victim or imply that his passing had been no loss. "Congratulations," she said tactfully.

"He was so fond of lawn tennis." Mrs. Barratt sighed. "He tried to teach me, but we used to quarrel so. He made up new rules all the time." The hair rose behind Mrs. Carlisle's ears. How had Bert Barratt met his death? Had he been clubbed with a racquet? Or felled with a wicked service? Or strangled with a tennis net? She moved restlessly away to the window. She found herself staring hypnotized at a notice over the piano. Onto the green baize was pinned a single, typewritten slip heavily edged in black. *The Management regrets to announce,* it read, *the demise of Piers Larsen. Suddenly, at his residence in Sweden, shortly after Mrs. Larsen's departure from these premises.* Under this statement was an enigmatic cipher written in blue chalk: D + 3F.

In the dining room, Flush passed a bottle of invalid port to Manelli. He noted with displeasure that the American bit the ends off cigars.

"I will interview you tomorrow, gentlemen," he said, "at your convenience. You may feel that this afternoon has been wasted. I assure you that it has not. You have been under constant appraisal from the staff. We have rechecked your references, acquainted ourselves with your circumstances and…" he allowed himself a faint smile, "assessed your capabilities."

He paused and glanced around the table. It always amused him to envisage the potential victims of new candidates. His deductions were, on the whole, reasonably accurate. Occasionally, he made an abysmal error. He remembered still the slight, soft-spoken companion who wished to inherit a sizable legacy too soon. To his chagrin, he had failed to recognize the sly reticence of the schizophrene and the woman had returned to her post and, for some curious motive, shot three policemen dead in Ecclestone Terrace.

The present batch of students, he thought with a tinge of foreboding, were all apparently decorous, the most difficult type to handle. He preferred the rough, rude, and predictable groups, the extroverts who took copious notes without shame, grimly intent upon getting their money's worth, who departed eagerly, making crude jokes about not sticking their necks out and seeing each other in hell.

He sipped his port. "Four points, gentlemen. First, we have found it psychologically helpful for any student entertaining unworthy thoughts about another to be fined five shillings. The money is to be placed at the time of the incident in the Benevolent Fund boxes which are in each room. Second, any disputes among you will be immediately reported to a member of the staff. Third, no firearms, spring knives or other lethal weapons are permitted in the house outside the gymnasium. And last, for those of you who are not taking the Creaker's part of the syllabus, the summerhouse is strictly out of bounds." He rose and pushed back his chair. "And now shall we join the ladies?"

He led the way to the drawing room. As he paused with his hand on the door, he heard a curious noise within which was half a gasp and half a groan.

"What was that?" said Bill uneasily.

"Bit uncanny, wasn't it?" said Cyril. He tried a laugh.

"Let's take a look," said Manelli.

Flush smiled. "It is nothing, gentlemen, I assure you." He knew that the Creaker had made his appearance and was being introduced to Mrs. Carlisle.

Across the lawns the shadows lengthened beneath the cedars under which the Lords of the Manor had once collected dues and tithes. A blackbird stirred in its nest on the bough from which disobedient serfs had once dangled. The crickets chirruped softly where, in years past, proud stags had raised their heads to the small night wind which blew between the Barrows. That night, there was no wind. The trees stood sentinel against the pinkish sky, stiff and silent, waiting for the threatened heat wave of the next day.

"Godalmighty," said Mrs. Carlisle, closing her bedroom door. "What a bunch!"

Cyril looked out of the window. The moon hung over an ancient oak, almost the same color as the fading sky. "Terrifying," he agreed.

"They all look so *normal*," she complained.

"Except that Creaker. He's...well, *really*!"

"I took one look at him," said Mrs. Carlisle, "and I'll never do it again."

"Did you notice the Colonel's eyes? They don't seem to have any pupils."

"Naomi Barratt, I must confess, gives me the barking habdabs." Mrs. Carlisle sat down at the dressing table, anointed her face with cold cream and began to massage the area around her eyes.

Cyril watched the mascara spread over her cheekbones. Over her astonishing hair, he caught a glimpse in the mirror of his own tilted eyes and small, sulky mouth. *Dina Parrish is quite lovely,* he thought. *Together, we would make a charming couple.*

Mrs. Carlisle passed a tissue over her lipstick. She glanced sideways at Cyril, guessing something of his thoughts. "Dearest," she said. "Let's go home before it's too late." With her misplaced sense of drama, she flung her arms wide and raised her livid face. "The price is too great."

"*Whose* home?" asked Cyril irritably. "Come off it, dear. You shouldn't have drunk that last brandy."

"You mustn't nag, angel, or Chloe smack." She picked up her comb. "I'm a child at heart," she said, tugging savagely at her hair. "I just want to live happily ever after, goddamn it."

Manelli climbed into his first four-poster bed and lay spread-eagled. The canopy was old and torn, but he still felt manorial. *God,* he thought. *I wish that Grossi hoodlum could see me now.*

In his small damp room under the eaves, Paget put on his night-shirt and combed his graying hair. *Oh, sir,* he thought upwards. *Once you said, in jolly mood, that I was the only constant in a changing world.* He poured cold water from the ewer into the chipped basin. *Those were the days, sir. Those indeed were the days!*

Blackie Rodden, Manelli's new bodyguard, had been forced to share a room with Al, the chauffeur. This angered him. "I take the kip by the window," he announced. He turned on the hot tap in the basin and held his finger under it.

"Who says?" inquired Al. He took off his jacket and dropped it onto the floor. "It's hot tonight and hot air rises. Who says you take the kip by the window?"

"I said."

"Ah, so *you* said?"

"That's right. *I* said, like I said."

Al considered this for a moment. "That's what I thought you said." He was bored with this discussion, but Blackie was a new member of Manelli's Boys and it was all wrong for him to get ideas of grandeur. "I'm sorry you said that," he said softly. "Honest I am. I want you to have this kip."

"Oh, you do?"

"Sure. I want you to be comfortable. You're a nice guy, we'll get along. Just so you don't sleep in my bed."

"Who says this is your bed?"

"I say."

Blackie's hand crept towards the inner pocket where he kept his razor. "That's my bed, punk," he snarled.

Al's hand leapt to his shoulder holster. "You shouldn't of said punk, lug," he said. His face dropped. "I forgot. That Paget took my piece."

"Mine too."

"Now *there's* a lug."

"What a punk."

"Why don't we move this other bed to the window, lug?"

"Okay, punk."

"That water hot, lug?"

"No, punk."

On the floor below, Bill looked out of his window. He could just see the swimming pool. The underwater lights were still brighter than the moon. Dina was floating lazily in the luminous water. Faintly, across the silent lawns, Bill heard her singing to herself.

He started to hurry around the room, throwing open cupboards, dragging open drawers, searching for his bathing trunks. He found them in the wardrobe, carefully arranged on a coat hanger. He seized them, grabbed a towel, tripped over the mat outside his room and rushed downstairs.

In the Mandrake Inn in Poxwell Regis, Antonio Grossi yawned, pushed his automatic under the pillow and got into bed. He was very tired. He had driven nearly three hundred miles. He lay down gratefully, then roused himself and, propped on one elbow, picked up the telephone.

"Gimme room service," he said.

A hacking cough answered him. "What number do you require?" asked a feminine voice when the paroxysm was under control.

"I want room service."

"Please replace the receiver and press button B."

"Who are you?"

"This is the Poxwell Exchange. Will you state what number you require please?"

"Gimme the desk."

"Your number please?"

"129. The desk at the Mandrake. Hurry it up."

"The number is engaged. Will you hold on please?"

Grossi held on. He could hear her coughing. Once she said, "Are you still there, sir? I am trying to put you through." Some five minutes later, she said, "They have only the one telephone. It is still engaged."

It occurred at once to Grossi that he himself was engaging the number. "Hey, you," he shouted. "Don't go away. Look, send them a telegram. Say Grossi wants coffee and a barber nine-thirty."

"That will be one and ninepence. Please insert the money in the box."

"Listen sister. This ain't no call box. I'm in the Mandrake."

"You are *in* the Mandrake?"

"I just said."

"And you wish to send a telegram to yourself?"

"Nope." Grossi's trigger finger whitened on the automatic under the pillow. "I want to send a telegram to the desk." He reasoned with himself. There was no percentage in shooting a telephone.

"I'm sorry," she said, coughing. "I am unable to send a telegram to you whilst you are still on the line."

Grossi hit himself in the temple with his fist. "Okay," he whispered. "Okay, okay. I'm signin' off. Coffee barber nine-thirty. Signed Grossi. Reverse the charges." He hung up.

He lay down, sat up and removed the automatic from under the pillow, switched off the light, lay down again and composed himself for sleep. *Old Manelli*, he thought once and just had time to lay hold of the automatic before he dozed off.

The telephone rang. Grossi groped for the receiver.

"Will you take a message to the desk please?" said the coughing voice. "Telegram. Barber coffee nine-thirty signed Grossi. I was instructed to reverse the charges. Will you please insert one and ninepence in the box?"

Chapter Four

The sun had not yet risen over Seven Barrow Down. The lawns lay in the blue shadow which would not retreat until eleven o'clock. The sprinkler revolved slowly in the rose garden. Beyond the pool, Barker was mowing the grass where once a Royalist spy had lain for fifteen years while the grass grew up through his bones.

In the library, Flush and Dina attended to the morning mail.

"What do you think of Bill?" asked Dina, tearing open an envelope. She did not wait for an answer. "Cyril's nice too. And both so different. It's interesting, isn't it?" She sniffed the azure notepaper. "Patchouli. A Greek. Can he pay in installments?"

"We regret. The usual thing."

"Here's another Distracted Husband. Money's no object, sponsored by Oswald Anson."

"Inform Mr. Anson that I shall accept no more of his proteges." Flush slit an envelope, glanced at its contents and threw the whole into the wastepaper basket. "Lined stationery," he said with a shiver of disgust.

"One from Mrs. Larsen. She's remarried and moved to Norway. She can't thank us enough and she hopes she'll never see us again."

Flush reached for the letter. Mrs. Larsen had been an exceptional pupil. "I will answer it myself," he said. He smiled. "She will be back."

"There's another one from that silly farmer in Northern Ireland."

"Ignore it."

Dina looked at him curiously. "Actually," she asked, "if it came to it, *could* you fix a whole herd?"

Flush frowned. He did not answer. "It is ten o'clock. Which candidate am I to interview first?"

Cyril stood by the window. A wasp was crawling up the pane. He followed it with the tip of his cigarette, forcing it to climb faster.

"We are in love," said Mrs. Carlisle aggressively for the third time. "Moreover, my husband is an intolerable bully."

Flush sighed. They all attempted to justify themselves. He allowed an additional half-hour for it. He glanced out at the lawns. The humped, threatening shadow of the Barrow had reached the azaleas. Time was up. He looked at Cyril. "Tell me," he asked, "do you intend to participate in this venture?"

Cyril moved restively. "As far as possible," he said. "Unfortunately my heart's not too strong."

"We have found it advisable, in the case of accomplices, to distribute the responsibility equally. Should there be any recriminations, both parties are equally involved. This is particularly desirable where any continued association is intended."

"I'll do what I can."

"Of course he will," said Mrs. Carlisle.

"I must warn you that I'm highly strung and inclined to be unreliable," said Cyril.

Flush studied him. *Once you have completed your repertoire of reluctance*, he thought, *you'll be a sterling pupil. You're a natural. Splendid balance, good hands, span of about an octave, useful spatulate thumb.* "Which of you," he asked, "proposed this particular solution to your problem?"

"We fell in love," said Mrs. Carlisle. "It seemed to follow quite naturally."

"Actually," said Cyril, "I believe Chloe first broached the subject."

Mrs. Carlisle laughed. "He's being naughty," she said. "He knows very well that it was him. I said I'd give him a lift home, and…"

"Be accurate, dear," Cyril interrupted. "You must remember that as we went into the tropical plant house at Kew you said…"

Flush raised his voice. "Would not a divorce be less hazardous?"

"Ned refuses even to consider it," said Mrs. Carlisle. She picked a piece of varnish off her thumbnail. "I've asked him again and again. He says that I've made my bed and he intends to sleep in it."

Flush made a note. "He is in good health?"

"I'm afraid so."

"Insured?"

"Oh yes."

"The policy should be allowed to lapse."

"That seems rather a waste," said Cyril involuntarily.

Mrs. Carlisle looked at him. "Dearest," she said, "if you don't stop tormenting that poor wasp, I shall scream."

Flush coughed, pulling at the lobe of his ear. "Will you describe the Intended please?"

"The Intended?"

"Your husband."

"Oh." Mrs. Carlisle fumbled for a cigarette. "He was quite attractive when we were first married," she said defensively.

"He has, as they do say," said Cyril, "run to seed."

"He is tall, about your height but heavier."

"A paunch, let's face it."

"Getting a little thin on top."

"Really, Chloe! He's as bald as an egg."

"He dresses soberly…"

"Except at the weekends."

"He's a Sunday golfer. He's…"

"Depressingly insular. Revoltingly selfish. An important bore."

"He's reasonably good-natured."

"He is very, very *jolly*," said Cyril. "He has a heart of *gold*."

Mrs. Carlisle turned round. "Dearest," she said, "aren't you being a trifle vulgar?"

Flush watched her. *Poor material*, he thought. *She has an ugly temper. I don't like the microcephalic development of the mandibular arch. Why is she infatuated with this promising youth?*

"He has a car," offered Cyril. "But he is a very careful driver."

"Does he suffer at any time from bouts of depression?"

"Oh, never. That's half the trouble."

"He drinks?"

"Like a crocodile."

"Suicide is out of the question?"

"Yes," said Mrs. Carlisle loudly.

"He has enemies?"

"He is a stockbroker," said Cyril.

"Anybody in particular?" This question was irrelevant but Flush still hoped, without hope, that one day somebody would answer it with a tentative, "Well, there's a bridge player named Armitage…"

"Not that I know of."

"Any tendencies towards—excuse me—extramarital adventures?"

"Certainly not," said Mrs. Carlisle indignantly.

Simultaneously, Cyril said, "Oh, I imagine so."

Mrs. Carlisle looked over her shoulder. Her smile was strained. "Jealous one," she said.

Rise and strike him, madam, Flush counseled her silently. *Take the globe.* "Does the Intended suffer from weak ankles? Eyestrain? Giddy spells?"

Cyril answered meticulously. "His ankles are cast iron. He wears spectacles for reading. He goes occasionally to Masonic dinners and becomes very dizzy indeed."

Flush pointed his pen at Mrs. Carlisle. "You have your own garage?"

"No. We hire a mews one."

"There is a gas jet," Cyril volunteered. "And water laid on."

Water? thought Flush irritably. *Do you propose to drown your rival in his own sedan?* "What of the lock?"

"A padlock."

"Three or four lever?"

"I don't know."

Flush looked up sharply. "You were asked to provide plasticine impressions of all relevant locks." He dug his fingernails into the pen. "Am I to understand that you have not done so?"

"We left in such a rush," said Mrs. Carlisle. "I had to pick up a pair of shoes and go to the cleaners and…"

Flush sighed through his nose. "Does your husband trust you?"

"He's met Cyril."

"I regret that I am obliged to ask you so impertinent a question, but have there been…other Cyrils?"

"Of course not." She stared at Flush with the passionate indignation of the practiced liar.

Flush turned to Cyril. "And you? Other Chloes?"

Mrs. Carlisle answered him. "One," she said. "One." She stubbed out her cigarette and lit another.

"Both of you can drive?"

"Yes," said Mrs. Carlisle. "I'm rather nervous."

"And endorsements?"

"Cyril was once questioned for being under the influence."

"Of luminol," said Cyril distinctly. "I had been, as prescribed by my doctor, taking luminol."

"And vodka," said Mrs. Carlisle after a slight pause.

"Chloe, I told you at the time…"

"Dearest, why *shouldn't* you drink vodka?"

"I had not been," Cyril's beautiful hands became fists, "drinking vodka."

"All right, dearest. It was luminol." She smiled at Flush. "No vodka."

Flush pulled at the lobe of his ear. Boredom swept over him. He stopped listening. *How I dislike them all*, he thought. *Their lunatic approaches to their absurd little problems, their amateurish blunders, their lack of confidence.* He remembered as the only shining exception the scrubbed, handsome face of Piers Larsen's widow; her eager, flashing smile, her minute improvements upon an already perfect alibi.

The sunlight had penetrated a few feet inside the mullioned window. The diamond-shaped shadows overlaid the intricate pattern of the Shirazi. Manelli paced the floor like a lion bred in captivity. Under certain combinations of circumstances, some animals will maul their keepers, yet they are uneasy without them. The same applied to Manelli and his familiars, particularly his bodyguards.

Flush indicated a chair. "Sit down, Mr. Manelli. I gather that you have had some previous experience?"

Manelli stood gazing at a framed lithograph of a woman's head. "Way back," he admitted. He tapped the glass accusingly. "It ain't signed."

Flush lit his first cigar of the day. "Some disapprove of the practice here," he said, blowing smoke.

"Yeah?" Manelli circled the desk, picked up a paperweight and replaced it exactly in its former position.

Flush pushed the box of cigars across the desk.

Manelli waved it away. "No thanks," he said. "I get mine special." He stared belligerently at a portrait of a man in a helmet. "I gotta Rembrandt," he remarked. "Signed."

Flush tapped his index finger impatiently on the desk. "Your full name, please?"

"Joe."

Flush made a note. "Profession?"

Manelli grinned. He recalled an occasion upon which he had been asked the same question by a federal prosecutor. So confused had he become by his own counsel's efforts to achieve a mistrial, that he had answered truthfully, "Hood."

"I got a florist shop," he said.

For a moment Flush said nothing. All candidates' histories were carefully checked and he knew that this claim was over-modest. He had already established that the American's enormous income was derived from intimidating bookmakers, extortion, protection, and generally throwing muscle around the east coast of the country which had adopted him; that he enjoyed a prominent place in the esteem of a dozen senators and was a power in several trades unions; that, these days, his most lucrative hobby was organizing strikes and later, for a consideration, breaking them. "I will put Industrial Consultant," he said.

Manelli's eyelids drooped. "Where do you get that?" he asked. He stood appallingly still. "I don't like no fairy tales. I am a florist."

Flush glanced at him, wondering without interest whether the man was breathing. He raised his eyebrows.

"You checked," said Manelli accusingly.

"Naturally."

Manelli moved with a jerk. He walked to the far end of the room, picked up an ashtray, replaced it and strode back to the desk. "Who from?" he demanded.

"Mr. Manelli," said Flush frowning, "your attitude is highly obstructive."

"That is why this dead man frisks me at the door?"

"Paget has instructions to search all prospective students."

"The others, too?"

"Certainly. In your case, obviously, I warned him to be thorough."

Manelli stiffened. "You did, eh?" He stopped breathing.

Flush looked at him. He asked himself whether, if he were to postpone his answer for sufficient minutes, the ex-gangster would die of suffocation. "Mr. Manelli," he said. "We are not children. We both know that you have been arrested nine times for homicide, fifteen times for assault and robbery, five times for grand larceny, three times for contempt of Congress, nineteen times for vagrancy, eleven times for consorting with known criminals, twice for…"

Manelli interrupted. "But did I get convicted?"

"I believe not."

"Not once."

"My felicitations. You must know all the wrong people."

Manelli watched his tutor for a long moment. Then, encouraged by a friendly gleam in Flush's eye, he suddenly roared with laughter. "Say, that's good. Wait till I tell Al, he'll kill himself."

"On these premises, that would be in the worst possible taste. What brings you here, Mr. Manelli? I understand that in America, provided that one has the necessary contacts…"

"Yeah."

"You have enemies in this country?"

Manelli pursed his lips. "Things are warming up over there," he said. "I don't like Ike."

Flush waited.

Manelli walked over to the window, pulled down the blind and allowed it to snap back again. He strode over to the desk and struck it with his open hand. "This Congressional Committee pulls me in," he said in a controlled voice. "Me. Like I am some cheap hoodlum. For questioning, is what they say. Well, that's okay, I got the technique, I almost enjoy it. I fetch my mouthpiece and we blow in. But this time it is different. You know what?" He scratched his head, the gesture of a barrister assuring the jury that he too is confused. "*We are televised.* I sit there and one hundred and nineteen times I say, 'I refuse to answer on the grounds that it may tend to incriminate me, incriminate me or by devious means tend to incriminate me.' The cameras are grinding and around one hundred million people are watching. I sit and sweat and I know that all over America the hoods are laughing."

"Barbarous," murmured Flush. "Trial by ordeal. Abolished in this country by Henry III."

Manelli was not listening. "So naturally I went out." He ran a hand through his hair. "Okay, here I am. I gotta expand. But these days I can't afford to take risks. I learn the law first and the cops ask questions later."

"Have a cigar, Mr. Manelli." Flush produced a humidor from a drawer and pushed it across the desk.

Manelli waved it away, feeling for his case. "I figured while the heat is on over there, I will open up some small business on this side."

"Perhaps a florist?"

"Maybe," said Manelli noncommittally. "Good address, quiet. You know. What do you think of this Throgmorton Street?" He took Flush's cigar from him and laid it in an ashtray. "Here. Throw that thing away and have one of mine."

Flush shook his head at the proffered cigar, then saw, mesmerized, that it was the brand which he smoked himself.

Bill Thurlow sat down at once. Without embarrassment or hesitation, he stated his full name, his age, his profession, his income and his prospective victim. He told his story clearly and concisely, without detail or comment. As it unfolded in its ghastly entirety, Flush rose from behind the desk and roamed restlessly around the room. "The blackguard," he said once. His hands shook. He dropped ash onto the Shirazi, stood staring down at it for a moment, then strode over to the window. "Enough," he said harshly. "Mr. Thurlow, I will deem it a favor if you will entrust this monster to me. He should be dealt with immediately. I will leave at once."

"No," said Bill. "It's very kind of you but I promised my father that I'd keep it in the family. I thought perhaps I would shoot him."

"No. It is too merciful. Allow me to summon the Creaker. When he is roused to anger..."

"No."

"I appeal to you."

"No."

"It would afford me great *pleasure*."

"I'm sorry."

Flush moved over to the decanters and poured himself a glass of sherry. "There will be others," he said. "Perhaps already…"

"I thought perhaps that you might do some sort of course in a nutshell. The time element's important."

"Permit me to drop but a hint to the Creaker."

"No."

"The course takes four days. During that time…"

"My father wanted to do it himself but he is crippled with arthritis."

"You have shown unusual self-control."

"Not really. I've taken three potshots at him, but I missed."

Flush drank the sherry and stood holding the empty glass. "I have attempted to solve many dilemmas," he said. "But never, in all my years of experience…" His voice failed him. He shook his head speechlessly. He drew a hand over his eyes and cleared his throat. "Mr. Thurlow," he said. "I insist upon your taking this course free of charge. I *insist*."

Paget knocked, opened the door and walked three feet into the room. He stood still and conveyed the impression that he had bowed.

"An American person has arrived, sir," he announced. "He claims that he is expected."

Flush was already roughing out a solution to Bill's problem. He laid aside his pen. "What name?"

"This person *says* that his name is Grossi, sir. From his general demeanor, I suspect that he may be traveling incognito. I relieved him of a sawn-off shotgun, a large caliber automatic, a long-barreled Colt Woodsman .22 and asked him to wait in the drawing room." Paget stared at Flush's left shoulder. "I did not care for his looks, sir. A very dynamic person."

"Show him in."

Paget left the room. He walked softly along the cold, flagged passage.

Oh, sir, he thought. *You would not have sat at the same table with one of them. Did you see this Grossi's tie, sir? Would you, sir, have sawn the barrel off that beautiful repeating shotgun?* He stepped into the drawing room.

"Will you come this way, please, sir?"

Grossi wheeled. Without appearing to move fast, he was across the room and through the door before Paget's invitation was completed. "Which way, which way?" he asked. His handsome head turned left and right so rapidly that the two movements were one. His feet twitched, eager to be in motion.

Paget walked slowly across the hall. Grossi bounded along slightly in front of him, glancing back over his shoulder. Paget allowed him to hurry into the dining room before he turned abruptly left and said, "Follow me please, sir."

Grossi sprang after him. Already he hated Paget. On arrival, he had mistaken the butler for his host and had offered to shake hands. Paget at the time had been attempting to relieve him of his coat and their hands had met inside the green homburg. "So," he said. "A funny man."

Paget stopped, his sad head tilted. "Sir?" he inquired.

Grossi gnawed his lower lip. "Skip it," he said. "Which way, which way?"

Paget, hating him, determined to show him the longest possible route to the library. "Follow me please, sir."

He led the way upstairs, along the west wing corridor and into a small, rope-operated lift.

"Why're we going down when we just came up?" Grossi demanded. Paget did not answer. He allowed the lift to descend a foot below ground level, took it up four feet too far, stopped and started as slowly as possible to inch it down again.

"Come on, come on," snapped Grossi.

Paget opened the rusty gate. His nostrils dilated as he got an astringent whiff of the other's shaving lotion. Grossi pushed past him. Paget stood still, fumbling with the gate. He glanced out of a small slit window which had known the whir of arrows and, later, the blast of the earl's rifle as he blazed angrily at his lazy gardeners. *Oh, sir*, he asked. *Would I exaggerate if I were to lead this beaver upstairs again?* Regretfully, he turned and led the way slowly along the passage to the library. He paused outside the closed door.

"What was the name again please, sir?"

"Grossi, *Grossi.*"

Paget tapped on the door, opened it and advanced three feet into the room. "Mr. Loss," he announced.

Grossi shouldered past him and by the time Paget had stepped backwards out of his way, was over by the desk.

"You Flush?" he asked. "Meet Grossi." He looked back at Paget. "Beat it, comical. We wanna be alone." He swung back to Flush. "Now about this Manelli," he rapped.

Chapter Five

The interviews were finished. There was half an hour before roll call. The sun blazed over the lawns. There was not a cloud in the colorless sky. Barker, off duty, swam slowly in the blue pool. He kept his head averted from the distant house, knowing that what he did was forbidden, hoping that should Paget see him, he would mistake him for one of the guests.

In the house, behind a door marked PRIVATE, the staff relaxed, drinking, with the exception of the Colonel, a mid-morning cup of coffee.

The Creaker was sunk into a sofa, his false leg stretched at ease before him. He ate wine gums and read an old copy of the *Police Gazette*. Mrs. Barratt, with several balls of brightly colored wool on her knees, was knitting a Fair Isle cardigan for the Colonel. Dina was mending a garment so small and so sheer that it was hardly visible. The Colonel was pouring himself a pink gin and thinking about the carburetor of his Bugatti. He was turning the mechanism over and over in his mind, refusing to admit that it had outwitted him. Flush stood immobile at the window, watching Barker in the pool. He could see for miles and he had instantly recognized the back of his chef's head. Was there, he wondered, some method of shortcircuiting the underwater lights and, by the flip of a switch, electrifying the pool?

Paget was suddenly in the room. Silently, he collected the cups and picked up the heavy silver tray. "Will there be anything else, madam?"

Mrs. Barratt looked up. "I think not, Paget."

"The students are entertained?" asked Flush.

Paget adopted his favorite stance, diplomatic, flatfooted. "I believe so, sir."

"What are they doing?" Since Grossi had revealed the name of his Intended, Flush had become increasingly uneasy.

"Mrs. Carlisle, sir, is typing. She summoned me and requested a bottle of gin and a quantity of tonic water. She informed me that she was about to write of an airplane crash and needed stimulant." Paget's gray eyebrows drew together. "She invited me to pinch her, sir. For luck, she said."

"Did you?" Dina looked interested.

"No, miss, I passed it off." Paget stared down at his feet. "I had reason to suspect that Mr. Cyril, sir, was concealed in the wardrobe. He was stumbling about among the shoes, sir."

"And Mr. Thurlow?" asked Dina.

"I passed him in the hall, miss. He requested me to inform you that he is to be discovered in the swimming pool."

"And Mr. Manelli?" said Flush.

"He is in the billiards room, sir, playing a card game with the two menservants who accompanied him." Paget hesitated. "I would be obliged, sir, if you would speak to these persons. Unless my authority is to be undermined, I prefer them to remain on the far side of the green baize."

"I will tell them."

"Thank you, sir. Mr. Grossi, when last I saw him, was attempting to transfer the fire in his bedroom into our Jacobean warming pan. It is being utilized, sir, as a flatiron. His manservant, who is upon overfamiliar terms with him, is pressing his suit with it. There was a bottle of whisky in evidence and both gentlemen appeared to be in the best of spirits."

"I see." Flush frowned. He asked casually, "Has Mr. Grossi yet, to your knowledge, met Mr. Manelli?"

"I think not, sir. Once, I was about to take the liberty of introducing them upon the grounds that they were compatriots, but when I turned, Mr. Grossi had vanished. He moves at great speed, sir."

Flush stared out of the window. Barker was drying himself at the edge of the pool. The towel, Flush noticed, was the one missing from the west wing. "Paget," he said.

"Yes, sir," said Paget. "I will upbraid him, sir."

"Good. That will be all."

Paget inclined his head and left the room as suddenly as he had come. "Dina," said Mrs. Barratt. "Are you flirting with Mr. Thurlow?"

"He's rather sweet," said Dina. "A bit slow, but he's got such splendid legs." She rethreaded her needle. "Who does he want to kill?"

"I intend to handle Mr. Thurlow's problem myself," said Flush. "I do not wish to discuss it."

The Creaker put a wine gum into his mouth. "'Orrible, eh?" he asked. His small eyes sparkled.

Flush nodded. "Later I may require you to show him one of your cruder routines."

The Creaker lurched to his foot. "Now?" he growled. He scratched his quadriceps nervously.

"No," said Flush sharply. "Sit down, please."

"I'll show 'im somethin'," said the Creaker. "I got a new one as would make you puke. See, I take this…"

"Creaker!"

"…bit o' wire an'…"

"Unless you are silent immediately, I shall ask you to leave the room."

The Creaker stared at Flush. Flush stared back with equal ferocity. The Creaker sat down. His crustacean hand descended into the box of sweets and removed four and some paper shavings. His eyes did not leave Flush. "I want a new sack," he said sulkily. He pressed the sweets and the shavings into his mouth and mumbled indistinctly, "An' urabberoshengroughera."

Mrs. Barratt looked up from her knitting. "I am not altogether happy about Mrs. Carlisle," she said.

"Nor I," confessed Flush. "Did you notice the prominence of the greater zygomatic? Have you Matron's report?"

The Colonel passed it. "Poor reflexes," he remarked.

Flush's eye sped down the page. "Mm," he said. "Longsighted…tendency to hysteria, heartbeat very irregular. After the last, Matron has added 'definitely hotchacha.' I hope that she has not started tippling again."

"What of her young man?"

"Bad type," said the Colonel. "Yellow streak."

"Cyril invited me to go to the movies," said Dina. "He asked me not to tell Mrs. Carlisle."

Flush turned a page of the report. "I see that his heart, contrary to his own suggestion, is in mint condition. The soles of his feet are ticklish. Really, Naomi, you must speak to Matron. Surely that is quite irrelevant." *Or is it?* he wondered. Had the woman innocently struck upon some subtle point? He knew that a man had died in Athens in 1902 from a paroxysm of laughter…

"Who's going to help an old lady to wind her wool?" asked Mrs. Barratt. "I presume that it is the husband who is to go?"

"Yes. It should be quite simple. I have a plan of his garage. I think that the puncture and faucet routine will meet the case."

"Operation Amen?"

"With certain modifications."

"Cyril will operate?"

"Yes. I propose to give him a course of manipulative exercises. Both of them will, of course, take anatomy. They can practice upon each other. As an alternative, Colonel, I shall ask you to take them quickly through Shotguns. Mr. Manelli will sit also. He brought with him a deplorable sawn-off pump model in a frightening state of neglect."

"Who's *he* after?" said Dina.

"I gather that he has not selected an Intended. Apparently he makes enemies rapidly and on a large scale. He confided that frequently he does not even know them. They are these days entrusted mainly to those of whom he speaks as his Torpedoes."

"What will you teach him, Clifford?"

"He claims that he knows rudimentary strangling, but is out of practice. It will do no harm to brush it up. I shall then hand him over to you, Naomi, for a comprehensive grounding in Forensic Medicine. He particularly needs a thorough legal training and instruction upon Candor or Concealment to Counsel and Etiquette in British Courts." Flush sighed, shaking his head. "I confess that my heart is not in Mr. Manelli's case. I fear that Mr. Grossi intends to settle all his problems at the first possible opportunity."

"Mr. Grossi asked me to go swimming with him," said Dina. "Did he want to shoot Mr. Manelli at once?"

"Immediately. I made it perfectly clear to him about the county limit. He appeared to agree, but he needs watching." Flush fingered his chin, gazing out of the window, noting Barker dodging from tree to tree with his towel-wrapped bundle. "I admit," he said, biting his thumbnail, "that I am profoundly uneasy about Mr. Grossi."

Mrs. Barratt laid down her knitting. "Clifford," she said, clutching at her locket. "You quite alarm me. This is the twenty-sixth course and the jackdaws are nesting again in the yews."

Flush gazed down at the medical reports in a preoccupied manner. "Let the staff keep on their toes," he said heavily. "I don't like this batch, I don't like them at all."

Upstairs, Paget tapped softly on Mrs. Carlisle's bedroom door. Cyril threw down his book and rushed into the wardrobe.

"Come in," called Mrs. Carlisle. She pushed away her typewriter and took off her spectacles.

Paget entered, stood in the doorway and bowed. "Roll call will be in fifteen minutes, madam," he said. He lowered his head and withdrew.

Cyril stepped cautiously out of the wardrobe. He was pale with rage. "I've never been so humiliated in my life," he said. "I'm fed up with running in and out of this bloody cupboard."

Mrs. Carlisle sniffed. "You're so good at it, angel," she said, coldly. "You must have had a lot of practice."

Cyril turned to the window breathing deeply. "Comb your hair," he said. "You look like a case of mistaken identity."

Mrs. Carlisle opened her mouth to scream at him, changed her mind and said instead, "What does that old zombie mean, roll call? *What* roll call? Angel," she said urgently, "let's go home."

Cyril sat down on the window seat and pulled up his socks. "Have you paid?" he asked.

"I wasn't taking any chances," she said, smiling at her own mild cunning. "I gave the Colonel a postdated check."

Cyril sighed. "My dear, don't you realize that if we do a bunk, you'll never live to stop it? Can't you understand that we've taken them for better or worse and worse and *worse?*"

Manelli did not like playing poker during the daytime. He threw in his hand, got up and wandered out onto the terrace. He was fumbling for his cigar lighter when he looked up and saw Grossi.

Grossi was leaning against the stone balustrade. He said nothing but the impact of his presence was in itself a shock. Manelli stopped, the lighter an inch from his cigar. For a full ten seconds he stood motionless. Then he lit the cigar and blew a funnel of smoke. "So," he said.

Grossi said nothing. He did not move.

"So," said Manelli again. He knew, with a surge of hopeless anger, that he was about to start behaving like one of his own torpedoes. Grossi inevitably had this effect upon him. Fifteen years ago, before their partnership had been dissolved, before the young upstart Grossi had decided to go West, they had behaved naturally in this manner because they knew no other; now, although both had learned better, they still reverted to type during their rare meetings. *Look out, boy,* said their relaxed shoulders and their steady oblique regards. *I'm still a hood at heart. One false move, that's all. One.* Manelli looked the other over carefully. The man wore tweeds of excellent cut, with none of the imperceptible slack of the middle period which allowed for a shoulder holster. Unless he had an icepick tucked into his sock, he was not armed.

"Old Joe," said Grossi. "Television favorite."

Manelli looked down at his shoes. "You got the Boys, Tony?" he asked softly.

"I got one, Joe. He *wanted* to come. He can't forget what you did to Bugs." Grossi tore a leaf off the jasmine and rolled it between his palms. "You got your Boys, Joe?"

"I got Al, Tony. Al keeps talking about that dirty thing you did to Vittorio. Also I have a likely young comer called Blackie. He does what I say."

There was a discreet knock on the French window. Paget took two steps onto the terrace and bowed. "Roll call is in ten minutes, sir, sir," he said. He nodded and disappeared the way he had come.

Both Americans stared after him.

After a slight pause, Manelli said in his normal voice, "Now that man *is* dead."

"And how," said Grossi. He rallied quickly. "You two should get together," he snapped. "But *soon.*"

Bill thrashed briskly through the chlorinated water. The pool was still cold on the surface. He climbed out. Drying his hands, he watched Dina swimming underwater.

She surfaced beneath him and stretched up a brown arm. "Pull me out," she said.

Bill took the wet hand and pulled. She slid out of the water and landed neatly six inches away from him.

"Dry me," she ordered calmly.

"No," said Bill. He turned away, found his case and lit a cigarette. "You're a big girl now. Dry yourself."

A brawny man in shorts and singlet burst from the summer-house and began to run at top speed towards the orchard. "Mornin'," he said as he flashed past. He disappeared behind the cedars.

"One of the Creaker's pupils," explained Dina. "He's not allowed out of the west wing except for training."

Bill glanced at her sideways for some echo of his own uneasiness. She was drying her hair, smiling at him. "What's he training for?"

"I don't know," she said. "His name's Hobson. He eats nothing but meat and eggs. We must hurry. Roll call's in five minutes."

"Dina," said Bill. "You don't belong here."

"Where else would I go?" she asked. She swayed against him and rubbed her wet shoulder against his ribs.

Flush stood with his back to the great fireplace. His benign expression did not betray that he always dreaded this ceremonial of the second morning of a course. He glanced around at the seated students. He fancied Cyril, Grossi, and Manelli, in that order. Bill and Mrs. Carlisle, he suspected, were stumers.

The Colonel read the roll call.

"Yes," said Mrs. Carlisle nervously.

"Here I am," said Cyril.

"Large as life," said Manelli, selecting a cigar.

"An' twice as natural," said Grossi, drumming his fingers on his knee.

"Here," said Bill, smiling at Dina.

"'Obson's doin' 'is run," said the Creaker.

"Now," said Flush, "you have all been introduced to the members of my staff, but I make it a practice, in order to increase your confidence, to tell students a little of our qualifications." He indicated Mrs. Barratt, who looked up from her knitting and nodded. "Your hostess was better known as Naomi Wottling. No doubt our British students know the name, but for the benefit of our American friends, I shall remind you that she was in 1939 unsuccessfully accused of administering a large quantity of powdered glass to her first husband. I myself was present during this battle of legal wits and I may say that her performance in the dock and on the stand was a pleasure to watch. The jury were out for a brief ten minutes." Flush smiled. "It was, by and large, an exceedingly unpopular verdict. Yet this gallant woman was undaunted. Within a week she married Mr. Barratt, whose testimony had played a prominent part in her defense. The implications of this match were widely commented upon after Mr. Barratt was found drowned in the lake at Aix-les-Bains."

There was a long pause.

"*Seen?*" asked Grossi.

"An open verdict was returned," said Mrs. Barratt.

"You will have noticed," said Flush, "her admirable change of tactics." He indicated the Colonel. "Colonel Quincey was tried in India for reversing over his wife in a highly powered car. His distinguished bearing and manly grief during the court martial secured a verdict of Death by Misadventure. More recently, he was obliged to drown a man in the Thames. There were several spectators, but his work was so polished that he was congratulated by the magistrate at the postmortem for an intrepid attempt to save his victim's life."

"Beggar swam like an otter," said the Colonel.

"He also," said Flush, "holds an engineering degree and has bagged an astounding number of large and small game trophies with a wide variety of weapons." He paused. Had his audience been entirely masculine, he would have recounted the episode of the panther and the homemade grenade.

"Wot about me?" asked the Creaker.

"Be quiet, Creaker," said Mrs. Barratt.

"Tell 'em 'bout me," insisted the Creaker.

"The Creaker," said Flush, frowning, "was tried and sentenced to death in 1937. His crime was…unattractive. Several attempts were made by the public to burn down the jail where he was in custody. However, owing to his comprehensive acquaintance with the underworld, he was able to produce certain spurious evidence which earned his reprieve."

"Tell 'em 'bout the..."

"Creaker!"

"...deck chair an' the..."

"Please be silent immediately."

The Creaker subsided, muttering.

Flush turned to Dina. "Miss Parrish," he said, "was recently affianced to a certain artist whom she had come to distrust. Her efforts to nullify the understanding did not meet with the gentleman's approval. She had the wisdom, on a certain day, to present herself at the local police station and report that her fiancé was missing and had flung off in a state of mind which smoothed the way to a verdict of suicide."

Bill stared at Dina. She pulled her skirt down over her knees and sighed heavily.

"We now come to myself," said Flush. "I do not wish to boast. I was once internationally known as the Balliol Butcher. I was accused of pushing three obnoxious women off fast-moving trains. The method, I now realize, is unsatisfactory unless put into operation over a viaduct. My fourth case survived. It was her evidence which acquitted me. I was of course obliged to marry her and she later threw herself off the Flying Scotsman, for which event I had an unshakable alibi."

"Genuine?" asked Mrs. Carlisle faintly.

"You will all, naturally, be required to pass in Alibis. Now will you please take a note? Mrs. Carlisle, I have you down for Anatomy, Firearms, Court Procedure, Jujitsu and Alibis. Have you got that?"

Mrs. Carlisle nodded speechlessly.

"Cyril, your curriculum is the same with the addition of Manipulative Exercises, Accidents and Electricity. Have you any knowledge of engines?"

"I haven't a clue," said Cyril.

"Then please add Automobiles." Flush turned to the Americans. "Mr. Manelli, your syllabus and that of Mr. Grossi are identical."

"Quite a coincidence," said Manelli. He knew now that Grossi intended to kill him, that he must be forestalled in the only method which either of them knew.

"You will study Firearms, British Law, Procedure, Court Etiquette, Forensic Medicine, Grips, Knots and Tourniquets, Single and Double-edged Weapons and Water. Manelli, I do not wish to be personal, but you are fifteen pounds overweight. You will be given a diet sheet to which you will rigidly adhere."

"I don't give up liquor," said Manelli.

"On the contrary. I have already given instructions to the domestic staff." Flush rose. "Timetables will presently be distributed to you. Please be punctual for your classes. This afternoon we have Anatomy, Jujitsu and Target Practice. You will all attend. There will be a lecture tonight after dinner upon Murder and the Classics, which is voluntary. You are now at liberty until noon when there is a general class in rudimentary Manual Routines in the gymnasium. Are there any questions?"

There was silence. The students avoided each other's eyes. Flush collected his papers, nodded and left the room, followed by Mrs. Barratt, the Colonel, and the Creaker.

"Mr. Grossi," said Dina. "Would you like to play tennis with me?"

Grossi had been intending to unnerve Manelli by following him around at a distance of about fifty yards, but he changed his mind.

"Sure, sure," he said. "I'll play anything with you, honey."

Manelli watched them go through the French windows. He knew that he ought to follow Grossi, to keep an eye on him, but this seemed to be a good opportunity to let Flush know that he had changed his plans and now had a definite victim in mind. He rose and set out after the staff.

Mrs. Carlisle gripped Bill's arm. "Bill," she said hoarsely. "Do you think we're *safe*?"

Bill misunderstood her. He glanced from her to Cyril. "I really don't know," he said uncomfortably. "I only met you yesterday."

"I was talking about Them," she said, annoyed.

Bill blushed. "I suppose so," he said. "I mean, surely this is the last place where they'd want a...any complications."

Chapter Six

It was very hot. In the comparative cool of the gymnasium, Manelli, already on his slimming schedule, lounged on the captive bicycle smoking a cigar and revolving his feet resentfully. Bill came through the door which led to the terrace and stood watching him.

"Hi," said Manelli. "Say, will you do me a favor?"

"What?" asked Bill cautiously.

"Climb on this fool thing and ride a coupla miles fast. Ten miles a day, this Flush tells me. Does he want to kill me?" He dismounted and gave the saddle a push. "As-aa-aah!" he said, disgusted.

Bill climbed onto the bicycle and started pedaling.

"That's swell," said Manelli. "You hear anyone coming, gumshoe off and I'm back. I'm not tangling with that bunch. Bump you as soon as look at you. Holy cow, that Creaker! What are you here for?"

Bill told him.

Manelli was profoundly shocked. "God, that's terrible. That's really awful. Say, let me stick Al on to this creep. He'll…"

"No, thank you."

"Be just routine to Al."

"No."

"Okay, take Blackie. He's new. I'd like to try him out."

"No."

Manelli slapped the rump of the vaulting horse. "My God," he said. "Some guys are mediocre!"

"Why are you here?"

"First, I just want to wise up on the legal angles. Then this Grossi shows up and, between ourselves, I've been forced to change my plans."

"You don't like Mr. Grossi?"

"I love that hoodlum like he is a two-headed cobra." Manelli sighed. "He was a nice kid once. Prohibition ruined his outlook. You know how it is?"

"I've ridden a mile," said Bill. "Is that enough?"

Manelli looked at the indicator. "Eight to go. Could you keep going a while longer? You ever chilled a guy before?"

"No."

Manelli suddenly had a pang of nostalgia for the days of his youth. Those, despite the fear and the violence, had been the days; the days when you were alive all the time because if you were not, you were dead.

Bill looked at him. Manelli was pushing out his lower lip, picking at the stitching on the vaulting horse. The menace was still there, but it was dulled, buried under the years of good living. The Manelli of the old days had been a household bogey. Now, he had reached the top and there was nowhere else to go...except, presumably, Britain. Bill said suddenly, surprising himself, "I'd still hate to meet you alone on a dark night."

Manelli sighed. "Thanks," he said heavily.

Mrs. Carlisle and Cyril came through the north door. Cyril held several sheets of manuscript paper and was tapping the top one with a pencil. "If you cut from 'licked around the fuselage' to 'deafening explosion,'" he was saying, "you gain speed. Cut, Chloe, *cut*."

"Cut yourself," snapped Mrs. Carlisle. "For my public, the ruddy thing's got to weigh three pounds."

Grossi appeared in the garden door. He wore brief white shorts and a cap with a green-lined visor. He had pushed Bill off the captive bicycle and mounted it before anybody else had turned round. He crouched over the handlebars and began to pedal so fast that his feet were a blur. "I gotta keep in trim," he said. "Haven't I, Joe?"

"You'll need to, Tony," said Manelli shortly.

"You should do more sports, Joe. Keep your eye on a fast-moving target. You gotta have the eye, you gotta get your bird on the wing."

"Not me, Tony. I will wait until my bird is asleep, then strangle him in his nest."

Grossi vaulted off the bicycle and climbed up a rope.

At twelve o'clock, the clock over the stables struck eleven. Seff White, the only man who knew how to advance it for Summer Time, was now too old to climb the belfry. As its chimes died away, Flush and Dina came in at the north door to take the class in Grips, Knots, and Tourniquets. Dina carried a basket which contained a number of lengths of rope, a ball of string, and several brightly colored silk scarves.

Flush sat down behind the table on the dais. The students drew up chairs. Dina began to distribute equipment.

"Each item, you will notice," said Flush, "is marked with your name. They will be kept in your lockers in the cloakroom. They are not, I repeat *not*, to be taken into the house. Will you number off from the left please?" He produced his own equipment from his pocket. "As I require you in pairs, Miss Parrish has consented to be number six. Will the odd numbers take the three-strand hemp in their right hands please?"

Cyril, Grossi, and Bill took the ropes in their right hands.

"Will the even numbers raise the right wrist?"

Mrs. Carlisle, Manelli, and Dina raised their right wrists.

Flush took his own rope. It was of superior quality, much worn and marked with an embroidered name-tape. "We shall start with a simple running bowline. Watch me please." He placed the rope around his foot and tied the knot in slow motion, intoning, "Left over right, right over left, turn, twist, tuck underneath." He completed the knot, making it appear absurdly simple. "I will run through it once again." He did so, with the same mesmeric rhythm. "Will you show us, number one?"

Cyril slipped the rope deftly around Mrs. Carlisle's wrist.

"Tighten the knot please," said Flush. "Slowly, but with a pronounced final jerk."

Cyril watched the rope sink into her speckled forearm. Over her shoulder, he saw Dina's upraised hand, slim and brown and infinitely...

"Not too tight, love," said Mrs. Carlisle.

"I'm so sorry. Did I hurt you?"

Flush watched them. He realized that Cyril already knew the knot. He liked his absorbed expression, his lack of polish. He noted the full use made of the nimble, spatulate thumbs. "Thank you," he said. "Will you demonstrate, number three?"

Grossi snatched the rope. He tied the knot more quickly, more expertly than Flush had done. Manelli sat looking at the noose around his wrist. He not only knew of old how to fashion it, but he had taught it to Grossi, the brash young Grossi who had needed but a single demonstration.

"Too tight, Joe?" asked Grossi with deadly tenderness. "I wouldn't want to bruise you." He glanced down at Manelli's feet and sucked in his cheeks.

Manelli knew that he was remembering the cruel device invented by Willy Spinner. Such a knot was placed around a victim's neck and attached to his trussed ankles in such a way that it was impossible for him to relax without strangling himself. "That is ideal, Tony," he said. "Just right."

"Number five please," said Flush.

Bill passed the rope around Dina's warm wrist. He felt her eyes upon him and determined to tie his knot as nonchalantly as Grossi had done. He started with a flourish, then fumbled. The rope uncoiled and slid onto the floor. Dina smiled at him and guided his fingers. As she touched him, he felt the same shock as once he had felt in the Mediterranean when he had by mistake laid hold of a high-voltage eel.

"Now," said Flush, "will the even numbers take the four-strand flex in their left hands? We are about to perform the spritsail sheet knot, for use only when we desire to cast suspicion upon a seaman..."

Mrs. Barratt sat in the shade of the weeping willow, relaxing before lunch. Flush appeared in the door of the gymnasium. He frowned up at the sun and strode across to Mrs. Barratt. He paused by the willow, mopped his forehead and sat down.

"I'm afraid," he said, "that this time we have a troublesome batch, Naomi. Mr. Thurlow, although apparently the scout-master type, appears to be incapable of tying the simplest knot. Mr. Grossi lost his temper with a tourniquet and Mrs. Carlisle claims that all the multiples make her eyes ache." He sighed. "An unfortunate course, Naomi, most unfortunate. It appears to be even more arrogant and unmalleable than the class of the second week in April. I feel that at any moment..."

Mrs. Barratt, troubled, patted his hand. "It is this heat, Clifford. It always unsettles you."

Flush stared across the lawns to the haze trembling over the swimming pool. "Naomi," he said. "Entirely between ourselves, do you ever feel that...?"

"Now, Clifford," chided Mrs. Barratt gently. "Come. Read *The Times* obituary. We have had another success."

Flush gazed moodily at Hanger Hill. "Cooper?" he asked without interest.

"Burton. Heart failure, no flowers."

Flush closed his eyes and rubbed his forehead with the tips of his fingers. "This infernal heat," he said.

Mrs. Barratt looked at him anxiously. He had never really been himself since the Armitage affair. But, surely, after all these years of retirement...?

"And you, Naomi?" he asked. "This unfortunate combination of personalities leaves you unruffled?"

Mrs. Barratt dug her knitting needles into a flower bed. "I like the heat," she said. "I am always at my best during heat waves."

"From whose point of view?" asked Flush automatically. It was an old joke, but neither laughed.

Flush leaned back and the sun blazed red through his eyelids. *Control*, he willed himself. *Control. Breathe from the diaphragm, count ten. One, two, three, Armitage, five, six, seven, Mrs. Carlisle, Grossi, ten.* He opened his eyes, appalled.

"Clifford," said Mrs. Barratt. "You were twitching all over."

Flush ground a daisy into the turf with his heel. "Naomi," he said slowly. "I have been a model of decorum for fourteen years…"

The Creaker brushed through the drooping branches of the willow, flopped onto the ground and pulled up a handful of grass. "'Ere," he announced. "'Obson's gettin' a proper 'eadache. 'E's browned off with trainin'. 'E's creatin' to go on an 'Op."

Blackie Rodden, Manelli's new bodyguard, was in disguise again; nothing elaborate, a simple impression of a night watchman. He held his tongue between his wisdom teeth and tested out the voice. "This'll cost me me job," he whined. "They went *that* way."

Paget came out of the pantry with a bottle of gin. He tugged at his wilted collar, looked at Blackie and curled his lip.

Blackie removed half a potato from inside his left cheek, peeled a rubber wart off his nose and put it into a matchbox. He pulled one shoulder upwards and forwards and studied the dislocated effect in the mirror. "Wouldn't fool a blind baby," he remarked. "It's this heat. I got no ambition."

Paget did not answer. He was concentrating upon preparing indifferent martinis. *Warm*, he thought. *Warm, sweet, shaky.* He glanced at Blackie. The man had put on Al's raincoat and was making himself appear incredibly small. Paget sneered. He acknowledged that it would probably pass on the far side of a high counter, but in profile it was ridiculous. He put the shaker onto a tray and carried it along the passage, across the hall.

The sun flamed through the great south window. A tie had been tossed over the giant carved fir-cone at the foot of the banisters. A hand-painted tie. Paget clenched his teeth. He went out onto the terrace thinking about the earl. *We had our little jokes, sir. Do you remember saying, sir, "You look very jovial, Paget. What's wrong?"*

He stepped from the shadow and the heat surged around him. The students were down by the swimming pool. Crossing the rose garden, Paget noticed with a tightening of the lips that Al and Barker, who should have been the far side of the green baize, were playing tennis with squash racquets. Mr. Grossi's bodyguard was crouching over a box of tennis balls, doing something to them with a nail file.

"Stop that, men," said Paget, passing. They took no notice of him.

"I said *stop* that," said Paget.

"Aw, go climb up your leg," said Al.

Paget walked away, trembling. He clenched his hands on the tray and a little martini squirted from the nose of the shaker. In front of him, the pool was blinding blue. He smelt the chlorine thirty yards away. He laid the tray on the diving board and withdrew, straightening his old back as he passed the tennis court, walking proudly as if he had a priceless vase balanced on his head.

Manelli was floating in the pool on a rubber mattress. He wore swimming shorts with flying fish painted on them and there was a cylinder of cigar ash wedged among the hairs on his chest. He berthed the mattress at the side of the pool and helped himself to a forbidden martini. He took a handful of olives and paddled away again. He found it difficult to hold the cigar, the olives and the martini in one hand, so he dunked the cigar in the water and held the glass between his knees while he ate the olives. Where were the staff? he wondered. What did they talk about when they were alone? Was it possible that the whole outfit was an expensive fraud? They had all been acquitted, hadn't they? Was it so unreasonable to sup pose that one or more of them were impostors? The thought smote him—the thought which had recurred as a nightmare throughout his adolescence and ricocheted around his rise to power—*Am I, somehow, being taken for a sucker?* And the old half-forgotten answer followed automatically, *If I am, somebody's going to be sorry, somebody's going to be dead.* He looked around aggressively and met Grossi's eyes.

Grossi was fooling about under the copper beech for Dina's benefit. He ran around the tree, sprang at a branch and pulled himself up until his chin was among the red leaves. He flicked his legs upwards and swarmed along the branch, running about in the tree, making loud jungle noises and scratching himself, pretending to be a monkey.

Manelli watched him. Perhaps, he thought, Grossi was some superintelligent animal; perhaps when Manelli killed him, the postmortem would prove that it had not been a capital offense.

Bill, lying on his stomach at the side of the pool, was also watching Grossi. *Fall down*, he willed him. *Fall down and break your bloody neck.*

From beneath a striped umbrella, Cyril was watching Dina. *She has exquisite legs*, he thought. *Her hair is almost the color of mine. Together, we would be quite spectacular.*

Mrs. Carlisle, sitting beside him, took off her smoked glasses and polished them vigorously. "Don't *stare*, angel," she said with dangerous calm. "It's so rude." She leaned forward to pinch him and her cigarette case fell off her knees.

The sun appeared to pause in the white sky directly over the pool. It cast squat, still shadows beneath the cedars as the warning gong echoed from the house and the five students separated apathetically to prepare themselves for lunch. The burning cyclops eye glared at them through the dining room windows; lit with equal impartiality the glitter of Dina's hair as she refused a slab of boiled cod masked in anchovy sauce and the greenish tinge under Paget's eyes as he circled the table pouring a rough Algerian hock.

A mile and a half away, the sun glowed red on the foil of a bottle of mead in the office of William White, the estate agent. The bottle was in its customary place in the wastepaper basket and had been, as time passed that day, a refresher at eleven, a cocktail at twelve, an aperitif at one and, now that the cheese sandwich was eaten, became a liqueur.

An hour later, the sun infiltrated stealthily across the wooden floor of the gymnasium as Mrs. Barratt instructed the five students in Anatomy. This, she explained, was closely allied to Manual Grips. As only Bill, Mrs. Carlisle and Cyril were taking the subject in full, she intended to confine herself that afternoon to head, neck and shoulders with the accent, obviously, on the neck. The sun flashed on her heavy gold wedding rings as she demonstrated a grip on the platysma of a life-sized papier mâché model. It warmed the backs of Manelli's hairy hands as he pressed a manicured thumb into the glazed sternocleido mastoid. It threw quick shadows around Grossi's grass-stained plimsolls as, unaffected by the heat, he leaped into the attack and expertly strangled the model sideways. It shone on Bill's left foot as he uncertainly laid hold of the superior vena cava.

Mrs. Barratt clicked her tongue. "I said the *carotids*, Mr. Thurlow." She raised her hands as if holding an invisible cantaloupe and Bill took an involuntary step backwards. "Now watch closely. First and second finger on the external jugular. So. Thumb on the internal jugular. So. Small finger on the subclavian, third finger falling comfortably onto the lymph nodes. Will you try it please, Mrs. Carlisle?"

Mrs. Carlisle jumped. She had been grinding her teeth, watching Dina smiling up at Cyril, touching his cheek and explaining that it was his buccinator. She stepped forward and seized the neck of the model. *Bitch*, she thought, glaring at Dina. *Damn him, damn him, goddamn him, I could kill her.*

"Splendid," said Mrs. Barratt. "That would have choked a gorilla."

The Jujitsu class took place on a mattress on the lawn. It was soon apparent that Grossi knew as much about the art as any Japanese samurai. Even as Mrs. Barratt was rolling up her sleeves and removing her rings, he grabbed Manelli, whirled him around and hurled him onto the mattress. Manelli sat up. His face was dark with rage. For an instant, his eyes were as inscrutable as those in his police portraits. Then he settled his lapels and said softly, "You will regret that, Tony." Grossi sneered and reached for him.

Mrs. Barratt took the outstretched hand, shook her head and without visible effort jerked Grossi onto his knees. "Let us always remember, ladies and gentlemen," she said, "that the aim of judo is not to kill but merely to incapacitate temporarily."

Grossi looked up at her. "You're breaking my ulna," he pointed out impassively.

Mrs. Barratt released him. "As you are already on your knees, Mr. Grossi, will you please remove the right shoe? I shall demonstrate a simple toehold. The main object of this is to persuade an unwilling Intended into a cooperative frame of mind." She smiled faintly. "Mr. Flush avers that after ten minutes at full pressure he would willingly submit to all his attacker's intentions and die smiling."

The clock over the stables struck three.

Half an hour later, the Colonel, taking Small Arms and Ballistics in the orchard, realized that he was hopelessly outclassed by Manelli and Grossi. The two mobsters had accepted their weapons in thoughtful silence, looked them over critically, squinted down the barrels and casually peppered the red heart on the man-shaped target.

The Colonel, trying to regain his prestige, threw a pear into the air and missed it with his Springfield.

Grossi accepted the challenge and drilled an apple with a Steyr. Manelli, firing from the hip, brought down a plum and invited the Colonel to shoot it on the ground. The Colonel, his blood up, screwed a telescopic lens onto the Springfield and braced himself against a tree.

Bill, Cyril and Mrs. Carlisle stood by holding their weapons nervously, delighted to have been forgotten.

The Springfield spat. The explosion echoed around the Barrows. The Colonel hurried forward to inspect the plum.

"Watch this, Joe," said Grossi. "See that garage wall?"

"Hundred yards, Tony. Any old lush can shoot a wall."

Grossi took a Schmeisser submachine-gun from the tray of firearms. He adjusted the large banana-shaped clip, bent down and fired three short bursts between his legs. Mrs. Carlisle clapped her hands over her ears and screamed. Grossi and Manelli set out side by side for the wall. Standing in the long grass, Manelli pursed his lips and nodded. Perforated in the wooden planks before him, a foot high and in a Runic script were the letters JOE.

"'Ot," observed Hobson at quarter past four.

"Shuddup," said the Creaker, listlessly searching through his toolchest for a pair of shears.

Hobson rose from the workbench. "*Wot* was that again?"

"Shuddup."

"Now look, cock," said Hobson, pointing a stubby finger. "Fer yer own good, don't argue wit' me. That's all. I beg yer not to argue wit' me."

"Shuddup."

"*A*ouw," said Hobson, his heavy face working. "So it's nasty, is it? I wouldn't talk to me like that, cock, not if I was you."

"Well, you ain't," said the Creaker. "An' never will be."

"Ho," said Hobson, advancing one pace and snatching up a bench. "Witty, is it? I don't want to 'ave to smear you all over the floor, cock, but enough's enough."

The Creaker found the shears and limped over to his pupil. "You got the right spirit, boy," he said happily.

Hobson stared at him for a long moment, then turned away, his overdeveloped shoulders slumping. "I 'pologize," he said. "I don't know wot gets into me."

"'S this bleedin' 'eat," said the Creaker.

"I'm like a tiger sometimes, I am honest."

"That's a boy," said the Creaker.

In the kitchen, the heat was appalling.

"'Oo wants a cuppa char?" asked Barker, throwing a dish-cloth at the smoking range.

"*Char*," sneered Blackie Rodden. He looked into the mirror, aimlessly practicing the "Asiatic Eye."

"Wat's wrong with char?" demanded Barker, instantly aggressive.

"Wat long wiff loo, flend?" inquired Blackie in a ludicrous imitation of an Asiatic voice.

"Aw, shuttup," said Grossi's bodyguard. "It's too hot."

There was a slight pause. Barker and Blackie turned on him slowly. Al, Manelli's chauffeur, stood up and stretched. "So he finds it hot," he remarked. "Imagine that."

"Okay," snarled Grossi's bodyguard. "It's freezing."

"You're a liar," said Al.

"You're calling me a liar?"

"Sure. You're a liar."

"Okay, I'm a liar."

"Yeah. That's what I said."

"You trying to start something? Just say. Whatever it is, I'll finish it."

Al laughed bitterly. "This two-bit farmer is threatening *me*! How do you like that?"

Grossi's bodyguard stood up and dropped his cigarette into Barker's cup of tea. "Watch your big mouth, brother," he said gently.

"*When* you've finished with my char," said Barker, also standing up.

Grossi's bodyguard took off his watch and laid it on the table. "Anybody takes one step forward, I'll tear his ass off."

Al took off his jacket and hung it over the back of a chair. Blackie fitted a spoon between his third and fourth fingers and clenched his right fist. Barker picked up a heavy skillet and weighed it in his hand. The three spread out and advanced upon Grossi's bodyguard from different directions.

A mile and a half away, Mr. White's latest client lay back in his chair and flapped a newspaper at himself. "Is Krunte Abbas *always* as hot as this in the summer?"

"Yes," said Mr. White. He glanced at the clock. The Wassail had been open for three minutes. Mr. White drummed his fingers on the axe-head which he used as a paperweight. "Now look, sir," he growled. "Either you intend to buy this heap of dry rot, or you don't. Which is it? I'm going home now."

At quarter to six, Flush woke on the couch in his dressing room. He lay still, staring up at a patch of discoloration on the ceiling. The dream was still vivid. Ingrid Larsen, her lovely face puckered with disapproval, floated towards him with a stopwatch in her hand. "Fourteen years," she said. "Fifteen years, sixteen years…"

Flush pulled at the lobe of his ear. It seemed to be hotter than ever. He went into his bathroom and turned on the cold shower. Three drops fell and lay brownly at the bottom of the bath. Either the cistern was leaking again or some madman had turned off the water. Flush bit his lip, dressed and went downstairs to conduct the class upon Electricity.

He was late. The students were already assembled in the outhouse near the garages. This was entirely constructed of asbestos in case of accidents. It contained a comprehensive range of electrical gadgets and was powered by a small dynamo.

The Colonel, who normally conducted the practical experiments, had not waited for Flush but had started upon the preliminary lecture. He was still ruffled by his humiliating experience in the orchard and was not doing justice to his subject.

"Much neglected," he was saying. "Domestic, universal, still baffles Einstein." He flipped a switch and stood motionless as if listening. There was complete silence. The class watched him uneasily. Twenty seconds later, an electric toaster on the far side of the room flung forth a piece of toast. "Gulla gulla," said the Colonel vaguely. "Now consider breakfast." He strolled over to the toaster, picked up a steel rod and applied it. There was a loud crack and a forked blue flash. "Electric kettles," said the Colonel. "Flatirons, television, radio, electric razors, radiators, stoves, vacuum cleaners, moist switches, burglar alarms, so on. Endless. Two vital points, ladies and gentlemen. Remember Intended may be revived up to four hours after your experiment. And," he tapped the steel rod on a broken telephone, emphasizing his point with a shower of sparks, "*earth yourself.* Form habit during slack period wearing rubber soles *always.* Thurlow, pass me that reading lamp, sir."

Bill looked down at his sturdy brogues. "I'm not earthed," he objected.

"Good," said the Colonel. He nodded approvingly, looking around at the class. "See the danger? Two-forty volts."

Flush strode over to the blackboard and picked up a piece of chalk. He wrote in large letters $2K + 2H2O = 2KOH + H2$. He turned away, pulled on a pair of Wellington boots and some heavy rubber gloves. "And now, ladies and gentlemen," he said. "Let us go outside and consider dynamos and lightning."

As the shadow of Hanger Hill slid over the whole valley, Barker slopped a bright pink blancmange onto a plate and tried to ignore the dogfight argument still in progress between Grossi's bodyguard, Al and Blackie. They were now discussing which was to escort the only girl in the valley who was not downright hideous onto the tumuli that night. The fact that this girl, the telephone operator in Poxwell Regis, had for some years had an understanding with Barker, did not interest them; nor did the fact that she had a hacking cough.

"That's *my* girl," said Barker for the ninth time. They took no notice of him.

An hour later, Paget appeared to fetch the after-dinner coffee. Seeing that it was not prepared, he looked about him.

Barker was holding a bloody handkerchief to his nose. Al's left eye was closing fast and his shirt was slit across the back. Blackie was lying on the floor, clutching his stomach and groaning. Grossi's bodyguard, apparently unharmed, was sitting on the table, cleaning his nails with the handle of a teaspoon.

Bill stood at a loss in the dark passage outside the dining room. He had planned to invite Dina to stroll with him in the grounds, but she was playing ping pong with Cyril. He stalked angrily across the hall, through the front door and into the sultry night. He sat down on the steps and glared around the garden, hating Cyril.

Twenty yards away, Mrs. Carlisle quivered in a deck chair on the terrace, thinking graphically about what she would like to do to Dina. Half an hour later, her thoughts were so vivid that her hands had become claws. When Cyril sloped through the French windows, she leaped forward in her chair and opened her mouth to scream at him.

"Chloe," said Cyril quickly. "She *asked* me to play. It was impossible to refuse without being flagrantly rude."

Mrs. Carlisle leaned back in her chair. "Oh, I think you were very polite dearest," she said brightly. "You accepted with such alacrity." She plucked a trailing branch of jasmine and started to rip off the leaves. "Come, angel," she said. "If you are infatuated with this murderess…"

Cyril raised his voice. "I shall attend this lecture in the library. Are you coming?"

Mrs. Carlisle laughed pluckily. "No, no," she said. "I must work. *Somebody's* got to earn our living."

Manelli walked into Grossi's bedroom without knocking.

Grossi, Al, Blackie and Barker were gathered around a small table playing poker. Al and Blackie, startled, sprang up at once. Seeing that the intruder was their employer, they sat down sheepishly, knowing that their acceptance of Grossi's hospitality was not strictly ethical. Grossi sat still, his hand nonchalantly in his empty dressing-gown pocket. He thought fast. His own bodyguard had deserted him for an assignation in Poxwell Regis. He had not yet attempted to corrupt Al and Blackie and they were presumably loyal. Was this a carefully planned chill? If so, Grossi was alone and outnumbered. In the old days, back in the Loop, he would have instantly shot out the light. Now, feeling curiously large without his automatic, he hooked his leg around the table in case of trouble and waited.

Manelli stood for a moment in the doorway with half-closed eyes. Then he blew cigar smoke up his nostrils, moved forward and drew up a chair. "Deal me in," he ordered.

Grossi plucked the cigarette from between his lips, dropped it on the carpet and put his foot on it. He picked up the cards. He dealt without taking his eyes off Manelli. He realized suddenly why the other was there; why he would sit in on all such sessions of this game which he had never enjoyed. He knew that from now on, Manelli would never be far away…

"Quit dealing seconds," said Manelli. He sounded bored.

Grossi gathered up the cards without comment. As he began to deal again, he noted his lack of anger. In the old days, such a challenge would have touched off a free fight, probably involved shooting it out until the first squeal of the sirens. Now it was different. There was more at stake.

In the west wing, Hobson lumbered up and down his room, gnawing at a button on the sleeve of his nightshirt. "Look, cock," he said. "I pulled up, sawed up an' chopped kindlin' out o' fourteen big trees. I eaten dozen eggs an' five pounds o' steak every day fer a week. I run 'undreds an' 'undreds o' miles an' I dug up a Norman bone orchard. I'm not bein' unreasonable, cock." He smashed a vast fist against the wall. "I'm just askin' fer a bit o' *practice*." The button broke in half. Hobson spat the pieces onto the floor and changed his tactics. "Now you're fair, tosh," he said persuasively. "Soon as I saw you, I knew you was a chap after me own 'eart. Now see 'ere, why don't we...?"

"'S against the flamin' rules," said the Creaker morosely.

In the library, Cyril was the only student to attend Flush's lecture on Murder and the Classics. At any other time, he would have been fascinated by such a subject, but now he found it almost impossible to concentrate.

Flush's pleasant voice droned on "...was Aristophanes...into Attica in the sixth century B.C....Susarion, Sophron...nucleus of the deathblow to the tragedy...Oedipus...Lear, Othello... Broadmoor...the McNaghten Rules...Poe, de Quincey... listening, Cyril?"

Cyril started.

Flush shuffled his notes together. "I fear that I am wasting your time," he said coldly. "What is it that so exercises you?"

Cyril coughed. "Well," he admitted. "As a matter of fact, I was thinking of Chloe."

Flush chose to misunderstand him. "Ah, Longus. Personally, I prefer the George Moore translation."

"I meant Chloe Carlisle."

Flush sighed. He rose and strolled over to the window. "I have been expecting you to approach me," he said, depressed. "I must tell you that I deplore your motives and that in any event I cannot help you until at least six months after the first calamity."

Cyril sat appalled. "No, no," he protested loudly. He added, a full five seconds too late, "I don't know what you mean."

Flush lit a cigar. He said nothing.

"I'm extremely fond of her," said Cyril indignantly.

Flush gazed out at the darkening sky. "But," he prompted, suddenly exasperated, "her intolerable jealousy drives you to distraction. I cannot imagine what a hell upon earth your life has been during the past…how many years?"

"Two. Really, I must…"

"She is revoltingly, cruelly mean with money. She is as rich as Croesus, yet she delights in making you beg for every penny. She humiliates you in restaurants. She denies you the barest necessities. She will not even allow you to use her husband's car. You have always been sensitive, due to an unhappy childhood. I cannot even begin to imagine what her deliberately brutal and malicious treatment has done to your delicate morale. She does not understand you. At one time, although you do not wish to boast, you might have been a considerable poet; now, in return for your niggardly keep, she forces you to dissipate your youth and your inspiration upon her own third-rate talent. Because she has altered her will in your favor, she imagines that she is entitled to treat you as an editorial Pekingese. You have your pride. Anything else?"

Cyril lay in his chair, incapable of movement. He knew that, in order to vindicate himself, he should at least hit Flush. But his tutor was looking out of the window and one could not with decency hit a man in the back of the neck. He knew that he must say something. It was now too late for a furious denial. Perhaps an admission, casual, worldly, as man to man? A contemptuous laugh? A solicitous pat on the shoulder, fearing for the man's sanity?

Cyril stretched his legs. "Aren't you a monster?" he said gaily. "I suppose one day somebody will bump you off."

In the stifling heat of the library, the Colonel was doing the accounts. Sighing, he placed an elastic band around the new students' checks, wondering as always whether any of them were forgeries. "Be relieved when this course is over," he remarked. "Troublemakers."

Mrs. Barratt rolled up her knitting. "I would feel happier if Clifford were himself."

"Bad blood," said the Colonel, wiping his pen on the end of his tie. "Never saw so many yellow streaks. Herd of zebras. Don't like it." He put the checks into a drawer. "Zebras," he muttered. "Chancy beasts. Hollow teeth."

Mrs. Barratt looked suspiciously at his glass. It was empty.

"Bit windy self," confided the Colonel. He wandered in the direction of the whisky. "Take Clifford. Commander slacks, troops play up. Mutiny, bloodshed, pity." He splashed whisky into his glass. "This course, nasty type of recruit, not an officer among them. Iron hand in velvet glove, Naomi. Clifford's not pulling his weight, absolutely not." He squirted soda down the side of his glass. "Only one thing to do prevent mutiny. Preventive measures, make an example of the sepoys."

"Between ourselves," murmured Mrs. Barratt, "I sometimes wish that Clifford had undertaken Mr. Armitage. That, let us face it, was when the rot set in."

The Colonel drank deeply. "Never fear," he said. "Rely on me. Prevented dozens of uprisings."

Mrs. Barratt looked at him doubtfully. "What do you intend to do?" she asked.

"First sign of trouble," said the Colonel, draining his glass, "fire over their heads. Second sign of trouble, make an example of a sepoy."

The second day of the course, the day always dreaded by the staff, drew to its oppressive close. Paget's soundless, painful feet padded around the rambling house. Slowly, he moved from window to window, locking out the night, locking in ten murderers and four homicidal students. Not for the first time, he wondered whether he, Matron, and Barker would ever leave the Manor alive.

He shook his head mournfully. He went upstairs and along the ill-lit corridor. As he paused to close the window on the landing, Mrs. Carlisle put her head around her bedroom door. Her expression was so murderous that Paget lowered his eyes.

"Have you seen Mr. Cyril?" she demanded. Her face shone eerily with cold cream.

Although Paget had summed up Cyril and knew that, at such an hour, it was the last place where he was likely to be, he said with gentle malice, "He is probably in his own room, madam."

Mrs. Carlisle bit her lip. She retired into her room and slammed the door. She trapped the sash of her negligee and for a moment Paget stood staring at the triangle of gray lace. He saw it jerk as Mrs. Carlisle tried to free it from the far side of the door. Fascinated, Paget saw that it had become entangled upon the metal surrounding the keyhole. He could hear Mrs. Carlisle breathing. Suddenly, he had the impression that she was watching him through the keyhole. Paget held his breath. The breathing on the far side of the door had also stopped. The triangle of lace was still. In the thread of light under the door, Paget saw a shadow and knew that Mrs. Carlisle stood there, waiting for him to go away. In case she was still watching him, he nodded briefly at the keyhole, then inched backwards until he reckoned that she could no longer see him. He crept silently down the corridor. As he reached the corner, he heard the door behind him open. Against his will, he looked back. But the triangle of gray lace had vanished. Paget nodded and turned the corner.

There was a loud and acrimonious argument in progress in Mr. Grossi's room. Shocked to the core of his being, Paget heard Al, who had no right whatever to be in a student's room, roar, "You lousy junkie! Since when do you take eight cards?" There was a crash, a thud, the tinkle of breaking glass. Paget heard Manelli asking somebody to go and climb a tree.

He closed his eyes and passed on.

The door next to Grossi's opened. Mr. Thurlow marched into the corridor in his pajamas. His hands were clenched and his mouth open to shout something. He saw Paget, swallowed, said "Good evening," and went back into his room.

Turning the corner towards the servants' quarters, Paget heard Hobson baying in the west wing. He had stopped and was massaging his eyeballs when Mr. Grossi's bodyguard cannoned into him.

"Get outa my way, egghead," snapped the American. His collar hung open and he had grass in his hair. "Okay, okay," he said aggressively. "I been on them tumuli. So what? Anybody else starts beefing, I'll bust 'em right on the nose."

Paget stood still, his face frozen with disgust. "Go to your quarters," he said.

"Drop dead," said Grossi's bodyguard. He bounded down the passage towards Grossi's room, slapping the walls with an open hand and whistling.

Paget stumbled into his small room and closed the door. Without turning on the light, he felt his way across the linoleum and leaned out of the window, breathing the quiet night. But there was no breath of wind and the hot dark air did not soothe him.

With trembling hands he turned on the light. He looked at himself in his cracked shaving mirror. *Paget*, he told his gray-faced image, *you are not afraid. The heat has upset you. You are not really afraid.*

He rallied. Head slightly on one side, he smiled at himself in the mirror. For a moment, he stared. Then, profoundly disturbed, he threw the mirror out of the window and admitted to himself that for the first time in his life he was afraid.

Chapter Seven

The morning of the third day of the course dawned still and hot. Long before the sun had penetrated the deep valley, the heat quivered over Dankry. The trees drooped motionless against the bright threat of the sky. The glassy surface of the swimming pool reflected a solitary curlew circling lazily, high in the sun. The petals of the wilting roses scattered and fell, as Mrs. Barratt snipped with her secateurs.

Walking back to the house, she hummed to herself, refusing to admit that she felt an absurd sense of reprieve. She had heard the uproar in Grossi's room in the early hours of the morning, and had concluded that only one of the Americans would appear for breakfast. But although they were clearly suffering from hangovers, both were present and apparently unharmed.

In the hall, she stood for a moment waiting for her eyes to become attuned to the gloom after the bright sky. She handed her basket of roses to Paget and told him to throw them away as they were heavy with greenfly. She slipped the secateurs into her pocket and hurried along the dark corridor towards the laboratory. Sighing, she realized that she was not in the mood for Forensic Medicine. Could she, just for once, skip the introductory discourse upon the primitive methods of the Borgias? Could she, just for once, confine herself to Narcotic and Convulsant? Need she, that glorious morning, go into Irritant and Corrosive?

The smell of disinfectant and formaldehyde greeted her at the bend in the passage. She pushed open the white-painted door and paused on the threshold.

Manelli and Grossi, the only students interested in poison, had already arrived. Manelli was sitting behind the scales absently weighing a cigar. Grossi was standing at the window examining a glass jar of curare. Mrs. Barratt noted the label and raised her eyebrows.

"Okay," said Grossi quickly. "I picked it up is all. I know it's comical."

Mrs. Barratt collected bottles of sulphuric acid, hydrochloric acid, nitric acid, prussic acid and vinegar. She placed these on the table with a Bunsen burner, a crucible, a retort and a six-inch square of carpet. "Curare," she remarked, "is no longer ludicrous. We must never forget that as soon as a poison is used by the medical profession as an anaesthetic, we too can take it seriously. Now, tell me, what do you know of our subject?"

Manelli glanced at Grossi. "I know most of the narcotics," he said casually. "I'm familiar with chloroform, ether, opium, chloral and henbane."

Grossi stiffened. He had never favored poison. He suspected that Manelli had not done so either, but had prepared a list with the intention of securing a psychological advantage. He congratulated himself that he too had had foresight. "Well," he admitted with a nice reluctance. "I know most of the Irritants. Arsenic, the oxalic group, sugar of lead and so on."

Manelli curled his lip. "Well, of course, any kid knows *that* stuff," he said.

Grossi was annoyed. Before he could curb himself, he had said explosively, "I know mercury, antimony, digitalis, trional, strychnine, fungi, yew, foxglove, monkshood, hemlock, privet, laburnum seed and mountain ash."

Manelli lit a cigar and blew smoke towards the ceiling. "Quite a guy," he said politely. "Remind me never to meet you in a forest."

"Let us not bicker," said Mrs. Barratt gently. She opened her notebook. "Let us start right on our own doorstep. Will you write down Tinned Meat, Shellfish and Sausages?"

The Creaker was sitting on a rustic bench outside the summerhouse. He was eating milk chocolates and idly throwing horseshoes up at the weathervane. As he saw Bill approaching to report for his class, he tossed up five at once, then rose and scratched himself.

"Yore late," he growled. "They're all late for me. Psychological, see."

Bill put his hands into his pockets. He did not want to go alone into the summerhouse with this monstrous cripple.

The Creaker guffawed. "Windy?" he asked. "'S orright. I don't turn yer stummick yet. First lesson's only clumsy."

Cyril draped himself over the bonnet of Grossi's fabulous Allard and lit a cigarette. The Colonel had removed one of the bucket seats from his Bugatti and Mrs. Carlisle sat in it, nervously picking at her nail varnish.

"Where's that damn murderer?" she demanded. "He's late."

It was exactly ten o'clock. The clock over the stables struck nine and Flush appeared in the garage door silhouetted against the light. He carried a notebook, a large plan of Ned Carlisle's mews garage, a hammer and a box of nails.

The Colonel crawled from the repair pit beneath his car and wiped his hands on his dungarees. "Always play the part of the Intended in these rehearsals," he explained. He added vaguely, "Miscast."

Mrs. Carlisle looked at him. Appalled, she realized that he was in fact much the same build as her husband.

"We are about to practice what is known here as Operation Tough Luck," said Flush.

"Said we were going to do Amen," protested the Colonel. "Spent nearly an hour fouling up exhaust. Never briefed properly these days." He glared at Flush, wandered over to a littered bench, picked up a primitive crash helmet and dusted it.

"Now," said Flush, "from the point of view of the coroner, the Intended has returned his car to the garage after an evening of overindulgence."

"He's invited to a Medical Dinner on fourth September," offered Cyril.

Flush looked at Mrs. Carlisle. "You are still unable to conquer your prejudice against suicide?"

"No," said Mrs. Carlisle loudly.

"She means yes," said Cyril helpfully.

Flush sighed. He could rouse no interest in Ned Carlisle's sudden death. He realized, horrified, that he did not much care if the stockbroker lived for years. He mopped his forehead. "A pity," he said coldly. "Accidents are considerably more tedious to construct." He glanced at his notes, musing that Tough Luck had already been practiced eight times and twice in London. Normally, routines were scrapped in any continent where six successful experiments had taken place. He knew that Tough Luck should not be tried again until at least December, but he could not be bothered to return to the house for the electric radiator which played so important a role in Amen. "The Intended," he said, noting and trying to suppress the singsong quality in his voice, "was in high spirits. He disembarked from his car, bent to inspect some slight damage to…" Flush consulted the plan. "To the right rear wheel, straightened up, stunned himself on the gas meter, fell obliquely and, so as to leave nothing to chance…"

"Can't we just shoot him?" pleaded Mrs. Carlisle. She sat tearing a cigarette to small pieces.

Flush ignored her. He moved over to Cyril and murmured in his ear.

"I see," said Cyril. He nodded.

"Do you also see the flaw in the sequence of events?"

"Yes," said Cyril instantly. "The light."

"Good. What else?"

"The doors."

"Unimportant. We have never had a comment yet."

"Presumably, I'm installed. How do I get in?"

"Mrs. Carlisle will have deposited you earlier in the day. I'm afraid that you will have a long wait."

"I'll take sandwiches and coffee." Cyril stiffened suddenly. *"How do I get out?"*

"There's no point in losing your temper already," said Mrs. Carlisle.

"You, madam," said Flush, "will of course have a comprehensive alibi for the period in question." He concealed a smile, remembering one overanxious graduate who had broken his leg and spent the danger hours in hospital and plaster of Paris. "The following morning *at an hour when the mews is full of witnesses,* you will be observed hurrying towards the garage. To your surprise, the garage doors will be improperly closed. You will enter, count three, scream. You will leap into the car, back out, damage a neighboring dustbin if there is one available, and drive wildly to the nearest police station."

Flush tapped Mrs. Carlisle on the shoulder. "Will you scream please?"

"Now?"

"If you please."

Mrs. Carlisle cleared her throat and screamed without conviction.

Flush clicked his tongue. "You will give up smoking for a month before the catastrophe and gargle night and morning. It is essential to achieve resonance."

"What about me?" said Cyril.

"You, my friend, will be in the back of the car adequately

concealed. You will descend in some deserted road or busy shopping center and will make your way immediately to your prearranged alibi. This, at first sight, will be highly unsatisfactory. Later, under duress, you will admit that the honor of a lady is involved. Your reticence will have been exemplary, your lack of concern disarming."

"*What* lady?" snapped Mrs. Carlisle.

"I recommend a certain Miss Murray. She is a member of my organization, reasonable and very reliable." He coughed. "Now, shall we consider technique?"

The Colonel handed Cyril a pair of cotton gloves and donned the crash helmet. He climbed into his Bugatti. Struck by a sudden thought, he paused. "Going to puncture the tire?"

Flush put his notebook into his pocket. "I shall probably indicate an incision."

The Colonel heaved himself out of the Bugatti and slid behind the wheel of Grossi's Allard. He tossed away his cigarette, laid one foot on the running board, leaned forward as if about to get out of the car and waited.

Flush advanced. "Cyril," he instructed. "Stand *here* please. Place your feet so. Are you relaxed and comfortable?"

Cyril swayed to and fro on his toes, testing the stance. "Not terribly," he said: "I once broke my right ankle."

"How can you be so selfish?" said Mrs. Carlisle, tugging at the fringe on her scarf.

Flush turned his back on her, drumming his fingers on the mudguard of the Allard. He stared up at the cobwebs among the rafters. A beam of light through a broken slate transformed them into a curtain of iridescent gauze. Behind it, for an instant, a ghostly Ingrid Larsen seemed to toss her jaunty head. "Stun her, my dear," she seemed to breathe. "You're such an old slow-coach." Flush clenched his hands and whirled upon Mrs. Carlisle.

The Colonel, alarmed by his expression, leapt up. "*Duck*, madam," he shouted. "*Duck!*"

Flush stared at him. "Are you mad?" he demanded icily. "Kindly return to your stance immediately. Cyril, I want you to take one pace forward and seize the Colonel by the anterior brachial... *thus.*"

Half an hour later, the students were gathered in the library. The room was darkened. The heavy curtains had been drawn against the morning light and over the portrait of the man in a silver helmet hung a large white screen. Facing it was a small projector flanked by several dusty boxes of glass slides.

The door opened and Flush strode into the room carrying a billiards cue. The Colonel was behind him examining a type-written list on a sheet of paper.

"Take your seats facing the screen, please," said Flush. "We are about to test our powers of observation and deduction. The Colonel will project onto the screen reproductions of the scenes of various *causes célèbres*. I shall ask you in rotation to discuss errors, in some cases flagrant errors, made by the Operators. We are ready, Colonel."

The Colonel turned off the lights. Bill, who was nearest to the door, saw the Creaker enter stealthily, escorting Hobson. The uncouth fellow was piloted into a corner and Bill heard the Creaker telling him that he was not to speak and that he was to leave the room before the lights were turned on.

The Colonel tinkered with the projector. A beam of light sprang across the room, hovered on a bowl of nasturtiums, skidded sideways and settled onto the screen. The Colonel grunted, selected a glass slide and slipped it into the stereopticon.

On the screen appeared a blazing armchair with a handbag and a pair of stockings on the seat.

Flush clicked his tongue impatiently. "I did not order Fox, Colonel," he snapped. "I distinctly told you that we would commence with Ruxton."

"Sorry," said the Colonel. "Not my fault. Put Ruxton in number fifty-eight, he's gone. Not here."

Flush tapped the billiards cue on a table. "We are waiting," he said coldly.

Muttering, the Colonel removed the slide and inserted another. Puzzled, he looked upon the interior of a dismal cellar, one corner of which was bricked up in a highly suggestive manner.

"Oh, *really*," grated Flush. "Where is *Ruxton*?" He slapped himself lightly in the forehead. "I ordered none of these colonial fol-de-rols." The Colonel began to root among the boxes. "Leave it, for God's sake, man." Flush struck the screen with the billiards cue. "Cyril?"

"*Madness*," said Cyril.

Flush nodded. "Will you tell us why, please?"

"God, these guys have patience," remarked Grossi.

"It's so jolly *obvious*," said Bill.

"The beast," said Mrs. Carlisle. "He could at least have made her look more like a disused chimney," she added shakily.

"You English," said Manelli, disgusted.

Flush peered at the shadowy outlines of his pupils. He was invariably fascinated by this section of the course. Protected by the gloom, the students seemed psychologically to expand, to loosen the rein on the demon which must necessarily be in them all. This was the moment, more than any other, when he classified them as Likely-to-Succeed, Doubtful, and Doomed. This was the moment, if ever, when they were off their guard and gave themselves away. He frowned across the months at the Italian specialist who had lashed himself into a fury when confronted with the same scene at the poor quality of the cement. "Can none of you," he asked, "spot the vital weakness?"

"Naturally," said Cyril. "The damp course."

"Thank you." Flush snapped his fingers. "Next please, Colonel."

The Colonel was still searching for Ruxton. Unable to find him, he substituted a bleary snowscape. A gutted and still smoking house lay in the background; in the foreground a trail of footprints led to the wreckage and disappeared into it. Otherwise, the snow lay around unbroken. In the center of the ruins were two downward-pointing arrows.

"Triangle case," explained the Colonel. "Husband, wife, other man."

"How awful," said Mrs. Carlisle. "Is it something to do with skis?"

"How about the petrol cans?" asked Bill.

"If you get a joint good and soused," said Grossi, "you can touch it off from a hundred yards with a Very pistol."

"Not for me," said Manelli. "I don't tangle with insurance claims, never."

"Well, I suppose he *meant* well," began Cyril.

"She," corrected the Colonel. "She was fed up with both of them."

"Oh?" Cyril was interested. "Where did they find the boots?"

"Good." Flush looked thoughtfully at Cyril. "Very good." He tapped the footprint in the foreground. "Let this be a lesson to us never under any circumstances whatever to try anything so fancy as walking backwards, particularly in snow, mud or sand. Now may we have Ruxton please, Colonel?"

"Tell you he's not here, sir," said the Colonel angrily.

"Find him."

"Got Smith here."

"*Ruxton.*"

The Colonel lost his temper. He snatched a slide at random and crammed it into the projector.

The screen returned its ghastly impact.

Five of the students sprang to their feet. A chair fell with a crash. Flush swore.

Mrs. Carlisle screamed.

"Dina!" shouted Bill. "Don't look!"

"My God," said Cyril, awed.

"Holy cow!" said Grossi and Manelli simultaneously.

"Lovely grub," said Hobson enthusiastically. "Just the job."

"Can't understand it," mumbled the Colonel. "Wrong box altogether. Staff only. Sorry."

Chapter Eight

At eleven o'clock, Paget carried a tray of coffee onto the terrace and set it down on the wrought iron table. He had heard the scream from the library and, although such an occurrence was not unusual, the atmosphere of this course was so tense that he counted the students quickly. Seeing that all were present and uninjured, he looked at them more closely. The five faces were expressionless, each silent, each withdrawn into his own thoughts. Paget sneered at their profiles and withdrew.

The coffee stood cooling on the table. A wasp settled languidly on the sugar. The silence had become so prolonged that nobody cared to break it.

Mrs. Carlisle's main preoccupation was that she had placed herself, so to speak, on the staff's Danger List. Leaving the library and the scene of the Colonel's crime, she had clutched hysterically at Manelli's arm. "Mr. Manelli," she had murmured wildly. "They should be put down like dogs." As at the time she was still suffering from shock and had not regained control of her vocal cords, the last words had emerged as a near shout. They had been clearly audible to both Flush and the Colonel and had visibly irritated them. Both had glanced at her with the curious intensity of certain basking lizards. Slumping into a chair on the terrace, she had decided hopelessly that one or the other would certainly put her out of her agony before the day was out...

Cyril, sitting next to her, was smiling faintly and trying to tie a double Flemish Loop in a piece of jasmine. He admitted freely to himself that the scene of the atrocity projected by the Colonel had intrigued him. He was now engaged in trying to sort this unexpected ghoul out of his complex personality. He glanced at Mrs. Carlisle from under his eyelashes, wondering whether she would pay a psychoanalyst's fee. His lack of horror was so discreditable that it seemed a pity to waste it. He turned to Bill on his left. "It's a wise man who knows his own grandmother," he remarked.

Bill jumped. "I entirely disagree," he said at once. He had not been listening but he knew that if he had he would have disagreed on principle. He was worrying about Dina. It had occurred to him that, living in such company, she was constantly in danger. At any moment, with or without a valid reason, one of the staff might go berserk and... He gritted his teeth. He found himself clenching his hands to prevent himself knocking Cyril down because Dina clearly liked him...

Grossi, next to him, looked at him curiously for an instant and immediately forgot him. He was thinking about Flush. The man, with his urbane good looks and his total lack of decent feeling, should be an asset to any payroll. Grossi pictured him reasoning with Waxey, who was a thorn in everybody's side; Waxey as usual surrounded by his armed escort, Flush armed only with a courteous smile; Waxey for once silent, listening respectfully as Flush persuaded him to shoot eight of his outriders...Grossi glanced at Manelli, wondering whether the same idea had occurred to him.

It had not. Manelli was puffing at a cigar, conscious of very little except a sense of relief. He had been haunted throughout the few days at Dankry by the thought that he was being swindled, that he himself knew more and had more experience than his instructors, that his hard-earned fortune was being squandered upon a training too insular to be of much use when he finally returned to Long Island. Now, in the light of the Colonel's blunder, he was convinced that the staff were indeed all that the prospectus had claimed. He was not being cheated...

As the clock over the stables struck the half hour, Flush came through the French windows with a timetable in his hand. "Now, ladies and gentlemen," he said, "we have a short examination paper upon the subjects which we have already studied."

"What happens to the ones who fail?" asked Mrs. Carlisle anxiously after a brief pause.

Flush did not answer. He said instead, "Tomorrow, we shall overhaul our Demeanor and see how we fare under impromptu cross-examination. A murder has been arranged." Mrs. Carlisle screamed. Flush shouted her down. "I assure you that nobody will be hurt. A member of the staff will oblige as the deceased and each of you in turn will be accused of his death. Behavior upon the scene of a crime is of paramount importance. Many an innocent man has been suspected for weeks because of a sloppy piece of footwork or an overelaborate hand routine." He noted the wasp on the sugar and swatted it casually, expertly with his timetable. "You will all of course be furnished with an alibi. I warn you that you will lose marks if it does not cover the hour in question." He rolled up the timetable and put it into his pocket. "And now shall we adjourn to the gymnasium?"

The students rose apathetically.

"*Exams*," grieved Manelli. "I always flunked at school."

"You didn't go to school," Grossi reminded him.

"This is one exam where I hope I fail," said Bill moodily as he followed Mrs. Carlisle through the French window.

"Why?" asked Cyril, surprised. "This is the one art where one has to be very, very crafty. Or else..." He spread his hands and raised his shoulders. "Well, *or else*."

Mrs. Carlisle walked ahead of him into the gymnasium. Five tables stood at intervals around the room. On each was an inkwell, a glass of water, a ruler, a sheaf of lined paper with double margins, a piece of blotting paper and a corked test tube containing a lock of hair. Paget was padding slowly around distributing typed sheets of questions. Flush sat on the rostrum reading *The Times*.

Cyril sat down and filled his pen. He loved exams. Smiling, he began to study the first question. *Discuss*, he read, *the finding of 0.193 grams of arsenious oxide in the exhumed soil beneath a two-year-old coffin where the lateral soil yields only phosphates.*

Manelli, sitting at the table to Cyril's left, produced his ostentatious gold pen and ticked off the questions he intended to answer. Not caring for the first, he turned to the second and nearly laughed aloud with pleasure. *What firearm*, it asked, *would you select to bag a (i) stationary (ii) moving target at (a) 3 miles (b) half a mile (c) 25 yards (d) point blank range? Why? Write 500 words upon any THREE of the following: the 4-bore, the .500 heavy express rifle, the P83 9mm. automatic, the Hammerli Automatic Olympic Model (Swiss), any shotgun featuring the Anson & Deeley action. At what range would any/all of the above penetrate (a) concrete, (b) armor plating, (c) bone? How?*

Grossi had already answered the ballistics question. He turned without a pause to the next problem. *Name twelve methods of liquidating and/or disposing of a well-known public figure. What are the disadvantages of each method? How would you overcome them? What do you mean by "cold blood," "hot blood"? Would you personally repeal the McNaghten Rules? Why not?*

Mrs. Carlisle was looking frantically around her for an ashtray. She caught Paget's mournful eye upon her. He indicated with a courtly gesture that she might throw her cigarette onto the floor and stamp on it. She averted her eyes hastily, fearing that he might smile at her. Her distracted gaze fell upon the fourth question. *As an accomplice*, it challenged her, *what would be your immediate gambit if surprised by (a) a constable (b) an inspector (c) your family lawyer (d) your best friend, under any FOUR of the following circumstances: (i) Eavesdropping (ii) reproducing the fingerprints of a false suspect upon some vital clue (iii) purchasing suspect drugs AFTER a successful experiment (iv) steaming open mail addressed to yourself (v) composing an anonymous letter to yourself?*

Bill sat chewing his pen and gazing out of the window. He could just see, if he stretched a little, Dina on the lawn. She was planting seedlings with the Colonel and wearing either a swimming costume exactly the color of her skin, or nothing at all. He tore his eyes away and stared at the fifth question. *To what use,* it inquired, *would you put the following: a four-inch length of three-strand flex, an electric hairdryer, half a gram of powdered chalk, a small tent, a wheelbarrow, 1 lb. of pork sausages, an anvil, a tweed scarf with a six-inch fringe, a handful of sand, a gas poker, a stream two inches deep and one foot wide, a small thorn, a Jeep?*

Cyril, Grossi and Manelli were writing furiously. Bill and Mrs. Carlisle met each other's eyes and simultaneously shrugged their shoulders. Paget moved dourly between the tables, silently distributing small booklets of pink litmus paper.

Flush looked over *The Times.* "No cheating, please," he murmured.

The staff took a glass of sherry before lunch under the weeping willow. "Have you looked yet at the papers, Clifford?" asked Mrs. Barratt.

"Cyril," said Flush thoughtfully, "wrote twenty-three pages. They appeared to be first class." He added with a trace of resentment, "Did you know, Naomi, that epileptics breathe partially through the retina of the eye?"

"What of Mrs. Carlisle?"

"She attempted one question only and wrote but half a page." Flush curled his lip. "I noted that if caught purchasing dangerous drugs, she would tell an inspector that they were for her window boxes. She approached me afterwards and inquired whether the hair in the test tubes was hers. Was it?"

"I really don't know, Clifford. The Colonel offered to secure the specimens."

The Colonel was pouring a pink gin. "Hadn't time," he mumbled. "Detailed Matron."

"Did she do it?"

"Suppose so."

Flush's hands whitened upon the arm of his chair. "You will kindly find out who put the hair into the test tubes and to whom it belonged. Do you realize that if no member of the staff attended to it, some unauthorized person had been cutting Mrs. Carlisle's hair without her knowledge?"

"Unless, of course," said Mrs. Barratt after a long pause, "she cut it herself."

"Find out." Flush lay back in his chair and lit a cigar. "Have you considered tomorrow's exercise?" he asked without interest. "Have you decided upon a victim?"

"I thought perhaps the Colonel might oblige again," began Mrs. Barratt.

"No," said the Colonel flatly. "Going into Krunte Newton."

"Well, perhaps Hobson?"

The Creaker was overcome by a gale of laughter. He struck himself several times on the knee and sprayed the area around him with half-masticated chocolate. He threw himself backwards and forwards in his chair, convulsed. The staff watched him, their faces expressionless. The Creaker produced a gray rag from his pocket and wiped his eyes. "Hoatshohorich," he guffawed. He succumbed to a further paroxysm. "Howaithoho-tilliellohohohobson!"

Flush frowned, trying to ignore him. "Have you approached Paget?"

"He declined. He has a touch of lumbago."

"Barker?"

"But, Clifford, what about the cooking?"

"Matron," suggested the Colonel. He said something to himself in Hindustani.

"Can she be trusted to lie doggo for so long?"

"Lapping up cowslip wine these days," remarked the Colonel. "Disgraceful state, should be court martialed. Guinea pigs dying off left and right."

Flush looked up sharply. "The snakes?"

"Ill," said the Colonel.

"The tsetse?"

"Dead. No steam." The Colonel refilled his glass and added, "Monsoon time and they know it."

Mrs. Barratt noted the slight tic beneath Flush's left eye and added hastily, "Don't worry about the victim, my dear. I will see to him."

"Going to stage show early hours?" asked the Colonel.

Flush nodded. "Unless there is a heavy dew."

"I would offer to operate," said Mrs. Barratt. "But I am never at my best at such an hour."

"I don't mind," said the Creaker without hope. This suggestion, as usual, was ignored.

"I'll do it," said Dina. She lay in a deck chair, sunbathing. "If I get the afternoon off."

Flush scowled at her. "I pay you a generous salary," he growled. "Why do you never appear to have adequate clothing?"

"What method are we to use?" asked Mrs. Barratt quickly.

Normally, at this point in a course, Flush had many ingenious schemes to offer. Now, he glared at his feet and said irritably, "Oh, shotgun or something."

"Right out of blanks," said the Colonel, looking at him with disapproval.

Flush dug his fingernails into his palms. "Well, blunt instrument then," he said through his clenched teeth. "I don't care. Anything that's handy."

Mrs. Barratt met the Colonel's eyes. He turned down the corners of his mouth. Both looked at Flush and quickly away.

"Let 'Obson 'ave a go," suggested the Creaker. "'E'll dream up somethin' original. If 'e goes too far, I'll rig up me new suicide. See, I take the weights off some 'eavy clock…"

Although nobody had seen him approach, Paget was suddenly behind the group. "Luncheon is served, madam," he announced.

"Meat?" barked the Creaker. He hobbled after Paget.

Flush offered his arm to Mrs. Barratt. "Naomi," he confessed in a low voice. "I am in vile mood."

Mrs. Barratt looked at him anxiously. "Clifford, surely not...?"

"Certainly not," said Flush without conviction. "Merely a slight headache." Climbing the steps to the terrace, he said irascibly, "This idiotic murder tomorrow exercises me. Who? By whom?"

"Now don't fret, my dear. I will arrange something."

"This confounded heat," growled Flush. "You note, Naomi, what happens when I feel under the weather? A general slackening of discipline. The staff have become impossibly lax during the past few days. Perhaps we are becoming soft and kindly. Perhaps we need new blood."

"*Clifford!*"

"Why do you deliberately misunderstand me? Whom can I trust, *whom?*" Flush's voice rose. "Can I never slacken my grip on the reins? Can I never relax? Must I operate tomorrow and also lie victim? Must I strike myself with some blunt instrument or singe my jacket with a shotgun, then fall into my prearranged pool of ketchup? Can I trust myself, in my present mood, *not to kill myself?*"

Mrs. Barratt patted his hand. She decided that for the general safety she would lock him into his room that night. And then remembered, with a pang of disquiet, that upon several occasions he had picked locks in his sleep. "You are hurting my arm," she said gently.

Flush bit his lip. He escorted her in silence along the dark passage to the dining room. On the threshold, he paused.

The students had already arrived. Mrs. Carlisle, her shoulders sagging, was seated at the table and, obviously unconscious of what she was doing, savagely and repeatedly stabbing a roll with a fish knife. Dina stood at the window between Bill and Cyril, smiling at each in turn with the satisfied air of a woman who knows that she is the cause of unrest between two men. Manelli sat staring at the salt and biting his thumb thoughtfully. Grossi stood behind him, staring with equal concentration at the back of Manelli's neck.

Flush glanced down at Mrs. Barratt. "Naomi," he murmured. "I cannot help feeling that a genuine murder would clear the air."

Chapter Nine

The conversation at lunch was dominated by the Colonel. He had consumed a large quantity of pink gin and was talking uncertainly but at length about the physical sciences and the wonders of nature. He waved away a dish of translucent whiting and said firmly, "Water, air. Too much, too little, too late. Embolism," he muttered, pouring Worcester sauce onto his empty plate.

"Not now, Colonel," said Mrs. Barratt.

Flush sat at the head of the table, eating little, saying nothing, his chin sunk upon his breast, his eyelids drooping. Apart from his other problems, he had slept indifferently, his dreams pervaded by an out-of-focus vision of Ingrid Larsen enjoying a champagne supper with Armitage. They had appeared to be surrounded by a thick glass wall, but he had heard their confidential whispers. "Poor old Clifford," murmured Mrs. Larsen with a fetching sneer. "Good as gold since 1939." Flush kneaded a piece of bread into a tiny mannikin of Armitage, rolled it into a ball and squashed it between his fingers.

"Gravity," said the Colonel. "Things dropped on people, people dropped on things."

"Not at meals please, Colonel," said Mrs. Barratt.

The fish was succeeded by a salad of dandelion leaves and some pieces of pastry covered with treacle.

The Colonel began to tell a story about a certain student named Goldhaus who was an international authority on Physics. The staff had hoped for a few tips on the byproducts of nuclear fission, but the professor had been unwilling to speak of anything except hypnotism. He had insisted upon giving a post-hypnotic suggestion to the Creaker who, under its influence, had charged into the garden and dug a hole under the cedars.

Paget laid a bowl of windfall apples on the table and handed around a platter in the center of which was two square inches of cream cheese. Finding that nobody wanted either, he stepped forward and cleared his throat with a sepulchral rattle.

"I hesitated to mention the matter before luncheon, sir," he told Flush, "but there has been an accident."

Flush closed his eyes and massaged himself between the brows with his small finger. "No, Paget," he said. "Not today. Tomorrow."

"I'm sorry, sir," began Paget.

"We will take tea in the garden, Paget," said Mrs. Barratt, rising.

"Yes, madam," said Paget. He turned back to Flush. "I fear that it is most serious, sir."

Flush opened his eyes and stared at his butler. "Leave us," he commanded. "Immediately."

Paget hesitated. "But, sir," he said unhappily.

"Go," said Flush.

Paget, who had never in his life disobeyed an order, went. He sat for half an hour clutching the arms of a broken chair in his pantry before he rose, shook himself, and set out with determination to find Flush. He traced his master to the library where he was speaking to Grossi and Manelli about the fundamental differences between English and American Law. Paget applied his ear to the door and stood listening.

"You must understand, Mr. Grossi," Flush was saying, "that there has been federal law in this country since the time of William the Conqueror."

Paget opened the door and took three paces into the room. "Excuse me, sir," he said. "I must speak to you."

"I disagree," said Flush frigidly. "You may go."

"It is most urgent, sir."

Flush threw down his pen and stood up. His eyes flashed.

Paget bowed hastily and retreated. He closed the door behind him and went along the passage to the sewing room where Mrs. Barratt was instructing Bill in the use of single- and double-edged weapons.

"Excuse me, madam," said Paget. "May I have a word with you?"

Mrs. Barratt clicked her tongue testily. "Later, Paget," she said. "*Later*."

She turned to the sack of straw upon which she was demonstrating a downward blow with a small kris.

Paget went in search of the Colonel. He found the drawing room occupied by Cyril and Mrs. Carlisle. The latter was reading a copy of *Country Life* and Cyril was doing some perfunctory revision on Bruises.

Paget did not speak. He bowed and retired. He set forth for the garages, but the Colonel was not there. Going under the rambler arch, he saw Matron throwing a bottle into the old well. She was wearing a blue hairnet and singing "From Greenland's Icy Mountains." Paget ignored her. He crossed the lawns to the summerhouse, but the Colonel was not there either. As Paget turned away, the Creaker opened the rustic window and threw out a large piece of cardboard, then disappeared inside, slamming the window. Paget heard him and Hobson roaring with rough laughter. He walked back across the lawns and climbed the steps to the terrace. Dina was there, lying in the sun reading a magazine, but her costume was so scanty that Paget averted his eyes and gave her a wide berth.

He went back to the library, jerked down his striped waistcoat, knocked and entered. "I insist upon speaking to you, sir," he informed Flush. "We have had a casualty, sir."

"Paget," said Flush, enunciating each syllable with care. "*Tomorrow* we have a casualty. Not today."

Paget coughed apologetically. "There may be another tomorrow, sir," he said. "But there is also one today."

Flush drummed his fingers upon his desk. "Send him to me," he ordered. "I wish to speak to him."

"I'm sorry, sir," said Paget. "I cannot send him to you. He is dead, sir."

"Will you leave us please, Paget?"

Paget considered this. It was not an order, it was a question. "No, sir," he said regretfully.

Flush rose. He collected his papers and turned to Grossi and Manelli. "I must apologize for this jobbernowl," he said. "Shall we continue on the terrace?" He went out of the window and pulled a small table into the shade.

The two mobsters closed their notebooks and followed him. Paget stood looking after them, clenching his hands. Grossi and Manelli were fetching chairs. Flush was already seated.

"Like I was saying," said Grossi, sitting down and crossing his legs, "I always send the judge some small token. For instance, a submachine-gun shell."

Paget finally lost his temper. He shambled forward and stood in the window. "Very well!" he screamed. "What do I care? What's one dead man here or there?"

Flush looked at him for a minute in silence. "Do not shout," he said eventually.

"I'm sorry, sir," said Paget. He passed a hand over his eyes.

"Have you been drinking, Paget?"

"No, sir."

"Are you unwell?"

"No, thank you, sir."

"Are you serious?"

"Yes, sir."

"You insist upon this calamity?"

"Yes, sir." Paget swallowed. "I'm afraid that it's genuine this time, sir."

Flush stood up slowly. "You mean somebody is *dead*?"

Paget nodded.

"Who?"

"Mr. Grossi's manservant, sir."

"Where?"

Paget swayed. "Pool," he said faintly. He gripped the window and steadied himself. "Sir," he added.

Flush pushed back his chair and strode down the steps onto the lawn. "Collect the students and Miss Dina in the drawing room," he snapped over his shoulder. "Alert the staff. Inform them to report upon the scene of the crime."

Flush stood on the edge of the swimming pool, staring down into the deep end with mixed feelings. Grossi's bodyguard lay at the bottom looking amazed. Flush, realizing immediately what this catastrophe might mean to Dankry, lit a cigar and flicked the match angrily into the blue water.

Mrs. Barratt hurried up behind him. She stood at his elbow, swinging her locket, her lips tight with disapproval, watching him.

The Colonel and the Creaker appeared together. The Colonel frowned at the pool. "Damned bad form," he said at a loss. "Who was he?"

The Creaker said nothing. He looked up at Hobson's window and saw his pupil changing into running shorts. Hobson, perhaps prompted by the intensity of the Creaker's silent accusation, straightened up and made a repellent face. The Creaker's tiny eyes narrowed. He scratched his false leg thoughtfully.

"Paget!" Flush shouted suddenly.

Paget was halfway across the lawn. He broke into a shuffling canter. He ran through a herbaceous border and stopped on the edge of the group. "Sir," he said, panting.

"Bring me that body."

Paget did not consider that such a task was fitting to his position. Moreover, he could not swim. He turned his head. "*Barker!*" he shouted towards the house.

Barker, still confused and dizzy from the poker session of the evening before, burst from the house and streaked towards the pool. Paget indicated the water. Barker did not hesitate. He hurled himself forward in an ungainly racing dive. He retrieved Grossi's bodyguard, dropped him unceremoniously onto the grass, then lay down on a bench to give his aching head a chance while his uniform dried.

Paget stood respectfully behind Flush. Having recovered from the initial shock, he realized that, due perhaps to the bloody history of his ancestors, he was not unduly shocked. His anxiety stemmed from a more personal difficulty. What was the etiquette upon such an occasion? Had he been wearing a hat, he could have taken it off, but he was bareheaded. Should he wait for orders or was this a time when initiative was correct? Should he fetch brandy? Pointless; the man was dead. Should he telephone to the police? Laughable, in such company. Should he fetch a stretcher? There had at one time been one in the dispensary, but the Creaker had attempted to use it as a hammock and had broken it. Paget cleared his throat.

"Shall I fetch a gate, sir?" he asked.

In the house, the drawing-room door burst open and Al rushed over to Manelli and seized his arm. "Say, Boss," he said. "Looks like the jerk was rubbed."

"Be your age," said Manelli.

"Honest," said Al. "A real sloppy cool."

Grossi seized him by the collar. "Quit horsing around," he snapped.

"Now take it easy, Tony," warned Manelli. "Let's get at the facts."

Grossi shook Al. "Spill," he said.

"Save your muscle," said Al. "I don't know nuttin except it's a *case.*"

He tore himself free and left the room at a run.

Mrs. Carlisle had half risen from her chair. "Was he implying," she asked, shaking, "that this creature has been murdered?"

"*Who?*" demanded Bill. "Who is it?" He had been asking this question repeatedly since he had been told to go into the drawing room and stay there. Nobody had answered him upon the previous occasions and nobody did now.

Grossi was striding up and down the room with clenched fists. Manelli sympathetically removed a chair, allowing his ex-partner a longer beat. Grossi stopped before him and stared into his eyes. "Okay, Joe," he said. "Very cute. Okay is all."

Manelli digested the implications of this remark. "Now, Tony," he began.

"I said all I got to say," snarled Grossi. "Okay, I said. So *okay.*"

"What an epitaph," murmured Cyril.

Manelli spread his hands in protest. Grossi's unspoken accusation, he realized, was not in fact entirely unjustified. In the fatal old days, he and Tony had liquidated each other's body-guards with almost domestic regularity. "Now, Tony," he said. "It hasn't been like that in years, you know that."

Furious though Grossi was, these words rang an almost obsolete bell in his memory. The last time, it had been he who had said them to Manelli as he led the older man towards an ambush on the outskirts of Salt Lake City. Manelli's life, ironically enough, had been saved by a cop who had arrested both mobsters and charged each with Consorting With Known Criminals.

"So I don't have no shadow," said Grossi. "Joe, you are a thinker."

"Why doesn't somebody send for the police?" asked Bill.

Grossi struck him on the head with a rolled newspaper. "Will you please stop asking damnfool questions?" he inquired.

Dina suddenly realized that she was the only member of the staff present. She asserted herself. "Sit down," she ordered Grossi. "We must all start thinking about our alibis."

There was a long pause.

"Must we?" said Cyril. "Isn't this one on the house?"

Down by the swimming pool, Flush straightened up and mopped his forehead with a silk handkerchief. "At a very rough estimate," he remarked, "this man has been dead for quite a long time."

Mrs. Barratt picked up an overturned wrought iron chair. "I imagine that he was struck with this," she said. "How dreadful, so clumsy."

Flush did not glance at her, but he knew that their thoughts were identical. Clumsy. The word in their small fraternity had always, in jest and in sorrow, referred to the Creaker. The Creaker also knew this. "Well, I dunno," he said, scratching the back of his neck.

Mrs. Barratt bent down and plucked a silver cigarette case from the body's wet pocket. Paget, sensing that his presence was no longer desirable, turned away, but not before he had noticed that the dripping case was monogrammed with a large C.C. "Come, Barker," he murmured and set out softly, as if he were afraid of damaging the grass, for the house. Barker, still groggy, lurched to his feet and marched through a rose bed.

Mrs. Barratt, speaking freely in the absence of her servants, indicated the body with her locket. "Clifford," she said. "I feel that the least you can do is to apologize."

"He is nothing whatever to do with me," said Flush coldly. "He is possibly one of Hobson's follies."

The Creaker sprang to the defense of his pupil. "Cock," he said firmly.

Flush sat down on the murder weapon. "Before we interrogate the other suspects," he said, pinching the bridge of his nose, "I suggest that we run through our own alibis." He pointed his little finger at Mrs. Barratt. "Naomi?"

"Really, Clifford!"

"Come, Naomi. The man was, I imagine, partially drowned. Your second husband was wholly drowned. There will be comment upon the recurrence of the water motif."

"As you well know," said Mrs. Barratt, "that was not murder, it was pure luck."

"Your alibi please, Naomi. I am waiting."

Mrs. Barratt studied her frail hands. "Offhand, I really don't know, Clifford. I haven't needed one for so long." She considered. Her standby, that she had been in the kitchen making a tisane with a reliable witness, would not fit the circumstances. "Of course, I would never have been up at such an hour."

"*Wot* hour?" asked the Creaker.

Flush turned to his Treasurer. "Colonel?"

The Colonel blew up his white mustache and muttered something in Pushtu.

"Creaker?"

The Creaker leered. He gave his standard answer. "Was with you, chum, 'cos if I wasn't where was *you*?"

"You appreciate that the gaucherie of the method is strongly reminiscent of your previous handiwork?"

"Bull," said the Creaker uneasily.

Flush stroked his chin, pondering. He was slightly comforted. At least these frank negatives were preferable to some of the preposterous and patently skittish alibis of the past. He reminded himself that these disarming admissions were not necessarily favorable and might indeed be deliberate. Had not Mrs. Barratt once convinced one of the ablest judges of her day that her ample, even flagrant, opportunity to tamper with her first husband's menu was most definitely a point in her favor?

"And you, sir?" asked the Colonel. "Any alibi?"

"Of a sort," said Flush absently. "At 12:30, I was obliged to have recourse to sleeping pills. I took four, enough to drug an elephant." He shrugged his shoulders. "Flimsy, I grant you."

"Can you prove it, sir?"

"Are my pupils not still dilated?" He did not wait for an answer. "Have I your assurance that none of you are responsible for this buffoonery?"

"He's not my type at all," said Mrs. Barratt.

"No motive," said the Colonel gruffly.

The Creaker took a handful of wine gums from his pocket and pressed them into his mouth. "Roogurrahoverrotive," he mumbled. He swallowed and added fiercely, "An' that goes for 'Obson too."

"I fear," said Flush irritably, "that in this case the motive will not necessarily lead us to the malefactor. In my opinion, the choice of victim suggests either a homicidal whim among the staff..." He bit his lip, frowning. "Or that one of our trainees has been practicing."

Some ten minutes later, Flush, Mrs. Barratt, and the Colonel, engaged upon fabricating their alibis for the benefit of the pupils, moved slowly towards the house. The Creaker was left to chaperone the body until such time that the domestic staff appeared to remove it to a less public place. He sat down sullenly on the bench where Barker had lain. The pools of water left by the chef's wet clothing seeped slowly through his corduroy trousers, but the Creaker barely noticed. He was persuading his brackish mind into the confusion which he regarded as thinking.

He was annoyed that the three senior members of the staff had all declined to substantiate his alibi. They knew well that he snored. Any or all of them could have agreed to say that they had heard him snoring all night long. It would have done him a slight favor and also strengthened the other's cock-and-bull story about his own alibi. But no, none of them would do it. They did not like him. Amongst themselves, they all talked about their trials, but they would never allow him to mention his. It was most unreasonable. Their cases had been premeditated, yet his...well, if the tide had been out, it would never have happened. Just because he had got rightly narked, and had…

Hobson appeared from the vegetable garden, running at top speed. The gravel sprang from beneath his huge, flashing feet.

"'Ere!" called the Creaker.

"Can't stop," shouted Hobson. "Timin' meself."

"Come 'ere."

Hobson stopped in an athletic attitude. He glanced at his watch. "Wot's up?"

The Creaker gave the body a nudge with his boot. "You did that," he said.

Hobson moved closer and looked down. "Topped?" he asked.

"'Sagainst the rules," said the Creaker. "You should of *asked*."

"I never saw 'im before in me life."

"You did."

"I never."

"An' wot's more," said the Creaker morosely, "it's downright casual, no imagination."

"Turn it up, cock."

The Creaker sucked his teeth. "'Imself's after alibis," he remarked. "'E doesn't care 'oo done it, but 'e's got to 'ave an alibi. I better be yours."

"Ta," said Hobson.

"An' that means you're mine, see."

"I'm not blind," said Hobson. He looked at his watch. "Got to take off eighteen seconds." He sprinted away in the direction of the shrubbery.

In the kitchen, Al, Blackie, and Barker were mourning the passing of Grossi's bodyguard.

"'E was a lousy, rotten basket an' I never liked 'im," said Barker. He sat steaming gently by the kitchen range, still confused. His sodden uniform dripped steadily onto the linoleum. "But this is fundamentally wrong. It's not right."

"That ain't 'ow you felt last night," Blackie reminded him.

"Last night was last night." Barker took a ten shilling note from his pocket and spread it on the stove to dry. "An' that was my girl 'e took out without my permission. I ring 'er up this mornin' an' 'er cough's proper chronic. Serve 'im right," he added.

"The 'igh Tosheroon took it calm," said Blackie disapprovingly. He got up and strode across the room, pretending to be Flush. "What a confounded nuisance! Fetch a boat hook," he mimicked.

"That poor stiff 'ad come from the far side o' the baize, wouldn't 'alf be 'ell to pay," said Barker sourly. "That ain't class 'atred, it's class indifference."

"'Ere," said Blackie. "That Grossi's not protected."

Al laughed shortly. "And, brother, that ain't no act of God." He raised his teacup. "I give you my Boss, kids. Joe 'Slots' Manelli, the guy who took the pin outa pinballs."

Flush strode into the drawing room. He stood with his back to the window, forcing the students to face the bright sunlight. "As you have doubtless heard," he said curtly, "there has been foul play. Will the culprit kindly step forward?"

There was a long silence. The students looked at each other doubtfully. "I expect it was a tramp," said Dina without conviction.

Flush ignored this suggestion. "So," he said, "our impetuous friend prefers to remain anonymous?" For a moment he wondered whether to dismiss them, to cancel the course, refund their fees and dispatch them to their problematical futures. He was silenced by the fact that were he to expel these amateurs there would probably result an outbreak of inefficient murders which would cause eyebrows to be raised in the wrong quarters.

"How about suicide?" asked Bill hopefully.

"If we accept such a theory," said Flush, "we must also accept the fact that the deceased was a remarkable eccentric. He was struck on the head with a chair."

Mrs. Carlisle screamed. Nobody took any notice of her.

Flush lit a cigar, drew upon it and added in a conversational tone, "I shall give the misdemeanant exactly ten seconds to confess."

He glanced at his watch. Fascinated, he mused that, unless one of the staff had suddenly gone berserk after all these blameless years, behind one of these anxious faces before him lurked the saucy *alter ego* of the Accused Unfit to Plead.

Out of the past, the nagging specter of Goonatilika raised its swarthy, smiling head. Flush controlled a shudder. *One...two...*Manelli was the obvious suspect, but long ago Flush had learned to discard the obvious. And why should the man attempt to cast suspicion upon Mrs. Carlisle? Surely the ploy of the cigarette case was too petty for a rascal of Manelli's caliber? One could imagine...*three*...him giving orders during a gang conference for an enemy to be mown down by submachine-gun fire; one could even imagine him saying, an afterthought as his henchman left the room, "Oh, and Al, frame the Carlisle dame, will ya?" But...*four*...so blatant a plant as the cigarette case was surely far too optimistic for men of such wide experience. Yet perhaps Manelli had indulged in a really tortuous piece of thinking; perhaps the double-take, so to speak, on the double-take...? But then again, admitting that these five students were unusually precocious, the...*five*...cigarette case, by the same reasoning, directly implicated Cyril. And who would wish to implicate this likely youth except possibly Mrs. Carlisle herself? And yet it seemed unlikely that a woman of her chancy temper would so *deliberately* fall between two fools. *Six.* The murder weapon was of wrought iron yet hollow, lighter than it appeared. Could a woman merely bent upon mischief have wielded such a weight? The...*seven*...blow must, with the difference of the passionate follow-through, have much resembled an overhand tennis service. Grossi had a powerful service and had indeed...*eight*...torn a hole in the wire netting surrounding the tennis court, but why should he slaughter his own bodyguard? *Nine.* To implicate Manelli? Ah, the dark, mad sanity of the gangster mind! Who knew? What came after the double bluff? *Ten.*

"Very well," said Flush easily. His tone gave no hint of his confusion. He resisted the temptation to tell them to take the afternoon off, to leave him in peace, to forget the whole affair. His own curiosity and a whimsical desire to play detective spurred him on. "Mrs. Carlisle," he said. "Your cigarette case was found in the pocket of the deceased. Can you explain this to my satisfaction?"

Mrs. Carlisle stared. "Mine?" she said. "*Mine?*"

Flush snapped his fingers testily. "All right, all right," he said. "You lost it yesterday, anybody could have taken it, you gave it to a man in a public house and you don't know his name and wouldn't recognize him again. I don't want to hear it."

"She has been framed," said Cyril.

Flush looked at him with interest. If, which was one possibility, Cyril were the brain behind the brawn of this calamity, then the move was a shrewd one, cool, daring, full of the gallantry which so often bemused policemen. "Have you," he asked Mrs. Carlisle, "an alibi?"

"When for?" She fumbled wildly for a cigarette. Flush passed her her case. She reared away from it. "Isn't it a *clue*?" she said hoarsely. "What about fingerprints?"

"No doubt there are many false leads on it," said Flush patiently. He breathed on the case. There were prints all over it. "There is also," he remarked, "a piece of fur caught in the hinge to which I shall pay no attention. Will you disclose your alibi please?" He polished the case with his handkerchief.

"I haven't got one," said Mrs. Carlisle. "We haven't done Alibis and anyway you said it would be tomorrow."

Flush pulled up a chair and sat down. "Take your time," he said. "An alibi for two or three hours around dawn or thereabouts. There is no hurry." Cyril laid his hand on Mrs. Carlisle's shoulder and raised his left eyebrow. He looked into her eyes and barely nodded.

The implications of Flush's question struck Mrs. Carlisle suddenly. She brushed off Cyril's hand. "Oh, no you don't," she said heatedly.

"*Chloe*," said Cyril. He shook his head reproachfully. He turned to Flush and said with an apologetic smile, "I hate to admit it, but I must confess that I can provide Chloe with an alibi until breakfast."

"You are a barking liar," said Mrs. Carlisle.

"Now, Chloe, *dear*."

"Look, angel," said Mrs. Carlisle. "If you need an alibi so badly, you can damn well go and..." She became slightly confused. "Go and browse in greener pastures."

Flush stopped listening. It suddenly occurred to him that he himself might have killed Grossi's bodyguard. *I was in restive mood yesterday*, he reflected. *Could I, under the influence of four sleeping pills, have been so goaded by my dreams...? Did not Naomi, a mere eight months ago, persuade me, still sleeping, away from the power plug in the Creaker's bedroom? Will I be obliged, for my own peace of mind, to resort again to tying my great toe to the bed?*

He pulled the lobe of his ear thoughtfully. Surely the sloppiness of the crime, the possibility of recovery or rescue exonerated the staff? Never would any of them have left so much to chance. And he himself, surely even in his sleep he would have provided himself with an alibi? And yet even the most gifted operator made mistakes. He himself had done so. He still recalled the thrill of horror with which he had heard his wife, whom he had pushed off an express train outside Bournemouth and who had lived to secure his acquittal, say, "Dearest Clifford, when you tried to save me, you looked almost *ugly*."

"And you, Cyril?" he asked. "Have you an alibi?"

"I'm not it," said Mrs. Carlisle. "Absolutely not."

Cyril sighed. "Chloe, how at a time like this can you be so suburban?"

"Suburban hell!" said Mrs. Carlisle, her eyes beautiful with rage. "If you had attempted to come into my room last night after that rodeo in the games room..."

"Yes?" Flush prompted, interested.

"What do you mean rodeo?" demanded Dina. She appealed to Flush. "Cyril and I were playing ping-pong…"

"*Ha!*" said Mrs. Carlisle explosively.

"Just because…"

"Exactly," snapped Mrs. Carlisle. "Just because, she said. Just because *what*, you may ask yourselves." She laughed bitterly. "As it happens…"

"If you imagine," said Dina, "that we didn't notice you crashing about in the bushes…"

Mrs. Carlisle blew smoke. "What a pity," she remarked sadly. "Such vulgarity in one so prematurely old."

"Dina," said Flush. "Please leave the room."

"And yet what can one expect," Mrs. Carlisle asked the ceiling, "from one with such an unfortunate past?"

"What about *your* past?" demanded Dina furiously. "And just look at your present. And I don't need any crystal ball to see your future." She left the room, slamming the door.

Mrs. Carlisle ground out her cigarette. "I apologize," she said surprisingly. "I have been accused of strangling somebody I don't even *know* and…"

"Drowning," corrected Cyril. "Wasn't it?"

"All right, drowning," said Mrs. Carlisle. "What *does* it matter? If he walked into this room *now*, I wouldn't recognize him. Yet I have been accused of shooting him. Not unnaturally, I resent it. I'm just a trifle nervous. I'm so sorry." She produced a handkerchief and blew her nose.

Flush watched her with disapproval. If, as he suspected, she was acting, it had been a remarkable performance, a *tour de force. I shall have to break her of that*, he thought. *Judges dislike it, juries hate it.*

"Chloe," said Cyril. "I was merely giving her my address."

Mrs. Carlisle screwed her handkerchief into a ball and hurled it on the floor. "What *for*?" she screamed. She leapt up and rushed towards the door. "If you think," she roared from the threshold, "that Chloe's going to stand for the role of *amie complaisante*…" This thought was too much for her. She laughed hysterically, pushing at her hair, and ran from the room.

For a moment nobody commented upon this embarrassing exit. All suspected Mrs. Carlisle of crouching outside the door waiting for them to do so.

"Dames," said Grossi eventually.

Manelli nodded. "Remember Marta?" he asked. "God! On that occasion, Tony, I coulda wrung your hand."

"Skip it," said Grossi. "She had it coming to her."

Flush interrupted. "I think that we can safely assume," he said, "that Mrs. Carlisle has no alibi. In which case, Cyril, neither have you."

Cyril stiffened. "Are you doubting my word?"

Flush noted the flashing eyes, the proudly upraised chin—a useful Court gambit if there were five or more women on the jury. "Yes," he said and was delighted to see that Cyril gave him the look again, exactly the same. He turned to the older mobster. "Mr. Manelli, is there any reason why we should not suspect you of this dastardly stratagem?"

"Sure," said Manelli. "I was playing cards with Tony here."

"No," shouted Grossi. "You don't cool my Boy and I'm your alibi. *No.*"

"Okay," said Manelli calmly. "I never saw you all evening, neither did Al or Blackie. Now where does that leave *you?*" He saw the flaw in this reasoning immediately.

So did Grossi. He sneered. Before both Americans rose the tipsy face of Barker, the cook, the only impartial observer of the night's session. Both knew that as soon as this meeting was adjourned, there would be a dignified race to get to Barker first.

"They haven't got any alibis," said Bill, glaring. "The game broke up at half past four and until then they were *all* there and the body was singing."

Flush nodded. "I shall assume," he said, "that none of you can account for your movements after half past four. *Rigor mortis* being the fortuitous matter it is, I am unable to say with any certainty when this maddening fellow was dispensed with. The staff, naturally, have comprehensive alibis. Therefore, between the hours of half past four and, roughly, eight this morning, one of the students took this step without my permission. I intend to ascertain which of you dared to do so."

"You'd turn this guy over to the cops?" asked Grossi.

"Certainly not. I do not intend to endanger the Manor's excellent reputation. Moreover, I am allergic to policemen."

"What then?" asked Manelli.

Flush clenched his hands behind his back. What then indeed? If the culprit proved to be one of the staff, he could fine him a month's pay; if he himself were the guilty party, he would make a handsome donation to the Benevolent Fund. But if one of the students had so thoughtlessly disrupted the course, what then? Flush wondered whether he could trust himself not to liquidate the fellow at once. Assuming that he were able to control himself, how would he punish the scoundrel? Turn him over to the Creaker for a spell in the summerhouse? Lock him into the basement without food or water? Tie the murder weapon around his neck and force him to wear it for a week?

"I shall expel him," he said slowly. "He will leave Dankry under a cloud."

Chapter Ten

The clock over the stables struck three. The four o'clock class on Gases and Their Uses had been canceled. The staff had retired to the library. Mrs. Barratt, with a knitting needle in her mouth, was counting stitches.

Her lips moved silently and the needle wobbled up and down. The murder weapon stood in the middle of the Shirazi. Flush, one hand on the back of his neck, his head bent, strode round and round the chair, willing it to offer up its secret. He snatched it up suddenly by one leg, brandished it around his head, then replaced it, looking depressed.

He glanced at Mrs. Barratt. She had been watching him. She looked away quickly but not before he had noticed the reproachful frown in her faded eyes. She suspected him. He drummed his fingers on the back of the chair, wondering whether she had any proof.

"I have never before seen you so upset by a murder, my dear," she said. She wound her wool around her little finger and began to knit.

"Mr. Grossi seems to have taken it very well," said Dina. "I thought he'd shoot Mr. Manelli at once."

"Do you think," asked Flush slowly, "that Mr. Manelli is the popular suspect?" He wondered whether in order to confuse Naomi it was worth framing Manelli in some inconclusive manner. For instance a broken watch strap, or a splash of chlorinated water upon a suit he had not been wearing, or a lock of the dead man's hair planted in Grossi's pocket...

"Put notice on the board," suggested the Colonel. "Invite blighter to confess anonymously, no names, no pack-drill."

"Bet *I* could make 'em talk," said the Creaker. His horny tongue flicked over his upper lip. "See, I'd take an ordinary bunch o'..."

"Please, Creaker," said Mrs. Barratt.

"...tintacks an' a white-'ot..."

"*Creaker!*"

"Orright, orright," growled the Creaker. "Only bein' 'elpful. We got to catch the chap, 'aven't we?" As soon as he had said this, he regretted it. He was convinced that Hobson was responsible for the disaster and whereas he intended to give his pupil a good talking to if his guilt were proved, he did not want him to be disgraced.

"Have we?" asked Mrs. Barratt. She gave Flush a flat stare. "Have we, Clifford?"

"Naturally," said Flush. "The pupils will expect it." If, he reasoned, at any stage of the inquiry it appeared that he was going to catch himself, he would scatter so many false clues and plant such a multitude of spurious leads that the whole issue would end in confusion. "Has the body been removed?"

"I suppose so," said Mrs. Barratt. "The Colonel offered..."

"Blast," said the Colonel. "Clean forgot." He turned on the Creaker. "You, sir. You said..."

"Well, I changed me mind," said the Creaker sullenly. He jerked a thumb at Dina. "She's the sekerterry."

Dina was reading the local paper. "Gregory Peck's on next week," she said.

"Clifford," said Mrs. Barratt, "if the body is still in position, do you not think that it would be splendid experience for the students to pick up a few tips from the scene of the crime?"

"Madam!" barked the Colonel, outraged.

"You are orful," said the Creaker idly.

Flush strode once more around the murder chair. "Had the affair been more polished, I might have considered it."

"Are you sure that it is *not* polished?" Mrs. Barratt eyed him. "We all know the Expert Oaf. It seemed to me that it might have been *very* nicely planned."

Dina folded up her paper. "Well," she said, adjusting the small piece of cloth around her bosom, "I'm going to meet my favorite suspect."

Manelli, the suspect favored by all but Dina, Mrs. Barratt and the Creaker, was in the kitchen reasoning with Barker.

"See here, boy," he said. He sat down on the table. "You're a good boy and I wouldn't want you to get snarled up with a louse. That Grossi, between ourselves, is a louse."

Barker made a futile, shaky attempt to cut the head off a large cod. He said nothing.

"Now I know that bum," said Manelli, lighting a cigar. "And here's what I think he'll pull. I think he'll proposition you to be his alibi, sorta say what *he* says, see. Now I know you got ideals. I know you wouldn't tangle with a bum. Am I right?"

Barker's hangover was now so intense that he knew that, were he to nod, he would probably fall over. He closed his eyes briefly.

"Sure," said Manelli warmly. He added with sudden suspicion, "He propositioned you already?"

Barker closed his eyes again.

"How much?"

Barker laid a finger on his lips.

"Can't speak, eh?"

Barker moved his index finger slowly from side to side, then pointed to his head.

"Gee, that's tough," said Manelli impatiently. "Was it in dollars? Hundred bucks?"

Barker rolled his eyes upwards.

"More? Hundred and fifty?" Manelli offered his gold pen. "Write it on the table, boy. Don't try to speak. Just write it down."

Barker took the pen and immediately dropped it.

Manelli frowned. "Too heavy, eh? Was it more than hundred and fifty?"

Barker dropped his eyelids.

"Okay," said Manelli. "Tell you what I'll do. Mind, I'm not propositioning you, I know you got principles. But I always say if a guy's got principles, well, that rates encouragement." He put a roll of notes into Barker's trembling hand and patted it encouragingly. "That's just so you don't let that Grossi make a sucker of you, see."

Barker raised one finger in acknowledgment. He took the notes and crammed them into the pocket already lined by Grossi's offering.

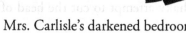

In Mrs. Carlisle's darkened bedroom, Cyril stood peering down at the sheet of paper in the typewriter. "Lady Diana," he read, "was sick at…" *Where*, he wondered, intrigued. In the last chapter, Lady Diana, Lord Peter, and the Hon. Terence had been in Paris. Now Terence had fallen victim to Chloe's ill temper and this absurd woman was being sick. Why? The smell of rich continental cooking? The sight of the waiter's thumb in her *bouillabaisse*? The croupier's yellow claw as he raked in the last of her travel allowance? And *where*? In her hotel, as she received the fatal telegram? In the Bois? On Lord Peter's manly waistcoat as he pressed her to his heart and kissed her—a frequent error of Chloe's—without removing the pipe gripped between his teeth? Where, where? It was fascinating. He glanced at Mrs. Carlisle.

Since her shameful exit from the drawing room, she had remained closeted in her room. She lay prostrate on the bed, her eyes covered with a dripping pad of cotton wool. The room was heavy with the smell of eau de cologne and sal volatile. In one hand, she held a bottle of eye lotion, in the other a tube of aspirins. She lay still, breathing heavily through her mouth. The extreme nobility of her attitude implied that, although she was in great pain, she wanted to make no trouble.

Cyril tiptoed over to the bed. He wondered whether she could see him through the cotton wool. He stood looking down at her, wondering what was the correct approach. Usually, when she made a fool of herself, it took her days to forgive him. Now, the process must be speeded up. He wanted an alibi before dinner.

He stroked her arm with the tip of a finger. "I'm so ashamed," he murmured.

"Don't bother about me," said Mrs. Carlisle bravely. "I'll be all right in a minute." She rolled her head away and grunted.

"Poor Chloe." He sat down on the bed and took her hand. "I shall never forget you standing in that door. You were magnificent. You *blazed*." He saw her squinting at him from beneath the wool. Her mascara had run. It gave her a rakish, dissolute air.

"You run along and play with your new friends," she said faintly. "Don't worry about me. It's only my silly head."

"Chloe," he said in a low voice. "Do you think that you'll ever be able to forgive me?"

She turned away, her shoulders shaking.

He was much relieved. Obviously, she was in tears. This usually meant that her resistance was crumbling. He stroked her hip. "I've been such a fool," he whispered.

She rolled over, quivering convulsively. Cyril saw that she was grinning. She lay on her back, helpless with laughter.

"You'll have to dream up a whole bunch of new tactics, angel," she gasped. She sat up, patting herself on the chest. She said in a shrill, whining voice, screwing up her face and wagging her head from side to side, "Chloe, do you think you'll ever be able to forgive me?" She started to laugh again.

Cyril, rigid with shock, stood staring at her. "You fabulous bitch," he said dully.

She made a ludicrous face and whined, "I've been such a fool." She added in her own voice, "I couldn't agree with you more. You needn't imagine that I've forgiven you. If I catch you hanging around that tarty blonde again, I shall…"

"What? Hit me on the head with a chair?"

"Ha!" she said with an air of triumph. "So *that's* the trouble? Wouldn't the horrid old bag give the poor wee fellow his little alibi?"

Cyril got up. He went over to the window and leaned his forehead against the cool glass. Appalled, he admitted to himself that there were still times when he did not understand her. His hands itched to slap her; but he was afraid that she might change her will again. He was haunted by the specter of a codicil. He controlled himself with an effort.

"I was merely attempting to keep you out of this squalid business," he said sullenly.

"Me?" she said. "Ah, yes, of course. Most gracious, too kind, so loyal."

He looked at her. How speedily discomfiture in her dear ones made her happy! Hating her, he said, "Well, of course, if you *want* to be involved in a working-class murder, wade in, wade in."

"Not wade, angel," she said, radiant with malice. "We will *paddle*, dear, hand in hand."

Cyril bit his lip and turned away. He went to the dressing table and combed his hair. Looking at himself in the mirror, reassured by his own bright beauty, he recovered some of his jauntiness. He composed his features into the plucky, suffering expression which he knew privately as *l'homme qui rit.*

"Tell me," he said lightly. "Where was Lady Diana sick at?"

"Heart, you fool," snapped Mrs. Carlisle.

The sun slanted over the swimming pool. The body and the murder weapon had been removed. The squat black beetles zigzagged again on the surface of the water. The trampled flowerbeds had been raked over. The rustic bench was dry again. There was nothing to indicate that, a few hours ago, this had been the scene of a crime.

Dina, wearing two small pieces of false leopard skin, rose on her toes, preparing to dive.

Bill ran towards her along the blue tiles. He had not seen her since she had flung out of the drawing room after her brush with Mrs. Carlisle. He had imagined that she had hidden herself away somewhere and wept tears of shame. He had decided to solace and comfort her. He had been looking forward to it. But clearly she had forgotten the whole episode. She was smiling, humming to herself.

"Dina," he called. "Are you going to swim *already?*" Confused, he wondered whether in some way the water was not evidence.

She dived. Her head emerged, her hair clinging. She looked, he thought with a slight shock, absurdly young to have murdered anybody. She laughed up at him, shaking the water out of her eyes. *Somebody ought to look after her,* he thought. *She's not wicked, she's just irresponsible.*

"Nobody seems to give a damn," he said. There ought, he felt, to be policemen milling about, the area roped off, people taking photographs.

"I think Clifford's rather annoyed," she said. She swam around in a small circle, splashing with her feet, making for an instant a tiny rainbow. "It's upset the whole afternoon. You're all supposed to be doing Deportment in the Witness Box."

"I wish I'd never come," said Bill moodily.

Dina looked at him. She floated on her back, lifted a brown, galvanizing leg from the water and pointed her toe at him. "Do you?" she asked.

"No."

She rolled over and swam a little closer. "Why, Bill?"

He stifled an impulse to dive into the pool in all his clothes. He turned away and kicked at a deck chair. He did not answer. When he turned back, Dina was sitting on the edge of the pool, watching him. "Could you untie this little bow at the back?" she asked.

He bent over her. As he touched her, he felt the same electric shock that he had felt before. He fumbled.

She smiled up at him, playing with his shoelaces. "I bet you've got an alibi."

"Why should I need one? I didn't even know the man's name."

"Nobody seems to. I expect he had lots. Those gangster people usually do."

Bill struggled with the small bow. His hands refused to obey him. He clasped them together for a moment, closed his eyes, opened them, and tried again.

"I bet you haven't even got a motive," said Dina.

"Of course I haven't."

"Clifford likes people to have motives. Otherwise it means Broadmoor."

"Have you?"

"Got a motive? Oh, I expect I could whip one up if I had to."

"Have you got an alibi?"

"Of course, I'm staff."

"What is it?"

She stood up. She was a foot away from him. "Why are you so interested?" she asked, straightening his tie.

Bill took her hands. "Dina," he said heavily. "I *want* you to have an alibi."

She moved about nine inches closer. "Do you, Bill?" she said. "I think I want you to have one too. I'll tell Clifford. He made me a *beauty*."

A hundred yards away, Manelli's bodyguards lounged on the tennis court. Grossi, lonely in his bereavement, had joined them. He leaned against the net, idly bouncing three balls at the same time. Blackie sat on the grass, hitting his bony knees with the strings of a racquet.

Al lay on his stomach, digging up a dandelion with a spring-knife. "Thirteen suspects," he remarked, "Ominous, ain't it?"

"You counted me?" Grossi jumped over the net and back again in the same movement.

"Sure." Al looked at Blackie along his sandy eyelashes. "But I figured us two are in the clear."

"Count yourselves," ordered Grossi. "I'm superstitious."

Al rolled over onto his back. "My dough's on the Boss," he said. "Put his alibi in your eye and you wouldn't even blink."

"That bum's motive would choke a horse," said Grossi.

"Nuts," said Blackie. "If the Boss'd wanted to put the chill on you, he'd of done it. He wouldn't of cluttered the joint up with a lot o' stray stiffs. Like to bet?"

"Don't like to rob you, boy."

"Even money. Five C's."

"I'll take some of that," said Al.

"Sort it out, sort it out," said Blackie. "I like Barker, this Hobson, Flush, and that Cyril, in that order." He added casually, "Present company excepted."

"I'll take ten bucks on Flush for a show," said Al.

"If I didn't know," said Grossi, "I'd fancy me. Nice twist."

Al put a dandelion leaf into his mouth and rifled it out at his foot. "I'd back that," he said. He smiled apologetically at Grossi. "A long shot, just for the hell of it."

"Help yourself," said Grossi. "Name your stake. I'll cover it."

"I mean, saying it wasn't the Boss." Al laughed. "Only kidding."

"Sure. No offense."

"Three grand is all I got."

"Three *grand*?" said Grossi. "That's a lotta jack."

Manelli walked towards them through the sunken garden, immaculate in gray. He bore down upon them, a plume of cigar smoke streaming behind him.

"I got a bet with me," said Grossi. "If it ain't Joe, I give five hundred grand to charity."

Manelli crossed the worn patch at the baseline. He sauntered up to the net. He stood in the sun, not quite squat, not quite hideous. He plucked at his lower lip and sighed. "Takes you back, doesn't it?" he remarked. "All this. Alibis and stuff." He suddenly remembered the night upon which he and Grossi had taken an inquisitive undertaker for the last ride in his own hearse; he and Grossi back in the room afterwards, toasting each other in rough Sicilian brandy, buddies. He shook his head, reminding himself of the elegant establishment on Long Island; the signed Rembrandt; the quiet dinners with the judges and the senators; the quiet, unarmed people; the hard-won, coveted, expensive, fattening, infuriating, boring security of it all.

Al watched him. He regretted again that on the occasion of the historic split, he had not thrown in his lot with the dynamic young Grossi. With Grossi, he would have seen life. He had been dissuaded by the fact that he would have also seen a lot of death, for in those days there had been many superfluous citizens between Grossi and his goal. "We been chewin' the fat, Boss," he told Manelli. "Saying who we like for this cool. Better be you, Slots. Grossi here's got five hundred grand on your nose."

Manelli stared at Hanger Hill. It was a long time since anybody had called him Slots; a long time since the cops had tried in desperation to frame him on an Income Tax rap; a long time since he had been even suspected of murder. "Yeah?" he said noncommittally. He pushed Al with the toe of his shoe. "Get up," he ordered without heat. "I like the Boys on my payroll to stand up when I enter a tennis court."

Al stood up. "Only kidding," he lied. "I know you wouldn't do that, not anymore."

Grossi sneered. He still shot his rivals personally. Manelli did not. The older man's slayings now took the form of a hint dropped by a peaceful fireside into an ear on the right side of the law; a hint which would lead to an investigation and finally lead somebody to the chair. "An *iron* chair," he said, "Made a change, didn't it, Joe?"

Manelli threw his cigar onto the grass and trod on it. "If this job turns out to be one of your funny jokes, Tony," he said coldly, "when I get back to the States, I'll dine out on it for the rest of my natural life."

"What makes you think you're natural, Joe?"

"Quite a joker, Tony."

"Or that you are going to live the rest of your life?"

"Ah, go jump on your foot," snapped Manelli.

"I'm mad at you, Joe."

"Okay, so you're mad."

Grossi picked up a racquet, threw a ball into the air and slashed viciously at it. In silence the four watched it soar into the air, over the cedars and the single-gauge railway line at the bottom of the grounds.

Al sat down again and began to dig up another dandelion. Blackie retied his plimsolls. Manelli lit another cigar.

"Well," said Al after a long pause. "This chill was not one of my babies. I hardly knew the guy." This, he realized instantly, was the weakest of arguments. He rarely knew his victims. Indeed in one case he had asked the man to wear a red carnation in order that he might recognize him. "Just wasn't me," he said feebly.

"Nor me," said Blackie. "I'd of used a cosh or a knife."

"I never used a chair in my life," said Manelli. "I don't like the idea."

"Of course, you could be lying," said Grossi. He took a tennis ball in his hand and allowed it to roll slowly down his arm. As it neared his shoulder, he flexed his biceps. The ball flew ten feet into the air.

"Sure," agreed Manelli. "We've all done some of that."

"I'd swear it wasn't me," said Blackie.

"Me too," said Al. "I'd bet on it."

"Okay, I swear," said Manelli. "How about you, Tony?"

"I don't have to swear, Joe. I know it was you."

"Go on," said Blackie. "Swear."

Grossi clicked his tongue impatiently. "Okay, okay, I swear. Where does it get me?" He raised his shoulders. "Does anybody believe me?"

"Include me out," said Manelli.

"Me too," said Al.

"I never believe anybody," said Blackie.

"So okay," said Grossi. "We all swore. We're all lying. Nobody can prove different."

There was a pause.

"We can't *all* of done it," Blackie pointed out reasonably. "The others would of noticed."

In the drawing room, Flush handed Paget a sheet of paper. "I wish to see the suspects," he said. "In that order."

"Yes, sir." Paget bowed.

"Oh, Paget," said Mrs. Barratt. "Before you go, pick up that chair, will you?" She indicated the murder weapon with her head.

"Yes, madam." Paget advanced upon the chair and laid hold of its arms. He tensed his old muscles, grunted and raised the chair an inch off the Shirazi. "It is very heavy madam... AIYEEEOOO!" he screamed suddenly. He dropped the chair. "I'm sorry, madam. It's my lumbago."

"Brown paper and a hot iron," said Mrs. Barratt. "You may go."

Paget left the room chewing his lip.

"You are a beast," said Dina. "You knew he had lumbago." She ruffled her damp hair. "Who's the first suspect?"

"Mr. Thurlow," said Flush.

"Oh, goody!"

"You wanted me?" asked Bill three minutes later.

Flush had been sitting on the wrought-iron chair. He rose. Mrs. Barratt laid aside her knitting. The Colonel turned with a siphon in his hand. The Creaker was asleep on the sofa with a newspaper over his face. Dina smiled encouragingly.

Flush indicated the chair. "Kindly pick this up," he said. "Wield it as you naturally would were you about to strike somebody."

Bill hesitated.

"Come along, Mr. Thurlow. I am waiting."

Bill picked up the chair gingerly by one front and one back leg. "It's quite light," he said, surprised.

Flush pulled at the lobe of his ear. "Surely, Mr. Thurlow, a man of your intelligence must realize that if you were to strike with the weapon held so, the victim's head would in all likelihood become wedged under the arm?"

Bill put the chair down. "To tell you the truth," he said with an attempt at sarcasm, "I'd forgotten that. I haven't killed anybody with a chair for weeks."

"I think he's *most* unlikely," said Mrs. Barratt as he left the room. "I see him having an accident with a lanyard or felling a tree in the wrong direction, but not this. No, not this."

"I agree," said Flush. "Unless…" He stopped. "Dina, how well did you know the body?"

Manelli came into the room without knocking. He was holding a cigar in a perpendicular position, balancing three inches of ash.

Flush pushed an ashtray towards him. "The chair, if you please, Mr. Manelli. Pick it up."

Manelli tapped the ash off his cigar. He picked up a small gilt chair. "This fella?" he asked.

"No, Mr. Manelli, not that one. *That* one."

Manelli picked up the wrought iron chair by its fluted back, raised it slowly above his head and dropped it behind him. "Sorry," he apologized. "It's so heavy. I'm right outa shape."

He was succeeded by Cyril and Mrs. Carlisle.

"How ghoulish," said Cyril. He picked up the chair by one back leg and staggered slightly. "I thought it was going to be heavy," he explained.

"I thought that you were left-handed," said Flush, interested.

"*Well*," said Cyril. "Actually, I hate to be difficult but I'm ambidextrous. Between ourselves, I can write with either."

"A different calligraphy?"

"Oh, entirely."

Flush nodded. "Mrs. Carlisle, please."

"I'm sorry," said Mrs. Carlisle. "I just *can't*."

"We are not accusing you. Just a formality."

"No, no, no!"

"*Yes!*"

Mrs. Carlisle swayed. "No," she insisted. "It's out of the question. I couldn't even touch it. I'd faint at once." She clutched her forehead and sat down heavily on the chair. "Excuse me," she murmured. "I'm just a trifle dizzy. So silly. I'll be all right in a moment." She sat for a moment, then lurched to her feet and, supporting herself on the furniture in her way, blundered out of the French window. "No, no," she said although nobody had spoken. "Don't try to stop me. Just a breath of air."

Cyril put his hands into his pockets and sauntered after her.

"Next," called Flush.

Paget ushered in Grossi. He stood in the doorway watching with tight lips as Grossi snatched the chair, tossed it into the air, caught it, balanced one front leg on the point of his chin, stretched his arms and raised one foot off the ground.

"Please, Mr. Grossi," said Flush. "This is no occasion for music hall antics."

Grossi swung the chair back onto the floor. "Whaddya want me to do?" he snapped. "Hit somebody?"

"Do you often hit people with chairs?"

Grossi raised his upper lip to indicate that he was not amused, pushed past Paget and left the room.

Paget, without turning round, sketched a motorist's sign to overtake. Blackie shuffled into the room and stood twisting a cap he had borrowed from Hobson.

"Honestly, sir," he said with the earnestness he usually reserved for the East London magistrates. "I know I got a record, but now I got a missus an' two kids at school…"

"You are not married and you have no children," Flush reminded him. "If you had, I should dislike them. Kindly pick up that chair."

Blackie took the chair by its arms and strained at it. "'Fraid you'll 'ave to 'elp me, sir," he said pathetically. "I was never much at 'eavy weights."

"You may go," said Flush.

"Thank you, sir," said Blackie humbly. He was a little disappointed. This was his favorite impersonation and he had not yet done the piece about his mother. "Thank you very much, sir. You're a good, just man. I 'ope the world treats you, sir, as generously as..."

Paget tapped him on the shoulder and jerked his head half an inch backwards.

Blackie shuffled towards the door. "My old mum, sir," he mumbled, "said you could always tell real..."

"Out," said Paget from the side of his mouth.

Blackie smiled sadly from the door. "I'm sure she'll write to you, sir." He twisted Hobson's cap and stumbled away.

"Paget," said Flush. "Has that man become smaller?"

"Yes, sir," said Paget. "He is always doing it. It is maddening, sir."

Al marched into the room. He picked up the chair by one front leg and twisted it around. He then put it down, dusted his hands together and started towards the French windows. "Sure I can whirl it around," he said over his shoulder. "So could a kid with the bends, so, so what?" He swung out onto the terrace.

"I believe, sir," said Paget, "that you will not wish to see Barker."

"Send him in."

"I advise against it, sir."

Barker stood in the doorway, bowing and smiling foolishly. He laid a finger on his lips and shook his head. He sidled up to the chair, strained at it, failed to move it, then clawed at his collar and staggered out of the room. The staff heard him cannoning down the passage.

"Paget," said Mrs. Barratt. "It appears that the staff is not itself."

"A temporary condition, madam. Will you see Mr. Hobson, sir?"

Hobson came into the room at a slow lope. "Last but not least, eh?" he said with a rough laugh. He looked at the chair. "Wot *that*?" he guffawed. He lifted the chair contemptuously with one finger. "*Now* look," he grumbled. "I gone an' bent the bleeder."

"It is perfectly apparent," said Flush ten minutes later, "that this chair must be weighed. Is it heavy or is it light?" He stood looking out of the window, watching and yet not seeing the rooks circling above the pine copse halfway down the hill.

"Of course, *Hobson*," began Mrs. Barratt reflectively.

The Creaker snatched the newspaper off his face and sat up. "No, 'e didn't," he growled. "Not 'is line at all." He could never resist imparting revolting information, so he added, "'E's got the 'ang o' me new one a treat. See, we take some magnesium ribbon an'…"

"That will do, Creaker."

"…an' a wonky geyser an'…"

"*Creaker!*"

The Creaker lost his temper. "Aou shuddup!" he bellowed. "*You* all talk shop, why not *me* ever? 'Snot *fair!*" He hurled his newspaper across the room and leapt to his foot. "Proper browned off, I am," he roared. "You watch out. I'm warnin' you." He hobbled rapidly away, kicking the couch as he passed. He slammed the door behind him. A shower of plaster fell from the ceiling.

Flush had not turned round. "Follow him, Colonel."

The Colonel put down his glass. "Alone?" Flush did not answer and he left the room unwillingly.

Flush sat down. "If the Creaker is in for another bout…" he began moodily.

"Do you think that he could have been responsible for last night's affair?" Mrs. Barratt poked at her hair with a knitting needle.

"Frankly, I don't know. There were one or two aspects which appeared to be…well, too studied. Did you notice that curious footprint on the tiles which apparently had two heels?"

Mrs. Barratt nodded. "And the slight skid at forty-five degrees? A splendid touch."

"By accident, Naomi, or design?" Flush rose and stood drumming his fingers on the back of the sofa. "It's infuriating. Are we seeking an expert or a lucky bungler? Is this a masterly illusion, planned down to the last slovenly clue? Or an impromptu bloomer, a blot on the name of Dankry?" He pulled Mrs. Carlisle's cigarette case from his pocket and hit it with the back of his hand. "Look at this damned thing," he said furiously. "What am I intended to deduce from it? An intelligent plant left by a gifted operator? A rapid attempt to confuse by a spiteful amateur? Or an oversight by a boisterous lunatic? Which, *which*?"

Mrs. Barratt studied him for a long moment. "Clifford," she said. "You walked again last night."

Flush sat down. "Where?"

"I found you in the passage. You were smoking a cigar." She hesitated. "My dear, since the Armitage affair, you have not been yourself. Are you certain that this case is not a recurrence of your old trouble?"

Flush's eyes flashed. "And you, Naomi?" he countered. "Perhaps you succumbed to your much-discussed desire to try a new line?"

Mrs. Barratt laughed gently. "Really, Clifford," she protested. "Do you see me, at my age, running about in my nightdress and a pair of borrowed boots?"

In his pantry, Paget pushed Grossi's bodyguard under the sink and began to prepare the martinis. He moved slowly, sorrow and shame as heavy upon him as a suit of armor. That such a degrading calamity should have happened at *Dankry*! Never in all the glorious years he had served the earl had there been a breath of scandal, a whisper of impropriety. Bloodshed, yes; but in the pursuit of sport. The gory hares, the matted partridges, the last of the stags. But this, no, impossible. His old mind boggled.

The gin overflowed from the shaker onto the back of his hand and ran up his sleeve.

"Drat," he said without heat. He undid his wet cuff, flapping his arm, hoping the gin would evaporate. Why, oh *why* had this presumptuous beaver elected to get himself assassinated *in the grounds?* There was the track, the dark and lonely track down to the village; the meadow to the east of the boundary, where arrowheads and forgotten currencies appeared after rain; the antique and reticent tumuli; the cliff to the northeast with its long, concealing grass and wreaths of buttercups. But no, it had to be in the grounds.

Paget looked into the shaker. It was full of gin. There was room for neither vermouth nor ice. He did not care. He blew his nose and with the other hand began to snatch glasses from the cupboard and bang them onto the tray. He dropped one and ignored it. Trampling on the fragments, he picked up the tray, shot a venomous glance at the body under the sink and pushed open the door with his shoulder.

As he reached the door of the library, he heard footsteps. He paused. The Colonel came round the corner, his eyes drawn to the shaker. His face was scarlet, his white hair ruffled. There was an ugly bruise behind his ear and a shred of linen dangled from his waistcoat button. He was feeling one of his front teeth.

"Are you all right, sir?" asked Paget.

"Oh yes." The Colonel took injury philosophically. The Creaker resented being followed. It was always the same. "That for the guests?"

"A draught of alcohol, sir," murmured Paget, "speeds up the bloodstream, prevents unsightly contusion."

The Colonel helped himself from the shaker. "By the way, Paget," he remarked, squinting into his glass, "decided not to call police. Lot of unpleasantness, so on. Good brew, this. Dry. Any objection?"

Paget leaned back against the lintel. His knees felt strangely weak. "No, sir," he said.

The Colonel looked at him suspiciously. "Why not?"

"The earl, sir, would not have liked a scandal."

"Count on you, eh?"

"Yes, sir."

"Water under the bridge," said the Colonel vaguely. "Don't want a lot of stuff. Speak to Barker, eh?"

"Yes, sir."

"Quite." The Colonel blew up his mustache and went into the library. Lightheaded with relief, Paget tottered along the passage. The Manor's reputation was safe. His own prestige in the village, the only comfort now left to him, was restored; his future stretched before him, unremarkable but proud and peaceful. There was, of course, the problem of the body, but the staff would make no mistake about that. Between them, they knew many fanciful disposal routines.

As he passed through the hall, he suddenly had the curious impression that somebody, a second before, had stood where he stood now. He stopped, uncertain, vaguely uneasy. There was no sound except the murmur of voices behind him in the library, the thud of a bee against the great south window. A shaft of light fell on the dingy parquet, the dust motes swirled placidly in the evening sun. A flower dropped with a soft little plop from a vase of wilting delphiniums.

Paget looked around him. His eye fell on the notice board. There was a typed slip pinned to it announcing a class upon Gases and their Uses across which somebody had written CANCELED. Below this, also neatly typed, was the Thought of the Day. *Gentle friends*, it read. *Let's kill him boldly, but not wrathfully; Let's carve him as a dish fit for the gods, Not hew him as a carcass fit for hounds.*

Stuck to the bottom of the latter slip of paper with a blob of sealing wax and shockingly askew, was a hairy piece of lined notepaper. On it, in sprawling capitals and written in lipstick, was the inscription DAINTY DOGS EAT DIRTY PUDDINGS.

Chapter Eleven

An hour and a half later, when the students filed into the dining room for dinner, the disgraceful message had been removed from the notice board. It had been taken to the laboratory and tested for fingerprints by the Colonel. He had found three of his own, but no others. He had reported this to Flush, who had laughed jovially and told him to consider himself gated. As the staff followed the students along the dim passage, Flush paused to attach a notice to the board announcing a compulsory after-dinner lecture upon Court Etiquette and Procedure.

"We shall carry on as usual?" asked Mrs. Barratt. She picked at the blob of sealing wax which had secured the anonymous message. "Clifford, do you imagine that this is a *clue?*"

"Who cares?" said Flush. He flicked it with his finger. It fell onto the floor and broke in half. Flush laughed and stepped on it.

Mrs. Barratt looked at him suspiciously. "You are suddenly very genial, Clifford," she remarked.

"Of course," said Flush. "I have only to prove that these two ribald crimes are connected to clear myself even in your eyes."

"Why?"

"Surely even you, Naomi, will allow that never, even under the most extreme duress, would I have used lined notepaper."

Mrs. Barratt looked thoughtful. "Clifford," she said slowly. "Provided that it was not you, do you much care who rested that fellow?"

"Frankly," began Flush. He stopped and cleared his throat. "My authority was flouted," he said.

Dinner, owing to Barker's indisposition, was a cold meal prepared by Paget. The rules of the establishment forbade any mention of homicide before the coffee and the students, feeling that other topics were inadequate under the circumstances, drank their iced Bovril in silence.

The staff were not so inhibited. Flush and Mrs. Barratt talked across the table about fainting in the dock, a subject upon which they had always disagreed. Mrs. Barratt maintained that one should faint just before an adjournment. Flush insisted that one should wait until all but one of the jurors had left the Court. Flush was in favor, when revived, of the classic, "Where am I?" Mrs. Barratt preferred, "Of course, it's just a horrible dream." Both agreed, however, as the argument broadened, that one should pass notes to one's counsel or ask for a glass of water only after the Accused had made some point slightly in favor of the prosecution.

The Colonel offered his system of Jury Control. He liked them to feel disgruntled and out of sympathy with all connected with the Law. He attended to this by complaining persistently of a draught or the heat according to the season. If the jury looked cold, open the windows. If they were hot, close the windows.

Manelli reminded Grossi of the occasion when the latter's counsel had failed to challenge an underling of Manelli's on the jury and Grossi had won four months in the penitentiary.

Flush interrupted smoothly to inquire whether any of the students admitted authorship of the message on the notice board. Receiving no answer, he nodded.

If, he mused, this new vexation were the work of the joker who had so presumptuously engaged Grossi's bodyguard, then the field of suspects had perhaps narrowed. The adage was not a common one and typically British. The flavor of the thing smacked of Cyril's sour humor. The lipstick in which it had been written had proved to be one of Mrs. Carlisle's large supply. The repeated desire to cast suspicion upon the novelist was interesting. Was it a personal grudge against the woman herself or merely a formal protest against her products?

He looked around curiously at his companions. They were trying to eat an undercooked cold roast goose. What part did diet play, he wondered, in the spiritual doldrums between the premeditation of murder and the deed itself? Were the energy-forming carbohydrates a deterrent or a stimulus to the moment of action? Did a balanced intake of starch inflame or stifle? Did a sudden increase of calories feed the Jekyll or the Hyde?

Paget circled the table, offering a white thing covered with raspberry jam. All refused it. Paget retired to the shadows. He decided against serving the cheese. It was the same piece. None of the students had ever eaten it and none of them ever would. He waited patiently until they left the room. They filed out in twos and threes. Their conversation was slightly subdued but apparently amiable. The murder seemed to have revived them. Paget stacked the plates on a tray and carried them along the damp passage to the kitchen. Passing his pantry, he pushed open the door with his foot and glared at the blanket-covered form under the sink. Tomorrow had been his day off and now, presumably, he would have to spend it helping to dispose of a corpse he hardly knew.

In the kitchen, Al was bending over Barker, attempting to rouse him. Barker lay in a basket chair, alternately pointing to his head and hitting out feebly.

"The jerk just can't take it," remarked Al. "I tried to rustle up that Matron, but she's soused too. Cowslip wine, she offers me. Cowslip wine! She sees me curl the lip, throws a glass in the fire and blows the goddamn grate out. Whaddya know?"

Paget laid the tray on the draining board. It ashamed him deeply that anybody, and especially these ill-bred foreigners, should see his staff in this degrading condition. In the old days, the voices in the servants' hall had rarely risen above a whisper. He himself had always been addressed, on pain of dismissal, as Mister Paget. Now, his staff had diminished to two; now, he was called "bub," "Mac," "sourpuss" and "fancy pants." Dankry had indeed fallen upon evil days and he had fallen with it. He straightened his back and pulled at the points of his waistcoat. Overhead, he heard Matron roistering in her room. Barker, as if to cap his sorrow, made a prolonged and echoing belch.

"Attaboy," said Al. He wandered over to the tray, snatched a leg off the cold goose and crammed it into his mouth. He chewed. Muscles moved all over his head. He dragged the bone out of his mouth and waved it at the pantry. "What goes with the stiff?" he asked.

"The master," said Paget stiffly, "does not wish this unfortunate accident…"

"Some accident," mumbled Al.

For a wild moment, Paget wondered whether to bang this young whippersnapper's head against the wall. "We do not intend to have the name of Dankry besmirched by scandal," he said. "The master has decided against summoning the police."

"Yeah?" said Al indifferently. He was in no way shocked. "Okay. No Law."

"The fellow is to disappear. After which, any reference to him on this side of the baize will meet with my displeasure."

"Yak, yak, yak," said Al, ripping the parson's nose off the goose.

Paget trembled. His rage threatened to choke him. "Put that bird down," he shouted. He turned away and blew his nose. "Can you be trusted to hold your tongue?"

"Brother," said Al. "Where I come from, one peep out of a big mouth an' you wind up in a block of cement."

"Very well," said Paget. "You may go."

Al stared at him, his lower lip slack. For a moment, he wondered whether to grab the old man by the tails of his coat and crack him in the air like a whip.

Paget smiled at him.

"Okay, okay," said Al, laying a hand over his eyes. "I'm going, I'm going."

In the library, the students settled themselves for the lecture upon Court Etiquette and Procedure. Grossi, as usual, prowled up and down the room, avoiding furniture at the last second by a swing of his lithe hips. There was, Manelli noticed, a pronounced bulge in the left-hand pocket of his ex-partner's jacket. As Grossi neared him, he reached out suddenly and grabbed it. He felt immediately that it was an orange. For a moment, the mobsters looked deep into each other's eyes. Both sneered.

"Got the jitters, Joe?" inquired Grossi.

The door opened and Flush entered holding a sheaf of papers. Dina was at his heels. Flush sat down behind the Colonel's desk. Dina selected a chair between Bill and Cyril.

Flush cleared his throat. "Before we begin," he said, "I wish to warn you that if there are repetitions of this morning's untidiness, I shall take the strictest possible disciplinary action." He opened a drawer and produced his humidor. "If any of you have any suspicion or clue to the identity of this practical joker, you may report to me *in camera* and without fear of reprisal." Rolling a cigar between his palms, he wondered what he would do if one of the students approached him and said apologetically, "Naturally, I'm not accusing you, but while you were taking your stroll at dawn..."

He lit the cigar. He leaned back in his chair and joined the tips of his fingers. "You have your notebooks?" he asked. "Please head your page *Etiquette for the Accused.*" He looked around at the bent heads, reflecting that, provided he himself had not had a brainstorm, one of his pupils was already practicing what he was about to preach. He wondered idly whether it was worth collecting their notes, studying the formation of their capitals. Probably not. The message on the board was almost certainly a forgery. He noted that Cyril was writing that evening with his right hand. The pens stopped scratching. The heads, with the exception of Grossi's, were raised. Grossi, one elbow steadying his notebook, was standing up, looking oddly boneless, writing against the wall. Without interest, Flush wondered whether it would be possible to strike somebody on the head if one were sitting down. "Mr. Grossi," he said. "Are you double-jointed?"

"Nope," said Grossi. "Why?"

Flush did not answer. He picked up his notes. "Our main aim," he said at dictation speed, "is clearly to disconcert our accuser. It is imperative to seize the initiative immediately. Therefore let our demeanor imply that the man cannot possibly be serious; in extreme cases, that he is insane. If the fellow appears to be slightly prejudiced in your favor, *inspire trust.* Why do you instantly act upon the advice of your lawyer or your doctor? Does it occur to you that the one may be in the pay of your enemy, that the other may have taken a dislike to you and be prescribing an untraceable poison? No. Their authority is undisputed. Study the bearing, tone and mannerisms of such professional men. Aim at quiet confidence. Remember that you too are an expert."

He turned a page. "Bear in mind that the thoughts of the average constable under forty turn repeatedly towards promotion, over forty, to his pension. Suggest *indirectly*—underline that please—that a charge of either False Imprisonment or of Malicious Prosecution will affect either prospect adversely."

He waited for the pens to catch up with him. "Do not forget the possibility—remote, I grant you—of a Common Law arrest by an officious civilian. If his meddling constitutes a serious menace, under certain circumstances you may feel entitled to silence him. *How would you do that, Mr. Thurlow?*"

Bill started. "You mean permanently?"

"Of course."

"On the spur of the moment, you mean?"

"Obviously."

"Well," said Bill diffidently. "I'd ask him to have a beer first and try to reason with him."

"And if he proved uncooperative?"

"Well, I don't know. I suppose I'd strangle him."

"How? With his tie?"

"Well, you can't say really, can you? I suppose I'd grab something. Whatever there was. A scarf or something."

"Later, you will learn that it is possible to choke certain stout individuals with their own lapels. Mr. Manelli, how would you deal with a busybody of this type?"

Manelli looked bored. "I'd take his address and send one of the Boys."

"*Which one did you send last night, Mr. Manelli?*"

Manelli yawned. "Can it, dreamboat," he said coldly.

Flush picked up his notes. "Remember always," he dictated, "that your immediate reaction after you are charged is admissible as evidence. *Cyril, I hereby charge you with the willful murder of last night or this morning.*"

Cyril jumped. "*Me?*" he said. "Are you serious?"

Flush studied him. "Try it again," he said. He glanced around at the other students. "Notice that his gambit, although promising, is ruined by the fact that he is sitting down."

Cyril laid his notebook on the floor. "Will you give me the cue again please?"

"I hereby charge you with the willful murder and so on."

Cyril got up slowly. He stood for a moment apparently bereft of speech, then laughed heartily. "For a moment, I thought you were serious," he said.

Flush nodded. "A nice try," he admitted. "The moment of suspended animation was well done and the *slow* rising was psychologically correct. The laugh was perhaps a shade prolonged. But, my dear boy, for heaven's sake *take your hands out of your pockets*." He turned to Grossi. "Would you, in this country, under such circumstances, make any attempt at bribery or any type of corruption?"

"Sure," said Grossi at once. "*Especially* in this country. I got dollars."

"An elementary mistake."

"Watch me," said Grossi. He put his hands into his pockets. There was a slight rustling sound. "If I see the whites of his eyes, it's going to be okay."

"Not in this country." Flush coughed. "Take a note please. Do not scorn a conventional alibi. See to it, however, that at first sight it is pathetically flimsy. In fact, of course, it is unshakable. Personally, I like the alibi which stands or falls upon the time element. Let us suppose that the crime has taken you, working at speed, twenty minutes. You will, ostensibly, have been with a companion for *half* that time. The remainder of the period is unaccounted for. Therefore, although your alibi is not comprehensive, it still appears to be manifestly impossible for you to have done the deed. Should the affair reach a Court, such an alibi gives your counsel an opportunity for the old-fashioned type of histrionics still much relished by juries. *Mrs. Carlisle, you killed this fellow sometime last night or this morning. Have you an alibi?*"

Mrs. Carlisle considered this, then went red with rage. "No," she shouted. "I have not."

"Excellent," said Flush. He wondered whether she could blush at will. "Provided, of course, that further questioning reveals that you were not alone during the hours in question."

"*Mis*-ter Flush," said Mrs. Carlisle clearly. "I have got no one. I was entirely alone all night long. I had ample opportunity to drown that character, *ample*."

Flush frowned. "An unusual finesse," he remarked. "And, unless you can prove complete lack of motive, foolhardy. Shall we consider motives? *Mr. Thurlow, will you tell us why Mr. Grossi saw fit to…er…crease his chauffeur?*"

Grossi froze. "*Smile* when you say that," he ordered.

Bill looked at Grossi, embarrassed. "Perhaps he didn't like him," he suggested.

Grossi clenched his fists. "I loved that punk like he was my own son," he said heatedly.

"Very well," said Flush. "It may calm you to suggest a reason why Mrs. Carlisle should have wielded the fatal chair."

Grossi shrugged. "Her?" he said. "How should *I* know? Maybe she's screwy."

Flush did not look up from his notes, yet he saw Mrs. Carlisle stiffen. "Will you indicate Cyril's motive please?" he asked, pointing his pen at her.

Mrs. Carlisle's spite immediately conquered her anger. "*Well,*" she said. "He was quite simply practicing. A knock-up, so to speak. He's a conceited little chap, aren't you, angel? He hates doing *any*thing unless he does it well." She warmed to her theme. "Look at his ping-pong. He spent hours practicing in the basement before he would play in public. Also, he's an opportunist. It's typical of him to grab the nearest chair."

Cyril sighed. "Dear Chloe," he said with a light laugh. "Fiction has her in a perpetual half-Nelson."

Flush pointed his pen at Bill. "Your motive please, Mr. Thurlow?"

Bill moved uneasily. He pondered for a moment, then shook his head. "I can't think of a thing," he said. "I'm dead against murder."

Cyril laughed. "Remember where you are, chum."

"Vendettas don't count," said Dina quickly. "I expect it was an accident. They happen, then you don't like to say anything."

Bill looked at her. The scene on Beachy Head at last emerged in its true perspective. Dina had not pushed her ex-fiancé over the precipice. It had been raining and he had skidded in the slippery clay. It had been an accident. If Dina confessed as much to Flush, she would not be eligible for the lavish salary she received at Dankry. She was not a murderess. He looked into her yellow eyes and reached for her hand. "Of *course,*" he said, knowing that he should not be smiling, trying to control his expression. "That would have been my motive if I'd had one," he said, beaming. "It was an accident. I saw this chap was going to fall or something and I grabbed the chair for some reason…and so did he, trying to save himself or some-

thing, but I'd let go and it whirled around his head and brained
him. That's not murder, it's just damned unfortunate." He
squeezed Dina's hand and added warmly, "It might happen to
anybody."

"You forget that the man was also drowned," said Flush.
He was not impressed by Bill's reconstruction. Moreover, he
realized tetchily, Dina was about to fall in love again. He recognized the primary symptom. Her infatuations were always
proceeded by a hint to the new suitor that she would not dream
of pushing anybody even off a pavement. Love made her moody
and unpredictable and played hell with her shorthand. "Are you
trying to confess, Mr. Thurlow?" he asked.

"No, no," said Bill. "I never even met him."

"He was a good hood," said Grossi sadly.

"Only one thing you can say about that creep," Manelli
remarked. "This is the first time he didn't do it."

Flush noted Grossi's expression and rapped sharply on the
table. "Shall we consider Judges?" he asked smoothly. "As most
of us will be detained upon a capital charge, we are concerned
only with High Court judges. Now how shall we address him?
Mr. Manelli?"

"Way back, I called 'em 'Judge,'" said Manelli. "These
days, I call 'em by their first names."

"Mr. Grossi?"

"My cases don't get to Court," said Grossi. "The witnesses
take a powder."

"Mr. Thurlow?"

"I'd call him 'Your Lordship.'"

"That, of course is the protocol. But *should you know the
protocol?* The jury probably do not. Therefore I like 'Your
Worship' implying that I too have no knowledge of legal procedure. You will of course be corrected. The next time you will
emphasize your ignorance with a confused and hesitant 'Your
Honour.' Never under any circumstances will you say 'M'lud.'
This term is used only by barristers and old lags. Do not attempt
any fancy titles of your own design. Goonatilika, in trying to

stress his ignorance of European customs, grossly exaggerated with a 'My Worship.' This enraged the Bench and when later Goonatilika weighed in with a chance 'Your Lud,' an adverse summing-up was assured."

There was a soft tap at the door. Paget advanced three feet into the room. "Excuse me, sir," he murmured. "The Colonel is driving into Poxwell Regis. He wants to know whether he should dispose of the body *en route.*"

Flush did not look up. "No," he said shortly. "I intend, since we have met with this misfortune, to afford the students the opportunity of practicing Disposal. *Sit down, Mrs. Carlisle.* You will have until tomorrow morning to consider ways and means. The most suitable suggestion will be adopted tomorrow afternoon. You may go, Paget." He tapped on the desk with his pen. "Now please write down and underline *Ripostes from the Bench and Judge-Control.* Mrs. Carlisle, will you kindly sit *down?*"

Chapter Twelve

Cyril knocked softly on Mrs. Carlisle's bedroom door and slid into the room without waiting for an answer. His bright hair was ruffled and exactly the same color as his carefully chosen dressing gown.

Mrs. Carlisle was sitting at the dressing table wearing her gray lace negligee and a pink hairnet. She watched Cyril in the mirror. "Yes?" she said icily. "What can I do for you? If you're looking for an alibi, you're in the wrong department."

Cyril took a pair of scissors from the table, sat down on the bed and began to cut his nails. "Peace mission," he said cautiously. "No alibi, no war drums, just a drop of peace."

"Where's your tarty little chum?"

"Don't know, don't care."

"Don't lie. What do you want? Money?"

For once, Cyril did not take offense. "You are vile," he said absently. "I was thinking about this Disposal caper tomorrow. I thought perhaps that we might get together. We need practice as a team."

Mrs. Carlisle wound a length of pink tulle around her head. "I refuse to have anything whatever to do with it," she said. "I didn't shoot him and I have no intention of burying him."

"Chloe, do try to remember. He was drowned and stunned." Cyril admired his hands. "What do you mean *bury* him? Bury him *where*?"

"I don't *care*," said Mrs. Carlisle. "He never meant more to me than a hole in the road. What's the matter with the tumuli? They were good enough for the druids."

"I'd thought of slinging him over the cliff."

"You are lazy. Anyway, you can't do that. Grossi's going to."

"Who said so?"

"Grossi."

"What's Manelli going to do?"

"He wants the cliff too, but Flush won't allow more than one."

"What about Bill?"

Mrs. Carlisle smeared skin-food over her face and neck. "He mumbled something about the old well. Typical, isn't it? No imagination."

Cyril got up and wandered over to the window. A thread of cloud was sliding across the round moon. "I'm not mad for this burying lark," he said thoughtfully. "The ground's hard as nails and anyway the whole area is stiff with bones."

"Well, acids," said Mrs. Carlisle impatiently. "Fire, quick-lime, trunks in cloakrooms, drowning…"

Cyril tapped his foot on the floor. "Are you *trying* to be irritating? I've told you eighteen times that he's already *been* drowned."

"Exactly," said Mrs. Carlisle.

"Of *course*," said Cyril. "Dear Chloe, what *would* I do without you?" The mere thought of such a prospect was so exhilarating that he was silent for a moment. As his eyes refocused, he found her watching him with a suspiciously mild smile. "Angel," he said, hurrying towards her, taking her into his arms.

"Be careful, you oaf," snapped Mrs. Carlisle. "You're bruising my thenar eminence."

In the room next door, Manelli, Grossi, Al, and Barker were playing poker. Each had a glass at his elbow and the air was blue with cigar smoke.

Grossi slid a card across the table. "Take one," he said. "Say, Joe, this finagle tomorrow. You know me, I don't work solo. Will you loan one of your Boys?" *That's not unreasonable*, added his sideways glance. *Seeing you ironed my sidekick.*

Manelli rose and strolled towards the whisky.

"I'll play these," said Al.

Barker raised two trembling fingers and shuffled up two cards.

"Twenty bucks says I filled my flush," said Grossi.

"I got thirty bucks says you're goddamn liar," said Al.

"Joe," said Grossi. "I'll make a deal. No Boy, no hooch."

"Okay. Take Blackie."

"I'll take Al."

"Blackie."

Barker belched. He pointed one finger at the empty fifth chair. He walked two fingers along the table, waved in a westerly direction, used two hands to describe a figure eight, made an undulating gesture with his left hand, pointed to the carpet and moved his jaws up and down.

"He means," translated Al, "that Blackie has gone into Poxwell Regis with this dame of Barker's. They will go onto the tumuli and Blackie won't be worth a damn tomorrow except to chew up carpets."

"Okay, okay," said Manelli. "Take Al. But I take the cliff."

Grossi sighed. "I already took the cliff, Joe. You take the hit-and-run routine. Nice U turn down in Krunte Abbas."

"I don't break my leg on that Roman junk twice," stated Al. "One cliff, *one*."

"Full moon," remarked Dina. "Isn't it splendid?"

Bill was on his knees on the mossy flags, trying to lever the top off the old well. "Wonderful," he grunted. The heavy round stone moved an inch. Bill sat back on his heels. The landscape reeled.

Dina leaned against the dank old bricks. She patted the grass beside her invitingly. "I wish you'd stop horsing around with that silly old well," she said with a trace of irritation.

Bill's jacket had somehow become trapped between the stone cover and the brick surround. He struggled silently for a moment, then gave up. He wriggled out of the jacket and sat down beside her. He had planned a slow maneuver of sliding his arm gradually off the bricks and around her shoulder, edging cautiously nearer and nearer so as not to frighten her; but before he could move, he found her on his knee with her arms wound tightly around his neck.

"That's better," she said with satisfaction. "About time too."

One by one, the lights went off in the gaunt old house. The moon climbed up the sky, throwing huge shadows among the towers and battlements. A bat flickered among the ancient oaks. The rooks on the copse on the hill fell asleep as the frogs woke up in the bogged water meadow.

As the tide went out below the red cliffs, the sea boiled out of the pool in the rocks known as Hardy's Cauldron. Hours later, in the still half-hour which preceded the dawn, the lantern went out on the buoy which marked the farthest of the treacherous underwater rocks.

At half past seven, it had already been light for some hours. In his little room which overlooked the quarry, Paget explored himself to make sure that he was still alive. He dragged himself out of bed, dressed and padded painfully downstairs to see whether Barker was in a fit condition to make the early teas.

Passing Grossi's room, he heard a groan. Another murder? Or the first agony of another hangover? Paget did not care either way. He shuffled on. As he neared Mrs. Carlisle's room, the door opened stealthily. Cyril, barefooted, clutching his bedroom slippers, crept into the passage. Paget stood still. Cyril took a full half minute to close the door. It did not make a sound. Then he stretched, rubbed his eyes and yawned so widely that for a second he shook all over. He started to tiptoe down the corridor towards his own room, then paused. He looked around over his shoulder and met Paget's fishy eye.

"Good morning," he said after a brief pause.

"Good morning, sir," said Paget urbanely.

"Yes indeed," said Cyril. He nodded and went into his room.

Paget proceeded along the passage and started downstairs. As he reached the hall, he was hailed from above by a hoarse whisper.

"'Ere, tosh!" hissed the Creaker. "Wot's for grub? I'll 'ave eggs. *Eggs*."

Paget ignored him. He crossed the hall, turned down the dark corridor and went into the kitchen.

Barker lay snoring in the basket chair. He was fully dressed and clutching an empty bottle of ginger ale. Somebody had put a lemon into his mouth.

Paget bit his lip and put on the kettle. Laying the tea trays, he thought about breakfast. Obviously, Barker would be unable to cook it. He himself—for whom once a staff had waited, around whose place had been ranged several hot, covered entree dishes ready for his approval—Mister Paget was about to cook for nine killers and four who were learning the art...

He blew his nose. So the Creaker wanted eggs, did he?

With a small, bleak smile, Paget went into the larder and carefully selected thirteen kippers.

An hour and a half later, the strong, stale smell of the fish still clung about the kitchen. Paget was washing up. Barker still lay in the basket chair. The lemon had fallen out of his mouth and he had stopped snoring. Overhead, Matron was stamping about, making her bed and singing "I Know a Bank."

Grossi came through the door and propped himself negligently against the wall. "Hey, Paget," he said. "Will you lend me a hand? This disposal gimmick this morning. Al was in with me, but he's still out. Me too, I got my head in a sling." He smiled ingratiatingly and made rustling noises in his pockets.

Paget, drying a plate, turned to look at him. "I understand, sir, that you intend utilizing the cliff?"

"Yep," said Grossi. "But there is no road and the going is tough. You got any ideas?"

Paget did not answer. He put thirty-nine potatoes into a bowl, sighed heavily and left the room.

Grossi wandered across and stuffed the lemon back into Barker's mouth. Ten minutes later, when he was wondering whether to abandon the cliff and switch to the U turn, Paget returned.

"This way please, sir," he said.

Grossi followed him out of the back door. A large black horse stood in the yard with its head lowered. It was an old horse. It raised its head and stared apathetically at Grossi. Over its back was a sack, full and yet curiously shapeless.

"Who's in there?" asked Grossi sharply.

"We always use the correct weight of sand, sir," explained Paget. He added patiently, "We cannot throw the Intended over the cliff, sir. The others will be needing him." He took hold of the bridle and led the horse slowly towards the vegetable garden. "Follow me please, sir."

Flush met the small procession as it crossed the upper lawn. "The cliff, I presume," he said. "The Cauldron?"

"I thought the point, sir," said Paget.

"What time is the tide high?"

"11:20, sir."

Flush turned away, then struck by a sudden thought, turned back. "How many sacks, Paget, have already gone over the point?"

"Quite a number, sir. When the tide is low, there is a small strand, sir. Samuel White's children…"

Flush frowned and strode away towards the house.

As the horse's hoofs clattered across the stable yard, the Colonel emerged from the garages. "Weighted?" he asked abruptly.

"Sir," said Paget.

"Good man."

Paget did not pause. Both he and the horse walked steadily, gazing at their feet. Neither took any notice when the Creaker came out of the summerhouse and asked, "You take my 'ammer?" Paget had never spoken to the Creaker and never would.

The horse pushed open the gate to the vegetable garden, turned left and went down the path between the late strawberries. He walked through a compost heap, trod on a marrow and pushed open another gate. Ahead, the tumuli stood silhouetted against the bright sky. The last of them was a mile away, on the edge of the cliff.

Paget and Grossi walked in silence, their feet tangling in the rough scrub and the long brown grass. A partridge rose with a whir of wings. Grossi jumped. He hated birds.

"Look," he said, nodding at the distant cliff. "That is going too far. Why don't we bury it here?"

"National Trust," said Paget curtly.

Some while later, the old black horse grunted and stood abruptly still. The sack fell off his back, slithered down a slight incline and came to rest against the broken astragal of a Roman column.

Half a mile away, on the point of the cliffs, Bill pulled Dina closer. Two minutes later, he said, "Dina, you ought not to be here."

She misunderstood him. "I have to show Grossi the cliff drill," she said softly.

"You don't know the cliff drill," he reminded her. "Do you?"

She sighed against his cheek. "Whatever I say, nobody believes me," she said pathetically.

"*I* believe you."

"That's sweet of you, Bill."

Bill swallowed. "Dina," he said.

"Yes?"

Bill drew a deep breath. "Dina," he said. "I love you."

Four minutes later, she murmured, "Just think how nearly we never met. If it hadn't been for…well, for one thing and another…"

Bill interrupted. "Everything's going to be different," he said, beaming.

She stirred in his arms. "Grossi's awfully late," she whispered. "Do you want me to go?"

"No. Yes."

"I don't want to."

"Please, Bill. I don't want you to…well, see me in action."

Bill stood up unwillingly. He looked down at the swell surging over the rocks a hundred feet below. A gannet plummeted into the waves, reappeared and flew away with a small fish in its beak. For an instant, the sea retreated, the foam creaming over the black rocks as a new wave reared. Bill took an involuntary step backwards.

"What were you suddenly thinking?" asked Dina. There was a hint of accusation in her tone.

"How awful people are," said Bill. "To think that you…I mean, *look* at you."

"I know," she said. "The beasts."

"Goodbye, Dina. Do be careful. Don't overbalance or anything."

"Look both ways crossing the tumuli."

Bill walked fast and straight. Smiling, he walked through a bog and a tangle of dead raspberry canes without noticing either. He picked up a stick and swiped at the buttercups. His life flamed ahead of him, a blaze of glory. When he and Dina were married and living in a neat little house in…

He stopped. He dropped the stick. The idea of marriage was in itself a shock. But he was a potential murderer, he had no right whatever to get married. Dina would never accept him. What of the children? Would he beget a tribe of assassins? Could he ask Dina to sit at home while their sons went to school, knowing that at the first caning the youngsters would almost certainly massacre their tormentors? He saw their small rosy faces, their beguiling smiles at the maimed rivals, the dead prefects, the headmaster lying in a pool of blood.

He moved on slowly, deeply preoccupied. In a small valley, he came upon Grossi, Paget, and a large black horse. The horse was cropping at the dry grass.

Grossi squinted up through the smoke of his cigarette. "Know any horse routines?" he inquired. "The animal likes it here."

"Bite his ear," suggested Bill. He added, too absorbed in his own problem for tact, "Have Paget smile at him."

For an instant, Paget looked astonished. Then his face curdled. He clutched at his sides and bent double, feebly stamping one foot on the ground. From him came a curiously high keening sound. Bill, horrified, started forward.

"It's okay," said Grossi unsteadily. "He's laughing."

Unnerved, Bill hurried away. Ten minutes later, he pushed through the swing gate into the vegetable garden. As he passed the summerhouse, the Creaker came out and emptied a bucket of some liquid which evaporated before it reached the ground.

"I got a treat rigged up in 'ere," he said, scratching his false leg. "Want to 'ave a dekko?"

"No," said Bill. "No, thank you."

"Come on. It's not 'alf mucky."

"No, thank you."

Bill backed away. The Creaker went back into the summerhouse. Bill heard him asking Hobson what he had done with the bag of nougat. Hobson roared with laughter. Bill hastened round the hedge. He did not want to hear any of the Creaker's jokes, ever.

Under the weeping willow, he came upon Mrs. Carlisle. Her typewriter was balanced on her knees and the grass around her was littered with paper.

"Have you Disposed?" she asked.

"Not yet. Have you?"

"No. We're after Manelli. I had a brainwave. We're going to re-drown him."

"What about the bump on his head?"

"Well, nobody seems to have spotted the original killer, so we're going to do it all over again, exactly the same."

"How do you know it will be exactly the same?" asked Bill suspiciously.

"Listen," she said. "If you're going to start being shrewd, I shall scream." She turned away and started to tinker with the ribbon on her typewriter. Bill walked away thoughtfully. As he went, he heard her roll another sheet of paper into the machine and begin to type again.

Crossing the courtyard towards the old well, he saw Manelli in the garages. The mobster was sitting in his huge black Studebaker, revving the engine and smoking a cigar. "Say," he called, leaning out of the window. "Did you see Tony? He's late. I'm way behind schedule." He reversed the Studebaker slowly out into the yard.

"What are you going to do?"

"Ah, shove him in the heap, dump him over the border, run over him, beat it. It's old, but it's still good."

"I wouldn't know," said Bill curtly.

"Don't be like that," said Manelli. "Here, have a cigar."

"No, thank you. Will you give me a hand with the well?"

Manelli got out of the car. Together they walked across the yard and under the rambler arch. Bill's jacket still hung over the brick surround of the well, trapped by the sleeve.

Manelli fingered the cloth. "Harris," he remarked. "Nice. Yours?"

"Yes."

Manelli laid hold of the large round stone, found a foothold and heaved.

The stone slid onto the grass on the far side of the wall.

Bill stared. "My God, you're strong," he said.

Manelli wiped his hands on his handkerchief. "Oh, I don't know," he said. "You get days." He picked up a pebble, held it over the mouth of the well then dropped it.

Both men stood motionless, waiting for the splash. Ten seconds later, Manelli picked up another pebble and threw it after the first. He stood listening. "Some well," he remarked.

"Deep," said Bill uncertainly.

"Bottomless."

"Wait. Did you hear anything?"

"Nope. Did you?"

"No."

They walked back under the rambler arch. Manelli stopped to pick a rose. He removed the thorns and put it into his buttonhole.

"Mr. Manelli," said Bill. "Were you ever married?"

"Sure."

"What happened?"

"It didn't take. She didn't like the Boys."

"She didn't mind about…well, about your career?"

Manelli raised his shoulders and made a gesture as if he were holding a large medicine ball. "The hours are too long," he said. "Suppose you have to blow suddenly. Suppose the Outfit wants to see you. Suppose the guy you want to cool doesn't show. Suppose you're a coupla days late. Suppose you never show up except in the morgue. What do you say? 'Sorry, honey. I got held up'? No, they can't take it. It's the hours."

"Suppose you don't make a habit of it?"

"Just the once?"

"Yes. What then?"

"No," said Manelli. He shook his head slowly. "Take me. I'd chilled but the one guy and my wife divorces me. They don't like it. I never saw it work out yet."

"Not even if it was…well, sort of honorable."

"Nope," said Manelli firmly. "They get crabby."

"Thanks," said Bill. He turned and strode away towards the house. Manelli stood under the rambler arch staring after him. Then he shrugged, collected a sizable stone from the rockery and started back towards the old well.

The four senior members of the staff sat in the library. Flush was correcting the examination papers. Mrs. Barratt was writing the next day's menu. The Colonel was oiling his Springfield. The Creaker lay on the sofa devouring a banana and reading a novel. On the dust jacket was a picture of a man burying his fist in another's face so savagely that it seemed unlikely that he would ever get it out again.

"Boiled mutton again," murmured Mrs. Barratt. "And perhaps sago. Surely nobody likes sago?"

"Kippers bad at breakfast," the Colonel accused.

"I'm so sorry," said Mrs. Barratt. "I will speak to the fishmonger."

"This paper of Cyril's is excellent," said Flush. "Quite outstanding. His camping accident is most ingenious."

"Practical?" asked the Colonel.

"Yes, and diabolically simple. All the others fell into the trap of the guyropes. Mr. Manelli, I am disappointed to see, offered the primus drill. Both he and Grossi tend to oversimplify."

"Mrs. Carlisle?"

"Hopeless, hopeless."

"Cyril will be on top?"

"Oh yes." Flush reached for a cigar. "Had he the necessary qualifications, I would be tempted to offer him a post on the staff."

"Be qualified September the fourth," pointed out the Colonel, "all goes well."

There was a loud knock on the door. Bill burst into the room and stopped abruptly. "Mr. Flush," he said in a determined manner. "Can I speak to you alone?"

Flush raised his eyebrows. "Some new method?" he inquired. "Is it repulsive?"

"No, no. Nothing like that."

"Then my colleagues will remain. Some flaw perhaps in your Disposal?"

"No." Bill hesitated. He put his hands into his pockets, then took them out again. "I've changed my mind," he said. "I'm not going to kill him after all."

"Really? Who?"

"My Intended."

Flush's expression did not change but he stiffened. "Come, Mr. Thurlow," he said coldly. "You are overexcited."

"No," said Bill. He added defiantly, "I won't do it. You can't talk me into it."

"I do not care for deserters, Mr. Thurlow."

"I know," said Bill. He put his hands into his pockets. "I realize that I probably won't leave this room...I mean, I know that you all hate me."

He clenched his hands. For a mad instant, he saw himself shot in the shoulder and Dina tearing up her petticoat to staunch his wounds. He controlled himself. Dina did not wear petticoats. "I'm sorry," he said feebly. "I know it's awful, but I just can't. Something's cropped up which changes everything."

"Indeed? I suggest that you are not yourself, Mr. Thurlow."

"I am," Bill insisted. "I'm terribly sorry."

Flush turned his back and stared out of the window. "So you propose to let this monster live?"

"Well," said Bill defensively. "He may get run over or something."

"And he may not."

"Well, he's quite old. And I'm only twenty-six."

"Yellow belly," mumbled the Colonel.

"Pure selfishness," agreed Mrs. Barratt.

"You may go, Mr. Thurlow." Flush hurled his cigar onto the terrace. "I advise you to go before I forget myself."

Bill nodded speechlessly and hurried from the room. The door clicked to behind him.

The Creaker dogeared a page and laid down his book. "Shall I get 'im?" he asked.

"No. Sit down please."

"Clifford," said Mrs. Barratt. "Are you never going to tell us what his Intended *did*?"

"Yes," said Flush. He leaned his forehead against the cool glass of the window and told her.

Mrs. Barratt stifled a scream. "*No!*" she cried.

"Gad!" said the Colonel. "By gad!"

"*Cor!*" said the Creaker, awed.

"He must go, of course," said Mrs. Barratt faintly.

"Obviously," said Flush.

"I'll show 'im somethin'," offered the Creaker.

Mrs. Barratt stood up. "I'm an old woman," she said. "I've been retired many years…"

"Needs a damn good horsewhipping," said the Colonel, "to begin with. Shall go myself."

"'Ere," protested the Creaker. "I said first."

"*I* shall go," said Mrs. Barratt. "Nobody notices an old woman."

The Colonel said something to himself in Hindustani, stabbing himself in the chest with his thumb.

"I'm goin'," announced the Creaker. "You can't stop me."

"Let us *all* go," suggested Mrs. Barratt. "First come, first served."

"Very well," said Flush. He strode across to an ashtray and ground out his cigar. "There is a train at 12:20. I shall be on it."

"'Obson and me'll go by coach," said the Creaker.

The Colonel looked at Mrs. Barratt. "Bus is in the yard," he observed. "Give you a lift, madam?"

"Thank you," said Mrs. Barratt. "I will fetch my coat." She touched Flush's arm. "It's really quite exciting," she admitted. "Just like the old days."

"I hope," said Flush heavily, "that none of us has lost our old flair…" He turned in the doorway. "Only the simplest routines," he warned. "This is going to be an accident."

Five minutes later, he crossed the yard.

Manelli, sitting on the running board of his Studebaker, raised one finger in salute and inquired whether Flush had seen Grossi.

Flush did not answer. He threw a briefcase onto the seat of the small staff car, climbed in, reversed into the yard and drove away towards the hill.

Manelli lit another cigar, sighed, leaned back and closed his eyes. He was roused by the triphammer roar of the Colonel's Bugatti. Mrs. Barratt, frail and tiny in a flowered toque and a black silk coat, was climbing into the front seat with remarkable agility. The Colonel, wearing a yellow waistcoat, crouched over the wheel. Even as Mrs. Barratt gathered her skirts, the Bugatti shot out of the yard and clamored down the drive.

Manelli frowned. Suddenly uneasy, he got up and stretched, made up his mind and strolled towards the house. On the terrace, he met the Creaker and Hobson. The Creaker was borrowing a silk scarf from Cyril and Hobson was pulling on a battered cap. The Creaker pushed Manelli out of his way.

"Gangway!" he roared. "We gotter job."

In spite of his limp, he walked extraordinarily fast. Hobson ran along beside him throwing up his cap and catching it.

Cyril raised his eyebrows. "Operation Kill or Curare," he remarked and went back into the house.

Manelli shook his head and started back towards the garages. As he went under the rambler arch, he saw that Grossi had arrived back from his Disposal. The younger mobster was sitting on an overturned rain butt with his head in his hands and his feet on the sack of sand. "Holy cow!" he said, breathing deeply.

"You are late, Tony," Manelli pointed out. "This annoys me."

Grossi raised bloodshot eyes. "Joe," he said quietly. "I am going to iron that horse."

Manelli looked at him without sympathy. "And who else?"

Grossi mopped his forehead. "That Paget is number two," he said. "You got yourself demoted, Joe."

Manelli laid hold of the sack and tried to lift it. "Holy smoke, that's heavy!" he complained.

"Yeah," said Grossi bitterly. "I should know. I just carried it in from the tumuli."

Manelli was shocked. "Gee, that's awful, Tony."

"On my back."

"God," said Manelli. "Didn't this Paget help any?"

"Sure, sure. He carried my cigarettes." Grossi took his head between his hands and shook it.

Manelli seized the sack, towed it across the yard and heaved it into the back of the Studebaker. He slid behind the wheel and started the engine. "I am going to Dispose by the U turn," he said. "I will probably drop off at this Pilgrim Ho! for a mead or three."

Grossi considered this unspoken invitation. He disliked accepting a favor of any sort whatever from Manelli, but the idea of a double mead was attractive and his morale was low. He lurched across to the Studebaker and fell onto the seat next to his ex-partner.

Manelli drove slowly between the overhanging shrubs in the drive, steered carefully through the gates and turned into the lane. The rocks exploded from the trees in the pine copse on the hill. The slanting rays of the sun had reached halfway down the opposite Barrow. The village lay below, still in shadow.

The mobsters did not look at each other. Both were slightly embarrassed. With the exception of the one famous occasion when both were under arrest and handcuffed to each other, they had not ridden in the same car for nineteen years.

"Sorta takes you back," remarked Manelli.

"Yeah."

"If Waxey saw us now!"

"He'd kill himself."

"He'd be no loss."

Manelli steered carefully between the potholes. The surging banks of cow parsley brushed against the flanks of the car.

"Nice heap," observed Grossi. "Bulletproof?"

"Sure. Yours?"

"Yep."

A rabbit hopped across the track and disappeared into the ditch. At the bottom of the hill, Manelli turned right onto the tarmac, drove across the road and parked outside the Pilgrim

Ho! Farther down the road, the Creaker and Hobson were waiting at the bus stop. There was a large, covered basket on the ground between them. The Creaker was wearing a bowler hat.

"Where are those goons going?" asked Grossi.

"Some cool."

The Americans walked side by side into the tavern. Grossi sank onto the stool where Cromwell had rested on the way to Corfe. Mr. White, the estate agent, rose from a dark inglenook and walked unsteadily towards him. "Welcome to this low bothy, sir," he said. "We are all Pilgrim Fathers under the skin. Will you accept a stoop of mead?"

An hour and a half later, Manelli and Grossi drove back up the hill. They had consumed a large quantity of mead and whereas they had not yet entirely sorted out their differences, both had wondered privately at least once whether it would be necessary to kill the other.

"Omaha," said Grossi. "Last time you bought me a drink."

"Pittsburgh."

"Buffalo."

"Yeah. Buffalo."

Lunch was nearly finished. Mrs. Carlisle, Bill, and Dina sat among the empty chairs of the missing staff. Paget, his shoes still dusty from the abortive excursion among the tumuli, was serving baked custard.

Mrs. Carlisle was clearly in a semi-hysterical condition. She half rose from her chair. "Where have you *been?*" she said shrilly. "Cyril and I were supposed to Dispose at 11:45. Where is everybody? Where's *Cyril?* Where's that damned *sack?*"

Manelli sat down. He met Grossi's eyes for a second across the table. He was unwilling to admit that, while drinking in the Pilgrim Ho! with Mr. White, the sack had been stolen from the back of the Studebaker.

Mrs. Carlisle did not wait for an answer. *Why*, she asked wildly, did nobody know where the staff were? Where had they *gone*? What were they *doing*? Why did nobody ever *tell* her anything? This was not why she had paid the exorbitant Dankry fee. She could hang around a dismal room and eat appalling food in any good hotel in Britain. And *where* was *Cyril*? Had the staff abducted him? Had they finally broken out and, well, in any way *maimed* him? It was all very well for Mr. Manelli to pull that idiotic face. It was not *his* accomplice who was missing and in such racy company. Even that rancid creature Hobson had vanished. Who even dared to think what Hobson might be up to *this very moment*? And what about Flush himself? She herself had seen Flush emerging from the armory, screwing a silencer onto a Colt .45 and *wearing a hat*.

Paget offered Manelli the baked custard.

Mrs. Carlisle savaged her roll and informed the company that she was not hysterical, merely, and God knew with good cause, alarmed. She did not wish to be in any way offensive, but after all Manelli and Grossi between them had probably wiped out a whole precinct. She personally found both of them charming, but surely they would agree that the staff had no right whatever to leave her alone with them? Mr. Grossi might well grin in that asinine way, but how would *he* feel if he were left alone with himself?

Grossi waved away the baked custard and told Paget to bring the cheese.

Mrs. Carlisle thumped on the table with both fists. She did not want to make a scene, she said, but how did she know that Cyril was not lying around *mangled*? She was well aware that he had his faults, and God knew they were legion, but he was her only accomplice and where she would be without him, she knew very well indeed. She wanted to make herself quite clear. She was damned if she was going to Dispose all by herself, course or no course, Flush or no Flush. Flush could take a running jump into the dew pond. That was all she wanted to say. *She would not Dispose.*

Paget cleared his throat and stepped forward. "I fear that, in any event, it will not be necessary, madam. The deceased has been stolen."

Manelli sighed. "Okay, okay," he said. "Some guy knocked him off while we were in this bar."

Paget shook his head mournfully. "I was not referring to the sack, sir. I too have been remiss, sir. I was speaking of…for want of a better phrase, sir, *the genuine article*."

Chapter Thirteen

"**W**ho took him?" Grossi was on his feet. "That's *my* stiff."

"When?" demanded Manelli.

"Really, Paget, you are careless," said Dina.

Paget stood holding the baked custard. "I left him in my pantry, miss," he said unhappily. "When I returned with Mr. Grossi from our errand to the tumuli, I was obliged to occupy myself with household duties normally performed by Matron. She is as usual not herself. I cannot be in two places at the same time, miss. I did not make my discovery until I had sounded the first gong. I repaired to my pantry with the intention of rubbing up a dingy cruet and felt at once that something was missing."

"Why didn't you report to me?" asked Dina.

Paget lowered his eyes. "You were on the terrace, miss. Your costume suggested that you wished to be alone."

"The staff had left?"

"Yes, miss. That was the last time I saw the deceased. I accompanied Mr. Flush when he went to test the degree of rigor."

"Perhaps he took him."

"No," said Manelli. "None of the staff. I saw them leave. Flush had a briefcase, that's all."

Mrs. Carlisle ran a hand through her hair. "In South America," she said in a choked voice, "there are tribes who shrink people to the size of pickled walnuts."

"We don't do that," said Dina.

Mrs. Carlisle pushed back her chair. "*I* know who took him," she said loudly.

"Who?" Grossi's hands whitened on the back of his chair.

"Who didn't like him in the first place?" said Mrs. Carlisle. "Somebody didn't want him around." She swallowed noisily. "I know that three of you are professionals. I try to look upon it like any other job. I'm a broadminded woman and I know that you have to earn your living. If you come to me and say, 'Chloe, I have killed three or four people,' I merely hope that you'll drop dead. But to kidnap a poor helpless corpse...! Well, *really*! Personally, I intend to lock myself into my room until those murderers return and I can feel reasonably safe again." She swept out of the room, across the hall and up the stairs.

Halfway up, she stopped, suspecting that somebody might comment upon her exit. She continued to move her feet on the wooden stair, lightening her tread so that each click of her heels grew fainter. She strained her ears, listening.

Grossi was the first to speak. "Gone?" he asked.

"No," said Dina. "I can see her feet. She's doing some sort of dance."

Mrs. Carlisle bit her lip and hurried upstairs. She went into her room, locked the door and looked around for something to throw. Trembling with rage, she decided to have a migraine.

"What can you expect from a pack of murderers?" she asked herself aloud. "Nothing. Obviously. Why should you? You're mad, raving." She bustled around the room collecting her props. "Ha!" she exclaimed, snatching the tube of aspirins. She ripped off her dress and clawed at her gray negligee. She pulled it on, her fingers fumbling wildly among the small buttons, and sat down before the mirror. "God, my *head*," she told her reflection, already believing the pain. She reminded herself that rage ruined her complexion, that it was absurd to endanger her looks when she was so shortly to become a widow. "Lot of flaming criminals," she growled as she climbed into bed.

Half an hour later, she heard voices on the lawn. She rose and tottered over to the window. Manelli was standing in the shrubbery and waving to Bill on the terrace.

"Find him?" Bill called.

"No." Manelli paused to light a cigar. "Did you?"

"I wouldn't have asked you if I had."

"You looking for the stiff?"

"Of course. Aren't you?"

"Just thought you might be after pantywaist."

"Who?"

"The creep, the creep," said Manelli impatiently.

"You mean twerp boy?"

"Come again."

"Cyril, I mean."

"That's what I said. You looking for him?"

"No. Are you?"

"Nope." Manelli turned and went back into the shrubbery.

Ten minutes later, Grossi bounded from beneath the cedars. "Any luck?" he called.

"No." Bill sat down on the steps. "You?"

"No."

"Tried the compost heap?"

"Yep. Straight compost."

"Anything nasty in the woodshed?"

"Check." Grossi sprinted away.

Mrs. Carlisle leaned out of her window. "Where's Cyril?" she cried.

Bill looked up. "I don't know."

"Look for him."

"Look for him yourself."

"*Why* won't you look for him?"

"I don't like him."

Paget stepped from the French window. "Have we met with any success, sir?"

"No," said Bill.

"I have inspected the lofts, the basement, and the boiler, sir."

"Try the stables."

Paget inclined his head and withdrew.

"Look for *Cyril*," Mrs. Carlisle shouted after him.

Dina emerged from the orchard and ran across the lawn. "Bill," she hailed. "I've found a little Roman coin."

"Anything else?"

"Not a thing."

"Keep trying."

"Look for *Cyril*," roared Mrs. Carlisle.

Al appeared around the corner of the house riding a bicycle. He rode across the lawn, through the vegetable garden, through the swing gate, skidded and fell off in the long grass.

Manelli strolled from the shrubbery and across the lawn. He sat down on the steps beside Bill. "Nothing there but a lotta leaves," he said.

"Did you search the outhouses?"

"No. You did."

"So I did."

"Whoever heard of *looking* for a stiff?"

"He's got to be properly Disposed."

"Seems he has been."

"We've got to be *sure*."

"Know what I keep thinking about?"

"What?"

"That well. That bottomless well."

Bill stared at him. "My God," he said. "Of course. *Come on!*"

Manelli yawned. "What *for*? If he went down there, he's in Australia."

"Where is *Cyril*?" bawled Mrs. Carlisle.

Bill was already running through the rose beds. He swung into the yard, under the rambler arch, along the small flagged path. He stopped within a few feet of the old well and looked at it. He picked up a pebble and tossed it over the lichened bricks. He waited without hope for the splash. There was none. He moved closer and bent over the edge. He could see for about thirty feet; beyond lay darkness and silence. He drew a deep breath. "CYRIL!" he bellowed. There was not even an echo.

An hour later, the searchers met on the terrace. Mrs. Carlisle sat above them in her window and, as always in moments of stress, daubed varnish onto her nails with surrealist abandon. "Poor boy," she said wildly. "He may be lying there dead."

"Lying where dead?" snapped Grossi. "Use your head bone."

"We've looked everywhere," said Dina. "They're not there, neither of them."

"Oh, so they're both dead now, are they?" yelled Mrs. Carlisle. "You murderers."

"Will you please shut up?" Manelli asked her courteously.

Mrs. Carlisle pointed a finger covered with crimson varnish at Grossi. "Him," she said. "That anthropoid. Get a rope and lower him into the well."

"Go chew a chair," said Grossi.

"I hope Clifford's all right," said Dina anxiously. "Honestly, when it's hot like this, he might do *anything*."

"To hell with Flush!" screamed Mrs. Carlisle. "*Where's Cyril?*"

Dina stood up. "If you say that once more," she said. "I shall...well, I shall lose my temper."

"You," said Mrs. Carlisle. "You cliff killer."

"You too," snapped Dina. "You old blunt instrument."

Bill picked up a concrete tub of begonias and banged it onto the ground. "We must keep CALM," he shouted.

An hour later, Al returned from the tumuli on his bicycle. He rode across the lawn with arms outstretched. "Look," he said. "No hands."

"Any luck?" asked Bill.

"Bones," said Al. He raised his feet onto the handlebars. "*Old* bones. Look, no feet." The bicycle went round in a large circle. "Want to see me stand on the saddle?"

"No," said Manelli.

"Bet I could do it, Boss. You watch."

"Beat it."

Al rode the bicycle at breakneck speed along the path. As he went around the corner of the house, he raised one foot onto the saddle.

Manelli rose and massaged his behind. "Stiff," he explained.

"Not that word, Joe," said Grossi. "If you don't mind."

"What are we going to say when the staff get back?" asked Bill. He dragged a hand over his face. "We haven't Disposed, we haven't written our essays and we've lost the body."

"One of you has Disposed," Dina pointed out. "And jolly well too."

Half an hour later, she shivered. "Clifford will be livid," she said.

"Perhaps we ought to write our essays," said Bill uneasily.

"How can we?" said Manelli. "Only Tony Disposed."

"I should write them just the same," said Dina. "You've never seen Clifford in a rage." She added, "You'd probably only see it once."

Mrs. Carlisle got up, closed her window and sat down before her typewriter. The migraine was forgotten. She reached for two carbons. She would make two copies of her essay. Later, perhaps she might write the work up as a short story...

As she lowered the lifeless form into the water, a tender breeze ruffled her hair. A tear glided down her cheek and fell into the... Mrs. Carlisle lit a cigarette and pulled her *Roget's Thesaurus* nearer. She looked up Limpid, returned to the typewriter. *Hyaline pool,* she tapped. *In spite of the torrid heat, the water was icy. From its pellucid surface, her own image gazed back at her; the wide eyes, the tumbled auburn hair, the pale cheeks. Slowly, tenderly, she allowed the dead man to slip through her slender fingers.*

Mrs. Carlisle went and fetched an ashtray. She collected her dictionary, found a new packet of paper, settled down and began to type in earnest.

In the library, Bill uncapped his fountain pen. He stared for five minutes at the sheet of white paper. He sighed. For some reason a pen had always felt like a walking stick between his fingers.

DISPOSAL, he wrote and underlined it.

He filled his pen from the inkwell and looked around for blotting paper. There was none. Feeling guilty, he opened a drawer. Inside lay a bottle half full of gin, a carton of air-gun pellets and a studio portrait of the Colonel in a major's uniform. Bill shut the drawer.

He decided to keep his essay short and to the point. *As arranged,* he wrote, *had intended to commence operation at 12:15 hours. There was, however, a technical hitch. The previous contestant, through no fault of his own…* He considered this for some time, then crossed it out. He took a fresh piece of paper.

DISPOSAL, he wrote. He sighed and wiped the nib of his pen on his handkerchief. *Had intended to weight…* He stopped. He did not know what the body's name was. He left a space and wrote *and drop him down the old well.* He chewed the end of his pen. Drop sounded very brutal. He crossed it out and put *lower.* But this, he realized immediately, would have meant ropes. Flush would certainly require to know the length used. But the well probably led into some fiery cave in the center of the earth; who knew how deep it was? Perhaps Flush did. Bill began to think about underground rivers.

He got up, walked across the room and opened the window. He walked back to the desk, sat down. *But,* he wrote. He added an elegant comma, then crossed out the whole. He threw the piece of paper into the wastepaper basket and took another.

He rewrote the first sentence. *However,* he wrote, and looked at it critically. Yes, *however* was better. But however *what?* He had known what he was going to say at the time, but now he could not remember.

Suddenly horrified, it occurred to him that should the body be found in the well, his essay would virtually amount to a confession.

He sprang out of the chair. He walked twice up and down the room before he returned to the desk, grabbed the piece of paper and burnt it in the grate. He collected the ashes and ground them into a fine dust. He sighed heavily and decided to go and ask somebody what the body's name was.

Manelli paced his bedroom. Al sat at the table, crouched over his notebook. "Shoot," he said, his pencil poised.

"Ah, I'm no damn good at this stuff," said Manelli. He clasped his hands behind him and stared up at the ceiling. " 'I place this stiff in back of my automobile. In Krunte Abbas, I pull in to refuel.' Kill that. 'In Krunte Abbas, I blow a tire.'"

" 'In Krunte Abbas, I run into a dame,' " suggested Al. "That's less phony."

"Okay," said Manelli. "That."

" 'So naturally I offer her a smoke.' "

Manelli blew smoke out of the window. "Al," he said. "You handle this. But I want nothing flash." He walked towards the door. On the threshold, he turned. "Make this dame around fifty, eh?"

In the drawing room, Grossi seized a piece of paper and pinned it against the wall with his elbow. Like Bill, he too had difficulty in writing, but for a different reason. During the time when he should have been at school, he was usually engaged in other pursuits. As others learned to form their pothooks, Grossi snitched fruit from the market. As less ambitious boys practiced their first signatures, Grossi helped his uncle to make bootleg whiskey in the basement.

He licked the point of his pencil and stiffened all over. *My name is Pete Kalder*, he scrawled. *I am a citizen of the United States.*

At half past five, Mrs. Carlisle finished her essay and typed THE END.

Beneath this and slightly to one side, she added *Krunte Abbas, 1954.* She took a fresh piece of paper and tapped NEVER AGAIN *by Chloe Carlisle* in the center of it, and in the right-hand corner the name and address of her literary agent. She stapled the sheets together, placed them in a large manila envelope and rang the bell for Paget. When he appeared, she handed him the envelope. "Have you found my fiancé?" she asked.

"No, madam."

Mrs. Carlisle clawed at her earrings. "Where can he *be*?"

"I couldn't say, madam." Paget waited. "Will that be all, madam?"

Mrs. Carlisle slumped into an armchair. "Paget," she said in a stifled voice. "I am beginning to think the worst."

"Quite, madam."

"You think that…?"

"I fear so, madam."

"*Dead*, Paget?" Paget bowed.

Mrs. Carlisle gripped the arms of her chair. "Who?"

"I really couldn't say, madam."

Mrs. Carlisle lost all control. "Oh, go and haunt yourself!" she screamed. "Go *away*! Go on, *avaunt*!"

Five minutes later, Manelli laid Al's essay on top of Mrs. Carlisle's bulky work. Bill appeared and added his brief contribution. "Seen Cyril?" he asked, sucking his inky fingers.

"Nope," said Manelli. "Did you?"

"No."

Manelli rasped a thumbnail over his bluish jaw. "I have a hunch," he announced.

"What?"

"I think maybe he chilled Tony's boy. I figure he threw him down that well and slipped or got sorta dragged in. These old wells, they make vacuums, play odd tricks. Bend over too far and *zoom*."

Bill stared at him. "That's awful."

"Yeah," said Manelli indifferently. "You sure started something when you dreamed up this well gimmick."

Dina toed the baseline and threw a ball into the air, preparing to serve. She changed her mind and the ball fell behind her. "Mr. Grossi," she called. "Do you think they're both in the well?"

Grossi was prancing about on his toes, holding his racquet as if it were a baseball bat. "Sure," he said. "Come on. Fifteen-thirty."

Five minutes later, Dina said, "Do you think that Cyril pushed your bodyguard, then somebody pushed *him*?"

"Maybe. Thirty-forty."

Dina picked up a ball. "Poor Cyril," she said. She laughed. "Fancy *him* getting caught out like that. I bet he landed on his feet."

Cyril sat in a first-class carriage in the dirty little train heading for Krunte Abbas. "The train is late," he remarked.

"Invariably," said Flush. He sat staring thoughtfully at his feet.

"Chloe will be snatching out her hair in handfuls."

"Doubtless."

The train rattled over a small bridge.

Flush glanced at his watch. "By this time, the news should be in the Stop Press."

Cyril looked out of the window at a motionless herd of black cows. "Who's going to break the news to Bill? He was so determined to kill him himself."

"He changed his mind. He cannot have his cake and eat it too."

"I thought I caught a glimpse of the Colonel," said Cyril. "On the escalator."

Flush picked a shred of tobacco from his lapel and rolled it between his fingers. "I like your work," he said abruptly.

"Work?" Cyril raised his eyebrows.

"When first I remarked you on the platform, I confess that I felt a twinge of resentment. But when I saw the turn of events, I gave you your head."

"Surely you can't think that I…?"

Flush flicked the shred of tobacco out of the window. "Of course not," he said smoothly. "I was wondering whether you would care for a position on my staff."

"But I'm not qualified," said Cyril. He leaned forward and grasped Flush's arm. "Really, I had no idea that the fellow was going to…"

"Yes, yes, yes," said Flush impatiently. He brushed off Cyril's hand and opened his evening paper.

Ten minutes later, Cyril ran along the platform at Krunte Abbas. "Mr. Flush," he said urgently. "You must believe me. I only wanted to see you in action."

Flush strode ahead, swinging his briefcase. "If you are going to join the staff," he said, "you may call me Clifford."

Ten minutes later, as the staff car turned into the Manor gates, Cyril said, "I insist that we understand each other."

Flush changed up into top gear. "You will receive a salary of twenty pounds a week, no mess bills, two months holiday a year, all expenses, and a substantial bonus if some assignment takes you abroad."

"Now wait a moment," said Cyril. "I'm going to be quite honest with you, Clifford…"

Mrs. Barratt and the Colonel had already returned. Flush found them in the library. Mrs. Barratt had changed into her lavender tea gown and was winding wool. "Ah, Clifford," she said. "You must be tired. A glass of sherry?"

Flush sat down. He glared at the Colonel. "You drive too fast," he snapped.

"We touched ninety-five on the Great West Road," said Mrs. Barratt proudly.

"Is the Creaker back?"

"Not yet, I met him in Tottenham Court Road. He was most upset. He had lost Hobson."

Flush's cigar broke in half. "Good God!" he said.

"I know," said Mrs. Barratt. "But, Clifford, it was bound to happen sooner or later."

"Told the Thurlow chap yet?" asked the Colonel, pouring three fingers of gin into a tumbler and squirting angostura onto the carpet.

"You knew that our mission was successful?"

"Was there," said the Colonel simply. "Wasn't in time to see everything. Got wedged behind ruddy great Indian chappie about eight feet high."

Cyril combed his hair, straightened his tie and looked anxiously at himself in the mirror of the downstairs cloakroom. He was wondering how best to approach Chloe Carlisle. When, some seven hours before, he had met the Creaker on the terrace and heard his horrible tale, he had thought of nothing but the imperative need to reach London before somebody made news. It was not until the train reached Gully Low that he realized that he should have announced his intention to Chloe.

He went upstairs slowly, wishing that he had bought some large, expensive present which might stymie her fury. On the landing, he bumped into Bill and instinctively recoiled. Had Bill learned of the afternoon's outrage? Was he too in a rage?

Bill was wearing plimsolls, carrying a flashlight and a huge coil of rope. For a moment, he stared at Cyril. Then he frowned and said, "So you're alive?"

"Yes," said Cyril. "I feel fine."

"We thought you were in the well."

"No. I'm not."

"Obviously. How did you get out?"

"I didn't. I haven't been in a well for ages."

"I was going to risk my life going down after you."

"Thank you."

Bill's face darkened. He had been looking forward to going down the dangerous well, to coming up covered with slime and reporting a gallant failure to an anxious Dina. "I call it jolly inconsiderate," he said angrily. "What have you done with the body?"

Cyril braced himself against the wall. "My dear boy," he said. "If you haven't the guts yourself…" He stopped, felt for his cigarette case and chose a cigarette. "Which body?" he asked, attempting to blow a smoke ring.

"Very, very funny indeed," said Bill. He dropped the coil of rope and went downstairs.

As he reached the hall, Flush came out of the library and pinned the examination results onto the notice board. Bill crossed to look at them. Cyril was top, Mrs. Carlisle bottom, Manelli and Grossi had tied. Bill's name did not appear.

"Did I fail?" he asked.

Flush did not look at him. "You have been disqualified," he said coldly. "Your Intended fell beneath an electric train this afternoon at Warren Street." He picked a dead leaf off a potted geranium, threw it into the fireplace and went into the library.

Bill stood motionless for a minute, gaping after him. Then he leapt forward and snatched open the library door. "My God, you've got a nerve!" he said, clenching his hands. "I've got a damn good mind to knock you down. Stand up." He dragged Flush to his feet and shook him furiously. "You selfish swine! What sort of a position am *I* in now? Everybody will say that I passed the buck. *What am I going to say to my father?*"

Hobson took off his cap and hung it on a nail in the summerhouse. He sat down on the bench, kicked off his shoes and put his feet up onto the table. The Creaker threw his bowler hat into a corner and tapped his pupil on the shoulder. "Look, boy," he said. "You can trust me. Where was you?"

"Lookin' at the shops," said Hobson.

"Orright," said the Creaker. "Just tell me this, boy. *'Ow many?*"

"Was a fruit shop, draper, fish shop, ironmonger…"

The Creaker sucked his teeth. "Look, mate," he said. "Let's 'ave it. 'Ow many did you clobber?"

Hobson scratched his bullneck. "Clobber?" he asked, frowning.

"Top. 'Ow many?"

"I didn't touch 'em."

"You was away an hour."

"Didn't touch nobody."

The Creaker drew up a packing case and sat on it. He laid a hand on his pupil's knee. "Don't you trust me, boy?" he asked.

"Bought you somethin'," said Hobson gruffly. He put his hand into his pocket and dragged out a huge penknife with many blades and devices. It was the first present Hobson had ever given to anybody.

The Creaker took it. He opened the tin-opener and felt the tip with his thumb. "You didn't 'ave no smash. You been on the dip."

"'S'not the smash," said Hobson. "'S the *thought*."

As the first gong sounded for dinner, Cyril met Mrs. Carlisle where he had particularly hoped to avoid her, in the dark passage outside her bedroom. He immediately hastened towards her, his arms outstretched. "Chloe," he cried. "You may spit in my eye. I'm a monster."

She jumped visibly. She opened her mouth to scream, then thought better of it. "Ha!" she said, clearly marshalling her reserves. "The prodigal." She stepped closer, peered into his face and raised her arm as if to strike him.

Cyril grabbed her wrists. "Angel," he said. "Were you worried?"

Mrs. Carlisle kicked him in the ankle. "No, no, *no*," she said. "I merely thought you were dead, that's all. Foully murdered, that's all. I've only fainted once and had two migraines. It's nothing, nothing at all. Don't give it another thought."

"Now Chloe, you've always been a generous woman. Here I am, back from the grave."

"Oh, so you have the effrontery to admit it, do you?" she snarled. "Where did you put him?"

"Who?" Cyril gripped her harder. "Angel," he said reproachfully. "Is this my welcome?"

"It's all very well," she hissed. "Look at me, you selfish, miserable, godforsaken little clunk. Can't you see that I'm *in mourning*?"

"For me?"

"I'll have to go and change, damn you."

"No. It's quite suitable. There's been another."

"Another what?"

"Well, body."

"Oh *no!*"

"Yes."

"Who?"

"I wasn't introduced."

"One of us?"

"No."

"Who did it?"

"It was an accident."

"I said who did it."

"He toppled under a train."

"*Who* did?"

"I tell you I don't know."

"Suicide?"

"The crowd sort of surged forward," said Cyril.

"So I'm in mourning for a complete stranger, am I?" she said angrily. "Why does nobody ever *know* these damn bodies?"

In the library, the staff sipped their drinks before dinner. Dina waited until the glasses were refilled, then cleared her throat and plunged into the story of the disastrous Disposal. When she had finished, there was a heavy silence.

"He disappeared *after* we left the house?" asked Mrs. Barratt.

"Yes," said Dina. She added, hoping to soothe them, "None of you could have done it. You've all got alibis."

"No idea who took him?" growled the Colonel.

"Well," said Dina unhappily, "I suppose only the operator would go to all that trouble…"

"Exactly," murmured Flush.

Dina looked at him anxiously. To her amazement, he was smiling. "Clifford," she said. "I thought you'd be *livid*."

"On the contrary," said Flush. "I am delighted. Do you not understand that this prankster has most effectively cleared the staff? None of us can have engaged the first case because at the time of Disposal we were all racing towards the second." He stood up and raised his glass. "Let us drink a toast to our vehement friend. He has done me personally a real service. I no longer suspect myself."

Chapter Fourteen

The last day of the course dawned hotter than ever. By break-fast time, the dining room, although still in semidarkness, was stifling.

As Paget removed the fishcakes, Flush produced a time-table and rapped upon the table with a spoon. "This morning," he announced, "you will revise your particular stratagem for the last time with your instructor. Remember, ladies and gentlemen, that this is your *final rehearsal*. The next time you run through these now familiar actions, it will be *official*.

"This afternoon, you will be free to prepare for your last exercise. This evening at six o'clock, the local estate agent will take cocktails with us. Each of you in turn will have the oppor-tunity to indicate to the rest of us a method other than the one in which you intend to specialize."

Mrs. Carlisle spilt her coffee. "I refuse to murder him," she said loudly. "I don't even know him."

Flush twanged the tines of his fork. "Mr. White has attended the last evening of every course since Dankry was inaugurated.

None has proved fatal and he has on no occasion suspected anything whatever. You will *indicate*, not engage." He picked up a crumb on one finger and looked at it. "I regret having to stress this point," he said slowly, "but in view of certain irregularities during this course, I must firmly insist that there will be no further demonstrations." He glanced around at the four students still under suspicion. "Mr. White will leave here this evening *alive*."

Two hours later, the shadow of Hanger Hill had reached the azaleas. The staff met in the library. Flush sat by the open window and fanned himself languidly with Mrs. Carlisle's essay on Disposal.

"The final rehearsals?" he asked without interest. "Did they pass muster?"

"Not satisfied with Mrs. Carlisle," grumbled the Colonel. "Latter part of operation *pukka tamarsha*. Backed out of garage like ruddy rickshaw wallah. Told her to step on it. Says, 'What's the hurry? Where's your hat?' Told her, 'Scream, madam. Scream, wake the witnesses.' Loses her temper, hooks front fender around hose, flood."

"A nice touch," said Flush thoughtfully. "We might incorporate that. And Cyril?"

"Top-hole," said the Colonel, enthusiastically. "One of us. Blighter struck me *with* the faucet. Definite improvement."

"The hold on the platysma?"

"A-1," said the Colonel. He stretched his neck and turned his head from side to side. "Not a mark."

"You blacked out?"

"Splendidly."

"Do you think that Cyril will join us?" asked Dina.

Flush nodded. "I believe so. Mrs. Carlisle really should be most grateful to us. Had Cyril no alternative future, he would certainly have engaged her."

"I don't believe he would even have waited the six months," said Dina. "He asked me whether I'd like to spend Christmas in Switzerland."

"Don't you think," asked the Colonel dubiously, "*she*'ll engage *him* when she learns what he's up to?" Nobody answered this question.

"I have several times," said Mrs. Barratt. She paused to pick up a dropped stitch. "Asked both Mr. Manelli and Mr. Grossi whether they intend to suppress each other in this country. Until today, both replied that they would respect the county limit and mentioned Wiltshire. Today, both hesitated. Mr. Manelli muttered something about his dentist. Mr. Grossi said who cared and that he had heard well of Kent. Their relationship appears to have improved."

"Mr. Grossi's terrifically confident," said Dina. "He told me that I was going to see Niagara Falls this winter."

"Clifford," said Mrs. Barratt uneasily. "Do you think that it is entirely *fair* upon this particular batch of students to entertain Mr. White this evening? Is it not much the same as leaving money around to tempt the servants?"

Flush shrugged. "I believe that we are entertaining a single paranoiac," he said absently. "We are left with only seven suspects. Manelli and Grossi, Mrs. Carlisle and Mr. Thurlow, Paget, Matron and Dina. They must be watched."

"*Me?*" said Dina, affronted.

"You have no alibi."

"Well, make me one. Just because you've suddenly got an alibi, I don't see why *I* should need one."

"What of Mr. Manelli's torpedoes?" asked Mrs. Barratt quickly.

"Paget assures me that they spent the morning at the telephone exchange in Poxwell Regis."

"And Barker?"

"He was, apparently, genuinely unconscious until late last night."

"Clifford," said Mrs. Barratt reasonably. "Do we honestly *care*?"

"Speaking personally," said Flush, "Frankly, no."

"And you, Colonel?"

"Under the bridge," said the Colonel.

"Soon as I knew wasn't 'Obson," said the Creaker, "just put it right out o' me mind."

"I'd like to know whether it was Bill," said Dina. "It's rather important."

Flush rose and tossed Mrs. Carlisle's essay into the Colonel's OUT tray. "Perhaps tonight's entertainment may stimulate our unknown into a further demonstration."

"Really, Clifford!" said Mrs. Barratt. "*Poor* Mr. White!"

Flush raised his shoulders half an inch. "In such a case, I hope to mark the culprit *before* he does any lasting harm to our guest. But I confess," he added with unusual candor, "that it is a gamble."

As the clock over the stables struck eleven, Bill decided that he could no longer postpone ringing up his father. He lifted the receiver and listened. He heard male laughter, then a slap.

"Shut up, *do*," said a female voice which dissolved immediately into a paroxysm of coughing.

Bill gave his father's London number.

"That's a trunk call," said the operator accusingly, and aside, "Leave *off*." She was about to add something further when she was overcome again. Bill heard her whooping and panting and shouting something unintelligible. Then Al's voice said anxiously, "Hey, fetch a glass of water."

"*Al!*" shouted Bill.

"Sip it, honey. *Sip* it," said Al. There was a metallic clang, a purring noise, then silence.

Bill replaced the receiver, went into the drawing room and helped himself to a cigarette. As he lit it, the phone rang. He ran along the corridor, across the hall and seized the receiver.

"I have a telegram for Thurlow," said the operator hoarsely.

"That's me."

"Southampton," crooned a new voice. "Are you there, Guildford?"

"Operator," said Bill. "Read my telegram. Hurry."

"Hullo, hullo," roared Bill's father. The old man hated and despised telephones and held the receiver to his deaf ear in order to outwit them.

"It's Bill, Dad. Have you seen the papers?"

"Operator," said Bill's father sternly. "Kindly clear the line." He added, "Damn silly woman. No idea these days."

"Three minutes," snapped the operator instantly. "If you wish to continue, kindly insert two-and-four."

"*Dad*," called Bill desperately.

"Who *are* you? Speak up, damn your eyes. I'm deaf."

The line went dead. Bill replaced the receiver, pressed it down convulsively, then lifted. "Operator," he said in a controlled voice.

"Get her head down," said Al's voice. "Give her here."

"I got her," said Blackie. "Open the window."

"*Blackie*," shouted Bill.

"Leave *go*!" said the operator in a snarling whisper. She cleared her throat, whooped once, then said, "Poxwell Exchange. Can I help you?"

"It's me," said Bill.

"The telegram?"

"Yes."

"Oh. Well, you read ALL DELIGHTED SUICIDE STOP GOOD LAD, signed THURLOW. Are you the party who was inadvertently cut off? Shall I reconnect you?"

"No," said Bill. "I've got to think." As he replaced the receiver the phone rang.

"London calling," said the operator, coughing. "Person to person. Thurlow to Thurlow."

"Get off the line, you nincompoop," roared Bill's father. "Bill, Bill!"

"Yes, Dad."

"Well, find him."

"*It's me, Dad.*"

"Oh, I see. Did he mention when he was coming home?"

"Dad, he's going to get married." It occurred to Bill that he had not yet proposed to Dina.

"Can't hear a word, blast you," shouted Bill's father. "Tell him we're expecting him tomorrow. Tell him red carpet. He'll understand."

"All right."

"What? Speak up, speak up. *Spell* it."

Manelli, Grossi and Mr. White sat in the dark inglenook in the Wassail.

Mr. White had been speaking for some time about his evening invitation to the Manor. "Every time I go there I expect it to be the last," he said, shaking his head.

Manelli met Grossi's eyes for an instant. "Why?" he asked.

"It must fall soon," said Mr. White. "It must. I have been expecting it for the past fifteen years." He drained his glass, belched gently. "They have an excellent white port, but I don't suppose that they will produce it. It seems a pity not to enjoy it before the dry rot attacks the corks." He rose and collected the empty glasses. He waved one at a dark portrait on. the wall. "Denzil Holles," he said vaguely. "Bewigged though in celestial company."

The mobsters watched him weave towards the bar. "He's nuts," said Grossi.

"The English," said Manelli. "How will you take him this evening?"

"I have a historical idea," said Grossi, over-intelligent from the mead. "I saw it in some book, kinda took my fancy. Seventeenth century, some jerk called Max Gate has an elm fall on him right near here. You saw that elm by the orchid house?"

"Max Gate is a place," said Manelli.

Mr. White returned from the bar with two misshapen glasses. "A special favor," he said proudly. "Used by John White the Puritan, founder of Dorchester, Massachusetts." He hurried away to collect his own drink.

"Joe," said Grossi. "I never worked on my own. Will I loan Al?"

"Nope."

"Okay, I'll take Blackie."

Manelli looked at him. "I'll go with you, Tony."

Grossi's handsome head turned. "*You*, Joe?"

"Sure. Like old times, Tony."

"That's swell of you, Joe," said Grossi uneasily.

Mr. White returned, his glass invisible in his huge fist. He sat down abruptly on the worm-eaten hexagon of wood reputed to have been part of King Sweyn's mounting block. He tasted his mead. "Vintage sack metheglin," he remarked smacking his lips. He proposed a toast. "John White!"

"John White," echoed Grossi.

"Max Gate," said Manelli, raising his glass.

Cyril, wandering in the garden, was trying to wrest the answer to his problem from the blazing sky and the shriveled lawns. Should he join the staff and for the first time have the dubious satisfaction of earning his own living? Or should he assist Chloe and cancel Ned, marry her and, after a decent interval, become a rich widower? The answer would have been obvious had he not realized that to erase a whole family and inherit its wealth was an action certain to attract jealous comment in the worst possible taste. Even if his work were unimpeachable, he would certainly be the target of a number of insolent implications...

By the circular pond where a single water lily wilted, he came upon Dina. She was lying face downwards on a large green towel. She had been swimming. The minute pieces of satin which passed as her bathing costume were wet and there were pearls of water on her brown back.

Cyril sat down beside her and lit a cigarette. "A friend of mine has a hypothetical problem," he said.

Dina turned her head sideways on her arms. "What a shame," she murmured.

"He is a fascinating case," said Cyril. He looked at her inquiringly. "Don't you think so?"

Dina's eyes roved over him. "I don't know yet."

Cyril lay down on the brown grass and kicked off his espadrilles. "What would *you* do if you were him?"

Dina stirred the duckweed in the pond with one finger. "I suppose he ought to take a job," she said. "But I hear he's been telling everybody that he hasn't got any qualifications."

Cyril blew a neat smoke ring. He did not answer.

Dina sat up and adjusted her shreds of satin. "My friend couldn't possibly give a proper answer unless she knew whether your friend had any qualifications."

"Has your friend any qualifications?"

"My friend asked first."

"Your friend is a lovely piece," said Cyril. "My friend would like to know her much, much better." He looked down into the pond. The two reflected heads smiled back at him, framed in a filigree of duckweed.

As Paget sounded the first gong for lunch, Bill appeared at the top of the stairs with a pajama jacket in his hand. "I had a piece of rope a moment ago," he said. "Who took it?"

"I couldn't say, sir." Paget struck the gong once more and went back into the passage.

Mrs. Carlisle came out of the armory. Inside, Bill caught a glimpse of the Colonel in an old bush-jacket and a yellow silk scarf. Then the door clanged to. Mrs. Carlisle had a small automatic in her hand. She was breathing on it and polishing it with a lace-edged handkerchief.

"Who's that for?" asked Bill from the top of the stairs.

Mrs. Carlisle looked up frowning. "This character this evening," she said shortly. "But that mad old soldier won't give me any bullets." She started upstairs.

"We're not meant to *kill* him," said Bill.

"Oh, be quiet," she snapped.

"Chloe," said Bill accusingly. He gripped her wrist as she passed. "You want to shoot someone else."

She looked at him, biting her lip. Then she drew him across to the landing window. She waved the automatic at Cyril and

Dina just visible beyond the tulip trees, lying side by side by the lily pond.

Bill scowled. "Shoot him in the foot," he said.

"What do you mean, *him*?" Mrs. Carlisle raised the automatic and sighted along the barrel. "What's the use? The damn thing's not loaded."

As Paget circled the table offering a suet pudding with a cicatricial sheen, Flush smiled benignly around at his students. By this time tomorrow, they would have left and taken their feuds, bickerings and suspicions with them. The staff would enjoy three days of leisure before the arrival of the next batch.

By this time tomorrow, he thought with profound relief, he would be eating a decent meal and drinking a distinguished claret. This irritating course with its anonymous body would already be half forgotten.

He waved away the processed cheese. In spite of the lapse on the part of one of them, the prospect of their imminent departure caused him to feel a sudden geniality towards his students. "Have you all decided upon your methods for this evening?" he asked, smiling around the table.

"Will you serve this white port?" asked Manelli.

"I need a saw," said Grossi.

"I need an accomplice," said Mrs. Carlisle.

"I suppose I'm not invited," said Bill.

"And somebody took my rope again," said Grossi.

"And mine," said Bill. "Mr. Grossi, did you take my rope?"

"What do I want with *your* rope? I got my own rope, nice rope."

"I had four *yards*."

"Brother, I had forty. I had forty *twice*."

"Am I to understand," inquired Flush, "that the joker among you has appropriated eighty-four yards of rope?" He rose with a short laugh. "That should, ladies and gentlemen, be enough to hang us all."

An hour later, the Colonel dispatched Paget to request Mrs. Carlisle's presence in the armory. When she appeared, he laid aside an ancient blunderbuss and asked about her plans for the evening. "Understand you intend to shoot the fellow? Alibi?"

"Not yet," said Mrs. Carlisle. Nobody had told her that she would need one.

"Range?"

"That depends," she said cautiously.

"Automatic checked?"

Mrs. Carlisle knew nothing about guns and would indeed not have noticed if the magazine were missing. "Later," she said firmly.

The Colonel muttered something to himself in Hindustani. He sucked in his cheeks and sighed. "Report here 1600 hours," he said. "Pukka plan of campaign."

Mrs. Carlisle went upstairs and knocked on Bill's bedroom door. He was sitting on the bed among a pile of scattered clothes. "Packing?" she asked brightly.

Bill threw a pair of socks at an open suitcase. He did not answer.

Mrs. Carlisle produced her case and offered him a cigarette. "Chloe needs an alibi," she said. He did not move. She sat down beside him. "Do *you* feel like an alibi?"

"No. Anyway, I don't count any more. Since they've bumped off my chap, I've been under a cloud." Bill took one of her cigarettes. "I can't understand it," he said moodily. "I thought they quite liked me. Now suddenly they all *hate* me."

"Do something decisive. Be my alibi."

"You know very well indeed that that's not decisive enough."

She patted his hand. "Are you man or mouse? Kill somebody."

He flicked the ash off his cigarette into a shoe, then lay back on the bed and stared at the ceiling. "I'd have to have a damn good motive," he said. "I'm that sort of chap."

She lost interest. "Sure you don't want to be my alibi?"

"Positive."

"Please, Bill."

"No."

She got up, kicked a brogue out of her way, stalked onto the landing and started downstairs in search of Cyril.

She found him by the orchid house. He was lounging on a wheelbarrow, watching Grossi balancing a ladder against the elm tree. "Personally," he was saying helpfully, "I think it's a lousy idea. Suppose it doesn't kill him. He'll sue you."

Grossi drummed one foot on the ground. "Look," he said, "*You* know it stinks. *I* know it stinks. We *all* know it stinks. Let's face it, it stinks. Now will you please leave me alone?"

"It'll take *hours*."

Grossi patted him once lightly on the shoulder. "Listen, brother," he said. "Antonio Grossi starts something, Antonio Grossi finishes it. Get it? Now I have got my teeth into this tree and it will fall down this evening at around six-thirty or else." He had realized immediately upon examining the elm that the project was not only absurd but also infinitely tiresome. He cursed the double meads in the Wassail which had given birth to the scheme. He had been prepared to abandon it in favor of the U turn in Herring Magna; but Cyril had jeered and that was a thing which Grossi would not take from anybody. Now he would fix this tree if it killed him, which, he thought angrily, stubbing out his cigarette in a woodpecker's nest, it probably would. He picked up the saw, climbed the ladder and looked critically at an overhanging branch.

"Not that one," advised Cyril. "It's hooked on to the one above." Grossi started to saw.

"Just look at all that sawdust," said Cyril. "How are you going to laugh *that* off?"

Mrs. Carlisle sat down beside him on the wheelbarrow. She remembered him lying by the lily pool with Dina and resisted an impulse to grab his ear and twist it. "Angel," she said. "Let us speak of alibis."

Cyril looked at her. He wondered how long it would be before he saw that same ingratiating smile in a dingy halftone under a banner headline in one of the evening papers. He thought suddenly of the melodramatic tantrums during the preliminary inquiry, the biting of the cuticles, the floods of hysterical tears. He saw the period of waiting, the intolerable meetings in the British Museum, the white hat which Chloe would wear for the registry office wedding…He gave a great sigh of relief. He knew then, positively, that he was going to abandon Ned Carlisle to a fate far worse than death; that he intended to join the staff and be rid of Chloe at a thousand a year. "Alibis?" he repeated politely. "I have one, thank you."

"I haven't."

"That's tough."

Mrs. Carlisle's hands twitched. "Aren't you being a trifle loutish, angel?"

Cyril got up and sat down again with his back to her. "Powder your nose," he said. "Unless you *like* looking like Rembrandt's mother."

Mrs. Carlisle reached for his ear then stuffed her hands into her pockets. "Sweetie," she said. "Be reasonable."

"I am," said Cyril frigidly.

There was a loud splintering of wood from above.

"*Look out!*" shouted Grossi.

With a series of sharp cracks, the elm branch bent and drooped down in slow motion. Its extremity hit the ground with a hiss of leaves. The other end remained suspended from the tree by a tendon of wood and bark.

Grossi swore, then climbed two rungs up the ladder and began doggedly to saw at another branch.

"I expect it's rotten right through," said Cyril. "They're often hollow."

"Mr. Grossi," said Mrs. Carlisle. "Would you care to exchange alibis?"

"Ah, shuttup," said Grossi.

"That branch is dead," said Cyril. "It has no leaves. Anyway, it'll fall on the conservatory."

Grossi climbed three steps up the ladder and started to saw at the branch above. He was invisible now, his presence suggested only by sudden showers of twigs.

"That branch ought to be tied up," said Cyril. "Unless you want the whole thing to drop apart."

Grossi backed down the ladder. He advanced upon Cyril, then poked his head forward until their noses were an inch apart. "Are you gonna shut up?" he asked.

From the direction of the garages came the purr of an approaching car. The Studebaker shot past the gap in the rhododendrons. Mrs. Carlisle fumbled for her compact, slapped herself in the face with the powder puff and headed for the yard.

The great black car stood glittering in the sun. Manelli was bent inside the back door pulling at a length of rope. He hauled it out with difficulty and hoisted it over his shoulder. Mrs. Carlisle considered him. He was clearly in a vile temper, but he was her last hope of an alibi. She saw that the loop of rope which hung down his back was about to uncurl. She hurried forward but she was too late. By the time she arrived, a single strand hung over the ex-gangster's shoulder and the rest lay around his feet.

Manelli took his face in the palm of his hand and squeezed it. With a convulsive movement, he brushed off the remaining strand, stepped out of the tangle of rope and strode through the rambler arch. Mrs. Carlisle plunged through a rose bed to join him.

"Mr. Manelli," she said. "I need an alibi."

He did not answer.

"Tonight," she said. "Only about ten minutes."

"I'm not in the mood," said Manelli.

"Only ten minutes."

"Sorry."

"*Five* minutes," she said desperately.

"No."

"*Please.*"

"Look, lady, I said no. Do I have to drive it into the ground?"

Cyril stood beneath the elm supporting the broken branch. Grossi was attempting to raise it, to attach it in some way to the one above.

"The whole approach is wrong," Cyril was saying. "You're barking up the wrong one entirely. Can't you understand that the whole *thing's* loose?"

"Hey, Joe," shouted Grossi. "The rope. Hurry it up."

"I'll get it," offered Mrs. Carlisle. Still trying to ingratiate herself with Manelli, she started, for the first time in years, to run. If she were to present him, pale-faced and panting, with his rope, surely he would relent and furnish her with an alibi? But when she reached the rambler arch, she saw at once that the rope had disappeared.

Bill, having tried for some time to close the lid of his suitcase without success, having rung his bell several times without result, went onto the landing with the intention of waylaying somebody to assist him. Halfway down the stairs, he met Dina. She was still wearing her little pieces of satin and she was eating a pear.

Bill grabbed her. Her back was warm from the sun. "Dina," he said. "I thought you'd been avoiding me."

"Did you?"

"*Have* you?"

"A bit."

"Why?"

"Clifford's told the staff not to speak to you."

"Because I didn't..."

"Yes."

"I did it for you, Dina."

"For me?"

"I'd do anything for you, Dina."

"But you *didn't* do anything."

"Are *you* angry too?"

She did not answer. She threw the core of her pear out of the window and said instead, "Bill, will you tell me something truly?"

He put his other arm around her. "Of course," he said earnestly. "Always."

"Bill, did you engage that first man?"

"Of course I didn't."

"Honestly?"

"Honestly."

"Swear?"

"Swear."

"It's rather important to me."

"Of *course* it is." He took her face between his hands and stared down into her eyes. "Dina, I solemnly swear that I've never bumped anybody off yet and I never will."

"Never?"

"*Never.*"

"You might meet somebody. You never know."

"No. Between ourselves, I don't believe I'd have even bumped my chap. I'm just not the type." He pulled her closer. "Dina, will you marry me?"

"No."

He gripped her in sudden anguish. "Why?"

"Well," she said as if this explained everything.

Bill's arms dropped to his sides. "Because I didn't...? Dina, not because I didn't...?"

She turned away.

"Dina! You *wanted* me to kill him!"

"Oh, shut up," she said.

"*Didn't* you?"

She lost her temper. "Oh stop nagging," she shouted. "Can't you understand, you fool, that you've got a splendid future and I've only got a past?"

As the clock over the stables struck three, Mrs. Carlisle reported to the armory. The Colonel was sitting at his heavy desk, dozing over the carefully-worded diplomas which each student received at the end of a course. He looked up, tugging at his mustache. "All fixed up?" he asked brusquely.

"Yes," said Mrs. Carlisle. "I shall not need an alibi. I intend to shoot him in self-defense."

The Colonel knew that he should challenge this proposition. Many students had tried to shoot Mr. White in self-defense, but the estate agent was a peaceful man and, unless he were denied a continuous flow of alcohol, refused to take offense at the grossest insults. The staff had agreed, however, that Mrs. Carlisle was a chronic bungler; whatever she planned for the evening was certain to be a catastrophic failure. "Right," he said, discouraged. "Dismiss."

Mrs. Carlisle found herself at once resenting his lack of interest. "My scheme," she said, thinking rapidly, "is to be as rude as hell. First, I shall upset his drink..."

The Colonel stopped listening. He drew a 16-inch naval cannon on a piece of blotting paper and shaded it carefully. When he had finished, she was still talking, so he added a pile of shells and wrote BANG. "Quite," he said. "Quite."

"And *then*," said Mrs. Carlisle. She drew a long breath.

The Colonel drew a bottle with a glass beside it. He drew a meniscus halfway down both and on the bottle he printed WHISKY.

"And then I shall faint," she said three minutes later.

"No," said the Colonel. "No."

"Why?"

"No fainting."

"All right. I need some bullets."

The Colonel sighed, wondering whether she was to be trusted even with the specially treated blanks which he normally issued on such occasions. Doubtfully, he gave her one.

"More," she said, clicking her fingers. "Suppose I miss."

"Meant to miss, madam," snapped the Colonel. "And kindly don't forget it."

At half past four, Mrs. Barratt donned a shady hat and went out into the garden to inspect Grossi's elm tree.

Grossi lay on the grass propped on one elbow. He was idly pulling the petals off a daisy. Manelli lay in a deck chair smoking a cigar. They were discussing the alarm system of a certain bank in Nebraska, and how they had outsmarted it in years past. The elm looked healthy and normal.

Mrs. Barratt put on her spectacles, frowning. She did not like tree work nor indeed any system of dropping anything onto anybody. She disliked the element of chance, the lack of the personal touch. She peered upwards among the leaves. The sun gleamed for an instant on two threads of nylon. "It seems very risky," she complained.

Grossi sat up, his eyes narrowing. He had come to hate the tree. But now that he had been somehow tricked into this false position, he knew that he must go through with it. The tree must work without a hitch. In the meanwhile, he would tolerate no further insults about it. "You want it should fall on you?" he asked shortly.

Mrs. Barratt looked at him for a moment in silence. Then she shrugged her frail shoulders and turned away towards the house. "Well," she said doubtfully. "Take care. Don't *you* get killed."

At five o'clock, the Creaker found Hobson sitting in the sun outside the summerhouse. His pupil wore running shorts and a grimy handkerchief knotted about his forehead. He was fingering a length of chicken wire. He looked up, his tiny eyes squinting against the glare. "I been thinkin'," he announced.

The Creaker performed the curious goosestep movement with his false leg which enabled him to sit down and lowered himself onto the rustic bench. He was already regretting that he had informed Hobson of the approaching exercise. He had done so in an expansive moment, thinking that Hobson had been pacified by his hour of freedom in Tottenham Court Road, that the two of them would exchange jokes about the soppy methods of the other students and that the matter would then be forgotten. But Hobson had not been amused. He had lowered his overgrown head and sulked, kicking at the flowers. The

Creaker had quickly assured him that his being excluded from the scheme was in no way a slight. The Creaker's trainees never took part in the final operation. It was Rules.

"I like you cock," said Hobson. "I'll miss you."

"Look, chum," said the Creaker. "You ain't gettin' up to no larks this evenin' an' that's flat." With a pang of irritation, he realized that even if he were to lock Hobson into his room during the period of temptation, the spirited fellow would immediately swarm down the wisteria.

Hobson touched the chicken wire gently with his huge foot. "Turn it up, cock," he said gruffly. "Be fair."

"No, boy. Won't do. S'Rules."

Hobson lost his temper. Without a word, he leapt to his feet, laid hold of the rustic bench and jerked the Creaker onto the ground. He placed the bench across his knee and snapped it in half. He then threw the two pieces halfway across the vegetable garden, stumped into the summerhouse and slammed the door.

At ten minutes past five, Paget came upon Manelli in the pantry. The American was feeling his chin as if to discover whether he needed a shave and studying the tray of glasses laid out for the evening cocktail.

Paget cleared his throat. "You are planning to utilize poison, sir?" he inquired.

Manelli nodded. He drummed his hairy fingers on the tray. "You going to serve this white port?"

"Yes, sir. Mr. White has a rare fancy for it."

"Anybody else drink it?"

Paget sniffed. "Not at such an hour, sir."

"Bring it."

"I must warn you, sir, that it has a delicate bouquet and it would be extremely unwise to tamper with it." He followed the direction of the other's eyes. "Mr. White does not take angostura, sir."

Manelli picked up a green glass vase, looked at it and replaced it on the shelf. "Never used poison," he remarked. "Doesn't come natural. How will I play this, Paget?"

"If I might make a suggestion, sir," said Paget slowly. "Mr. White's taste for alcoholic beverages is notorious. Should one glass, sir, be slightly larger than the others…"

"Here," said Manelli. "Have a cigar."

"Thank you, sir. We normally use a pinch of sodium bicarbonate in place of the…the real thing, sir."

Manelli laid a hand on the old shoulder. "See to it, will you?"

Paget bowed. "Sir," he said.

Manelli strolled away. "You didn't see me," he said. "I wasn't here."

Paget did not turn round, nor give any indication that he was not already alone. He whistled silently to himself as he took a large crystal goblet from the shelf and set it on the tray with a jaunty little flick of the fingers.

Five minutes later, Cyril hurried into the library and, before he had time to change his mind again, formally accepted Flush's offer of a post on the staff. The idea of earning his own living was still startling in its novelty. But, he comforted-himself, should his duties prove too arduous, he could always resign. There would always be a Chloe and he was an impresario, a virtuoso of Chloes…

Flush shook him by the hand. "I'm sure that many will regret your decision," he said, smiling. "I have every confidence in you."

"Good man," said the Colonel. "Swear you in tomorrow."

"You may have the round room in the tower," said Mrs. Barratt. "The laundry goes on Friday."

"I'll show you me wire joke," offered the Creaker.

Dina said nothing. She gave Cyril a secret smile.

Flush sat down by the window. "Have you informed Mrs. Carlisle of your decision?"

Cyril raked a hand through his hair. "Not yet."

"Shindy, eh?" asked the Creaker.

Cyril laughed nervously. "If there's only a shindy, I shall be delighted. I only hope and pray that she doesn't…well, do anything idiotic."

"Do you think," began Mrs. Barratt.

"I don't know," began Cyril. "I don't know at all."

Flush drummed his fingers on his knee. "Do you wish to participate in this evening's exercise?"

"Oh yes," said Cyril eagerly. "Do you mind if I make rather a dashing experiment?"

The clock over the stables struck the half hour.

Manelli and Grossi appeared first. Both were smiling. They sat down together on a sofa and Grossi passed Manelli an ashtray.

Mrs. Carlisle arrived on Bill's arm. She glanced at Cyril and pursed her lips, then selected a chair as far as possible from him. Flush gazed out of the window. "There is one in this room whose presence is superfluous," he stated.

Bill looked at Dina. She avoided his eyes. "All right, all right," he said angrily. "I'm going." He left the room and closed the door behind him.

Flush turned round. "I presume," he said, "that you are all prepared for our last exercise?"

"Sure," said Manelli. "He'll never know what didn't hit him."

"I'm fine," said Grossi. *Long as the wind lays off,* he thought, spitting on his thumb for luck.

"I've only been given one bullet," said Mrs. Carlisle. "If I miss, it's not my fault."

"I'd like five minutes alone in the drawing room," said Cyril.

"Couldn't 'Obson 'ave a go?" asked the Creaker. " 'E's keen as mustard."

"No." Flush studied his students. "Then it remains only for me to instruct you in the code words. When you intend to go into action, you will remark, 'What a *pleasant evening*.' At the successful conclusion of your maneuver, you will declare, '*I fear a drought. The crops will suffer.*' If you are foiled in some way and forced to abandon your scheme, you will complain of a *draught*, which will entitle you to one further attempt. Is that clear?" He glanced around the room. "All of us," he said clearly and distinctly, a slight threat in his tone, "will do our utmost to see that Mr. White spends a pleasant evening."

Chapter Fifteen

Mr. White, wearing a dinner jacket the color of a bruise, was propping up the bar in the Wassail. He watched morosely as the publican, Amos White, filled his flask with liqueur mead. He invariably carried this secret reserve on his visits to the Manor.

"'N dëay gnöo mwore'll zee yure fëace," Amos warned him. "Thik ëat Dëankry en awl be clouties."

Mr. White ignored this prediction. He belonged to the school of thought which held that the newcomers on Hanger Hill were either psychical researchers or something to do with the Foreign Office. He picked up his flask, scooped his change into his sagging pocket, raised one finger in farewell and shambled out into the sunshine.

Halfway up the long hill, he paused to refresh himself. He looked around at the parched fields, savoring the possibility of an agricultural disaster. At the top of the hill, he paused again to examine the Manor gates and their crumbling heraldic beasts. He found a small stick and poked at the cracked cement until a brick fell, then shook his head and started up the drive.

At the door, he pulled the bell, then leaned against a folded shutter and picked at the blisters in the paint.

Some five minutes later, Paget opened the door. He disliked Mr. White intensely and, as usual, looked around and through him, managing to convey the impression that nobody was there. Then, also as usual, with a slightly theatrical start, he noticed his master's guest. He stretched his hand for the hat which he knew that Mr. White never wore and murmured, "Of course, no hat. Will you step this way, sir?"

He preceded the agent through the gloom of the hall, along the passage and threw open the drawing-room door. "One of the Whites to see you, sir," he announced. He stood directly in the doorway so that Mr. White had to dodge around him, then nodded and withdrew.

Flush rose and advanced with outstretched hand. "My dear fellow," he said. He loathed Mr. White.

The agent bent one knee and lowered his left shoulder, an embarrassing habit of which he had never been able to break himself. Flush took his arm, led him across the room and introduced him to Mrs. Carlisle.

"Ah," said Mr. White. "The famous novelist?" He had borrowed many of her books from the library in Krunte Newton, diligently correcting her punctuation in the margins and adding such comments as "Not a fact," "Yus?" and, on the flyleaf, "Silliest book I ever read."

Mrs. Carlisle warmed towards him. She loved all her readers, even the ones who wrote and asked her for old clothes. Yet her program demanded that she insulted him immediately. "What of it?" she growled.

Flush frowned and led Mr. White away.

"Good evening," said Mrs. Barratt.

"Hullo," said Dina.

"Meet again," mumbled the Colonel.

"'Ot enough for you?" asked the Creaker.

"Hi," said Grossi.

Manelli bowed.

"I've heard so much about you," said Cyril with a charming smile.

Bill, sitting in a corner, was not presented.

Paget returned with a bowl of ice and a bottle wrapped in a napkin. He noted Flush's raised eyebrows, tapped his little finger against the bottle and pointed his head at Mr. White.

Flush bit his lip and turned away, attending again to his guest who was describing how the Roman legions had been seen and heard again the previous night on the road between Bindon and King's Hill.

Paget approached Mrs. Carlisle and lowered the tray. She glanced at it and, realizing that her scheme of calculated hostility would be tiring, reached for the largest glass. As her fingers closed around the stem, she saw that Paget's bloodless thumb was planted firmly on the base. He shook his head and raised his chin in Manelli's direction. Mrs. Carlisle nodded and accepted a smaller glass, then shut her eyes quickly, knowing that Paget was about to smile at her. He shuffled away and hovered at Mr. White's elbow.

"Thirteen eighty-four," Mr. White was saying. "The headless skeleton of a Carmelite friar." Some sixth sense informed him of the presence of alcohol behind him. He swung around, his eye racing over the tray.

"The white port, sir?" murmured Paget.

"Try the brew," suggested the Colonel. "Dry."

"The port, sir?" said Paget. He frowned at the Colonel.

"What a pleasant evening," remarked Manelli.

"Brew," said Mr. White. He respected the Colonel's opinion on such matters. His hand closed gratefully around the large crystal goblet.

"I feel a *draught*," grumbled Manelli. He glared at the Colonel.

Flush clicked his tongue testily. He was always contemptuous of students who demonstrated a poison routine. Most pupils seized the opportunity of the last evening to indicate more ambitious schemes. Manelli had not only displayed no interest whatever in his maneuver, but the planning had clearly been done by Paget. Moreover, between them, they had ruined a bottle of irreplaceable white port.

Manelli shrugged his shoulders and strolled away from the scene of his theoretical crime. He sat down again, trying to yawn with a cigar between his teeth. Paget sidled over. "Many a slip, sir," he murmured philosophically, "'twixt the cup and the lip."

Mr. White was advancing a suggestion that the west wing of the Manor had been built by Inigo Jones as a jest. The rafters, he said, even when new must have been alive with bolies. Now, of course, they were of the consistency of melba toast. Mr. White shook his head and remarked that the numbers of bolies in the woodwork must now be astronomical. They bred by the million, swarmed in all directions, destroyed all before them.

Paget refilled his glass.

"Here I go," said Mrs. Carlisle. "*What a pleasant evening.*" She stubbed out her cigarette, finished her drink and walked over to Mr. White. She lunged clumsily against him, upsetting his glass.

The agent looked at her in amazement. "I'm so sorry," he said politely, puzzled.

"Ha!" she sneered, wondering whether she should stamp on his foot.

Mr. White decided that she was drunk and must be humored. He was accustomed to dealing with drunks. "Of course," he said. "Of course."

"I don't understand you. Are you mad?"

Mr. White spread his huge hands. "Aren't we all?" he asked gently.

Mrs. Carlisle stared at him, baffled. She knew that she would lose her temper long before he did.

"Madam," said Flush. His eyes were narrowed to slits. "Will you kindly sit down?"

She took a step backwards. "I haven't finished," she mouthed over Mr. White's shoulder.

"Sit *down* please."

Mrs. Carlisle capitulated with bad grace. "Well, of course, if I'm going to be constantly interrupted," she said. She flounced away.

Mr. White, who had himself made many such embarrassing gaffes, smiled sympathetically after her. He began to speak tactfully of the curious manner in which the entire western substratum of Hanger Hill was sliding at the rate of nine inches a year towards the sea. The dew pond at Moigne Herring was already at such an angle that after rain the cottage beneath it was flooded regularly.

Mrs. Carlisle sat down next to Bill. "I didn't have a *chance*," she said fretfully. "Five minutes more and I swear that he would have hit me."

Bill tore his eyes away from Dina's brown legs. He roused himself from a doldrum of misery. He knew that if he had avenged his family like a man, Dina would probably have accepted him. One righteous moment, he thought hopelessly, had ruined his entire life. And he still had to explain to his father that the family problem had been solved by a complete stranger; more shame, more ridicule. "Shoot him now," he advised Mrs. Carlisle savagely. "Shoot them all. Give it to me. *I'll* shoot them."

"You know very well it's not loaded," said Mrs. Carlisle. "You impostor."

Paget bent over her, refilling her glass. "Bad luck, madam," he breathed. "May I suggest that you try Misadventure?" He straightened up and slid away.

Mr. White was swinging his empty glass pointedly at his side as if it were a croquet mallet. Paget trapped it neatly, raised it into a perpendicular position and filled it with white port. He looked over at Manelli, but the gangster was deep in conversation with Grossi. "What a pleasant *evening*, sir," he hissed.

Mr. White took a large gulp from the glass, then hesitated. He drank again, raising his head like a bird. "Ah!" he said. "As I feared. The cork has gone." He added mournfully, "Ah well! The bouquet is still quite amusing."

The Colonel, who was in charge of the cellar, stiffened. He poured himself a glass of port and tasted it.

Mr. White watched him. "Muck?"

The Colonel nodded. "Muck," he agreed.

Flush strolled over to Manelli. He said softly, "You realize, of course, that had your gambit been official, you would also have poisoned the Colonel?"

Mr. White began to discuss the Manor's poltergeist. What the bolies tore down, the polter threw up. The new rectory at Gore Crichel had harbored the same unholy alliance and where was it now? The Colonel replied with a long and unsatisfactory tale of the ghost of a coolie which haunted the cantonment at Lucknow.

"What a pleasant *evening*," crooned Cyril.

Flush turned and looked at him with interest. From this new member of the staff, he expected a ploy of fiendish ingenuity. Cyril lit a cigarette and leaned back in his chair, gazing at the ceiling.

Mrs. Barratt, provoked by his smirk, laid down her knitting and said, "You have something up your sleeve. I can see it."

"Absolutely not," said Cyril. "No."

A wasp flew into the room. Flush followed it with his eyes, then turned to Cyril. "Yours?" he asked.

"No, no."

The Colonel refilled Mr. White's glass and embarked upon the history of how his great-great-grandfather had distinguished himself during the Battle of Assaye. Mr. White countered with a description of how a tame stag belonging to an earlier White had pinked John of Gaunt.

The door opened suddenly with a loud click. Everyone turned to look at it. It blew open two inches and was still.

Flush raised his eyebrows at Cyril.

Cyril shook his head with a faint smile.

Flush pulled at the lobe of his ear. "I thought you said that it was a pleasant evening."

"I did."

"You meant it?"

"Of course."

"Perhaps you feel a draught?"

"No, thank you."

"You're perfectly comfortable?"

"Ideal."

Flush studied the room. Everything was apparently as usual. He tapped a fingernail on his teeth and looked at Cyril sideways. "You are finding the weather clement *now?*"

"Delightful."

Flush lit a cigar. He looked at Cyril through the flame of the match. "And *now?* The climate still suits you?"

"Yes indeed."

Flush bit his lip and, forgetting discretion, began to roam around the room scrutinizing every movable object. He returned to Cyril frowning. "Have we been exchanging pleasantries?" he asked.

"No," said Cyril. He glanced at his watch. Two seconds later, he said smugly, "In fact I fear a *drought.* The crops will *suffer.*"

Flush wandered across the room to Mr. White, examined him covertly, then wandered back to Cyril. "I frankly don't understand you."

Cyril grinned. "It's revolutionary," he said. "The timing's important but otherwise it's pathetically simple."

"I don't believe you. You are too proud to admit that a draught is bothering you."

"I'm as warm as toast."

"Gas," said Flush.

"No."

"Some sort of poisoned dart nonsense?"

"You insult me."

"Poison?"

"No, no."

"Electrical work?"

"No."

"Gravity?"

"Well, in a roundabout way."

"Gravity up or down?"

"Neither *quite*."

"With some form of delayed action?"

"Well, in a *way*."

"Fuse work?"

"No. I'll explain later."

"I suggest that your arrangements would become obsolete if Mr. White were to move two inches to the left."

"Did you address me?" asked Mr. White.

"No, no," said Flush. He stepped closer to Cyril, lowering his voice. "Well? Am I right?"

"Certainly not. In fact, I could sit here without moving a muscle and pick you off one by one."

Flush blew smoke. "Indeed?" he said coldly.

"Yes. Not swanking."

"And you definitely fear a *drought*?"

"Yes. The crops have practically had it already."

"True, true," said Mr. White. He slopped over and joined the group. "My small plot is in sorry plight. What the Colorados started upon, the drought will terminate."

Bill suddenly rose in the corner. He marched over to Dina and sat down beside her. He seized both her hands. "Dina," he whispered desperately. "If I said I'd killed the first body, would it make any difference?"

"No," she said. "Don't go on and on."

"If I promised to kill somebody soon?"

"Who?"

"Well, I don't know offhand."

"No."

"I *will*, Dina," he said wildly. "*Any*body. Just say a name."

"Mickey Mouse," she said. She freed her hands, got up and walked away.

By the empty fireplace, Mrs. Carlisle looked at herself in her compact mirror, laid her handbag on her chair and stood up. "*What* a pleasant evening," she said cheerily. She smoothed her dress over her hips and made for Mr. White.

The agent was explaining to Mrs. Barratt that it frequently took several centuries for an old house to "settle." The Manor, particularly the west wing, had settled long ago. The disturbing creaks and sighs, the mysterious opening and shutting of doors, the sudden gush of water from the scullery tap, were not the work of the polter nor the bolies, but simply another spasm of the dry rot. Mrs. Barratt was annoyed. She had come to like her home and she had never liked Mr. White. She claimed that the door had opened a moment ago quite simply because a breeze had risen.

Grossi looked up sharply, his cigarette halfway to his mouth. "Breeze," he said. "Joe, did you hear that?"

Manelli was already on his feet. "We gotta go!"

"Excuse us," Grossi said to Mr. White. He ran through the French window.

Manelli hurried after him. Crossing the lawn, he watched his ex-partner clear a flowerbed, skid around the corner of the conservatory and pause at a respectful distance from the elm. A minute later, Manelli joined him. He looked up at the tree. The leaves were fluttering in the small wind. "What are you waiting for, Tony?"

"Joe, I have no faith in this tree."

"Me neither."

"I say let it fall."

"Okay. It's your prestige."

"You scared?"

"Plenty. You?"

"Sure. Come on, let's get it." Grossi stepped under the elm and dropped onto his knees among the roots.

"Pleasant evening," remarked Manelli.

"Ah, go on," said Grossi uneasily. "The tree feels a draught."

"You hope."

"I hope."

Manelli advanced and knelt down. He took one of the nylon lines and looked up anxiously at the heavy branch above.

He reflected that if it fell now, he and Grossi would die on their knees, which would set the hoods laughing from New York to San Francisco.

"If I kick off," said Grossi noncommittally, "Fernandez takes over."

"That would be too bad," said Manelli. Fernandez loved trouble. "I got Cantril."

"Ed?"

"Sam. The cousin."

"That gopher," said Grossi.

They began cautiously to tighten the lines. Conscious of their perfect teamwork, Manelli found himself wondering whether a new merger would have the old success. Perhaps a readjustment of frontiers, a division of the more lucrative unions; perhaps with his brain and connections, and Grossi's brawn and gruesome reputation…

"Joe," said Grossi. "While the heat is on, I will be here and points east."

"Me too," said Manelli.

Grossi hesitated. "Maybe we should come to a little understanding."

"Maybe."

"Only one thing. Fernandez just can't take Cantril."

"Tony," said Manelli. "Truth now, is Cantril generally thought to be a gopher?"

"Sure."

Manelli looked thoughtful. "Fernandez," he remarked, "is known as a skinful of hop."

"Yeah?" After a slight pause, Grossi added, "Fernandez is getting ambitious. If anything happens to Fernandez, Gig Ferrari takes over."

"Alex Gotha's after Cantril."

"Gig likes Alex."

"Yeah, I know."

The tree wheezed.

"Watch it," said Manelli.

"What do you say, Joe?"

"I don't want a lotta rough stuff, Tony. I grew outa all that."

"Me too. Say you take France, I take Italy. I take Britain, you take Africa."

"You take Africa," corrected Manelli. "I take Britain. Every year millions of pounds of stuff is lost on the railroads alone."

"Chicken," said Grossi.

"Sure. The guy up there has no know-how. Take me. Look what I did for Wool."

"Yeah, but who balled it up with the strike?" Grossi leaned forward and tapped Manelli on the kneecap. "Joe," he said. "Let's get together. Let's move in and get Europe on a sound financial basis."

Manelli faked a punch at Grossi's chin. "Little old Tony," he said. "Smart as they come when you were knee-high to a rattlesnake."

"Is it a deal, Joe?"

"It's a deal, Tony."

"Shake."

"Shake."

They shook hands. Even as Manelli let go of the nylon line, he saw what was about to happen. He sprang to his feet. He gave Grossi a savage push which landed him six feet away.

The sawn branch fell with a crash. Its heavy base missed Manelli by inches. The outer twigs snapped around Grossi's feet.

For a moment, both mobsters lay where they had been thrown, their faces pressed into the grass, their arms flung upwards to protect their heads.

Grossi was the first to recover. He sat up and ran a hand over his hair. "Holy cow!" he whispered. "That was close." He stood up and dusted himself down. He bent, stretching a hand to help Manelli, then paused and straightened up slowly. "Joe," he said, puzzled. "You tried to crease me."

Manelli rolled over and retrieved his cigar. "You're crazy," he said shakily.

"You shouldn'ta *done* that, Joe."

Manelli clambered to his feet and spat out a twig. "Look," he said. "I saved your life is all."

Grossi stared at him "Oh?" he asked politely. He drew the syllable out, his tone sliding down a full octave. "That is your story, Joe?"

Manelli mopped his forehead. "Forget it."

"Going to tell it on television, Joe? I wouldn't like that." Grossi remembered what had happened to Tiggy Sierra. After Tiggy's life had been saved by his uncle Salvadore, it had not been worth living. Tiggy had become generally known as "Junior" and, after years of shame, had been assassinated by an old hood of poor repute.

Manelli blew the ash off his cigar. With a sudden spurt of rage, he realized that he too was compromised. He remembered what happened when Nick "the Enforcer" Caldera had been nearly drowned in attempting to save the life of Willy Spinner off Morgan's Wharf. Among the hoodlums, it had been the best joke in years. Nick, unable to face the ridicule, had taken a powder to Mexico. It was told that he now sat all day on the shore waiting for a tidal wave to drown his sorrows.

"I do not like heroes, Joe," said Grossi steadily. He clenched his hands, turned on his heel and strode away towards the house.

Manelli stood watching him. He knew now that until either he or Grossi lay in a cement overcoat at the bottom of the Channel, they would be obliged to stay within yards of each other. The world was no longer big enough to hold both of them. He tossed away his cigar and began to run.

On the terrace, he sidestepped to avoid the Creaker and Hobson. The Creaker was sitting on the steps talking to his pupil in a heated undertone. Hobson was in shirtsleeves, shorts, and plimsolls. "But *why*, cock?" he was muttering. "I won't 'arm 'im."

"Get back, boy," pleaded the Creaker. "Go an' feed the ferrets."

Hobson arched his neck. "Fork the ferrets," he growled. "Let me pass."

Manelli went through the French windows into the drawing room and looked around.

Mrs. Carlisle was leaning heavily on Mr. White's arm, showing him a small automatic and inviting him to examine it. Grossi, as Manelli had suspected, was talking to Flush in a corner. Manelli joined them hurriedly. "I heard a crash," Flush was murmuring. "Am I to understand that you are feeling a draught, Mr. Grossi?"

"I'm leaving," said Grossi. "I want my stuff from the gunroom."

"Me too," said Manelli.

"Now?" asked Flush.

"Yup."

"Yep."

Flush's eyelids drooped. "You are leaving *together*?"

"Yeah," said Grossi. "At first."

Flush sipped his drink. "I see," he said. He looked at them with a flicker of interest. "You will not wait for your diplomas?"

"Nup."

"Nope."

"Have you…er…any presentiments about the outcome of this journey?"

Manelli shrugged. "He's quick," he admitted. "But he gets excited. I'm steadier, but I'm outa practice."

"Take your pick," snapped Grossi. "Come on. The *key*!"

Flush considered them. He reassured himself that neither would shoot the other in the presence of so many expert witnesses. "I trust that neither of you gentlemen will forget the county limit?" he murmured. "You will not, naturally, be so ill-bred as to settle your differences on the premises?"

"Come on, come on."

Flush put down his glass, excused himself to Mr. White, who was gingerly examining the safety catch on Mrs. Carlisle's automatic, and led the way out into the passage.

"The post office at Creech Minster marks the county border," he said. He added helpfully, "Two miles past it, there is a turning to the left which leads to the remains of a Roman amphitheater, the scene no doubt of many an ancient gladiatorial combat." He stopped outside the armory door, produced a key and fitted it into the lock.

Grossi pushed past him into the room. He ran a finger along the lockers until he found the one marked with his name. He opened it and took out his sawn-off shotgun, his large-caliber automatic, and his long-barreled Colt Woodsman .22. He dropped the automatic into his pocket, tucked the shotgun under his arm and screwed a silencer onto the Colt. He glanced at Manelli, wondering what firearm the older man would favor. Manelli was testing the action of his Thompson submachine-gun; there was also a huge bulge under his left arm which he kept adjusting irritably. He had not worn a gun for years.

Paget advanced three feet into the room. He looked from one mobster to the other. With the clairvoyance of all good butlers, he had seen the conversation beneath the elm and had correctly assessed it. "I have taken the liberty, sir, sir," he said, "of placing your bags in your motors."

"Where are the Boys?" demanded Manelli. "Send them."

"They have not returned from Poxwell Regis, sir."

Grossi sneered. "It's you and me, Slots."

"You or me, Pete."

Paget backed away. In the doorway, he collided with Cyril. "Have a care, sir!" he barked. He jerked down his waistcoat and retired.

Cyril hurried into the room. "Clifford," he said. "Hobson is in a rage. It looks as if things may become rather *al fresco*."

As if to support this statement, there was a muffled scream from the drawing room. It was followed almost instantly by an oath and the tinkle of breaking glass.

Flush pursed his lips. He picked up a Steyr automatic, slipped it into his pocket and left the room.

Cyril looked over the tray of pistols, chose a small, pearl-handled Swiss model and hurried away.

Grossi and Manelli were left alone. They ignored each other. Grossi opened a drawer and helped himself to four boxes of hollow-nosed, high velocity .22 bullets. Manelli opened another and began to fill his pockets with submachine-gun slugs. Grossi shouldered past him, opened a small cupboard and started to count out twelve bore cartridges. Manelli fitted a clip into his automatic, wedged three more into his breast pocket, then took a grenade off a shelf and looked at it. It was silver-plated, a paper weight.

Along the stone corridor rang the explosion of a single shot. Mrs. Carlisle's voice, shrill with hysteria, cried, "It just went off! I didn't even *touch* it!"

Before the echo of the shot had died away, Manelli's automatic was in his hand. It was a purely reflex action. So was the tightening of Grossi's trigger finger upon the gun in his pocket. Involuntarily, he fired through the cloth.

The bullet went nowhere near Manelli. It plowed through the table and embedded itself in a leather armchair. But the elder mobster had not waited. He had not heard a shot fired indoors for many years, and he panicked. He fired a wild burst at Grossi, plunged out of the room and flattened himself against the stone wall behind the door.

Grossi, who had instinctively flung himself to cover behind the Colonel's massive desk, crawled cautiously through the kneehole and fired two shots into the corridor.

The bullets ricocheted off the Portland stone. One struck an African shield directly over Manelli's head. Manelli looked rapidly around him. Paget was standing at the far end of the corridor, holding a tray of glasses and staring.

Flush came out of the drawing room. "Stop that noise immediately," he snapped.

Another shot came from the armory. An arrangement of Zulu spears fell off the wall behind Manelli. Manelli fired twice through the open door, dropped his automatic into his pocket, turned and ran upstairs clutching the Thompson.

Grossi streaked out of the armory, across the hall and hurled himself behind a heavy brass gong at the foot of the stairs. He raised the repeating shotgun and fired four times at the upper landing.

A stream of bullets from the Thompson clanged off the gong.

The Colonel marched along the passage. He went into the armory and reappeared with his Springfield. He advanced into the middle of the hall. A bullet from the landing cracked past his head. "Yellowbelly!" roared the Colonel, his face magenta with rage. He leveled the Springfield and took careful aim.

Grossi seized the opportunity to race up the stairs and arrive sprawling behind the cedar chest on the half landing where Mrs. Barratt kept the spare eiderdowns.

The Colonel, his blood up, fired one shot at the chest, one at the upper landing. Two shots answered him almost simultaneously. One raised splinters in the parquet a foot in front of him. The other smashed a vase of roses to his left. The Colonel made a tactical withdrawal.

Flush, Cyril, Paget, and Bill stood in the passage. Flush glanced around the corner into the hall. A bullet clipped the end off his cigar and smacked into the wall. Flush's face darkened. "Organize the staff, Colonel," he growled. "Silence those lunatics."

Cyril raised his eyebrows. "Bring 'em back *alive*?" he inquired.

Flush looked down at his ruined cigar. "Not necessarily," he said.

Bill ran along the passage and into the drawing room. Mrs. Carlisle was tottering around the room, wringing her hands and moaning, "It just went off. Nobody told me about any safety catches. It just went *off.*" Dina was on the terrace arguing with the Creaker and Hobson. Mrs. Barratt sat on the couch knitting unperturbed. And Mr. White lay on the floor with one leg twisted underneath him and one hand still clutching the large crystal goblet.

"Good God!" said Bill. "Who did that?"

Mrs. Barratt turned her knitting around and started at the beginning of another row. "He has fainted," she said. "Most considerate of him."

"I shot him," babbled Mrs. Carlisle. "I'm a *murderer!*"

"My dear, do sit *down*," said Mrs. Barratt irritably. "As you well know, it was only a blank. You have merely singed his tie."

"Dina," called Bill. "The Colonel's mobilizing the staff. In the hall." She trotted past him. Bill ran onto the terrace. The Creaker and Hobson were lying on the tiles, deadlocked in a terrible, tigerish, Cornish All Purpose. Bill left them. He shot through the drawing room and back into the passage.

"Kindly shut the door," called Mrs. Barratt. "I am in a terrible draught."

Bill shut it and ran along the passage. As he reached the far end, Dina came out of the armory holding a box of large cartridges.

Bill seized her arm. "What's that?" he demanded.

"Tear gas," she said. "Let go. The Colonel wants it."

"Where are they all?"

"Manelli made a break. Then they all tore upstairs. Can you hear anything?"

"Not now."

"I expect they're all digging themselves in."

"Dina," said Bill. "If I…if, quite accidentally, I…"

"No," she said firmly, turning towards the stairs. "Will you bring the riot gun?"

On the half landing, she met Paget. He was brushing plaster off his coat. He stood aside to let her pass. "The front line is now in the tower, miss," he said. "The master requires me to mount the roof and create a diversion in the rear."

Dina, appalled, stared at him. "You can't do that! You'll never even…"

"It was an *order*, miss."

There was a sudden burst of firing from upstairs. Dina clutched the tear gas cartridges and ran upstairs. On the third

floor, she tripped over Cyril. He was sitting on the floor with a
Sten gun beside him. He was holding his right arm and trying
to rip the tail off his shirt with his teeth.

"I'm bleeding to death," he announced with satisfaction.
"The Colonel admits that the tower is as bad as the Khyber Pass
and he knew it *when*."

The window on the landing splintered. A bullet thudded
into the stuffed head of an eland on the wall behind. Cyril and
Dina flattened themselves on the floor.

"It's Manelli," said Dina. "He's got the range from the top
of the tower. I can see him jumping around in the battlements."

Bill raced upstairs carrying the riot gun. "You'll see," he
told Dina as he flashed past. "You'll just see."

On the top landing, he found Flush sitting in an armchair
and fitting a new clip into a repeating rifle. Facing him, the
Colonel was leaning against the angle of a slit window and
sniping at the tower with his Springfield. The floor was littered
with cartridge cases. At the bottom of the spiral staircase, a
heavy couch stood on end to form a barricade. As Bill watched,
three bullets raised dust in it. Another bullet whined down the
stairs, ricocheting off the circular stone walls.

Bill sprang behind the couch. "Grossi," he shouted. "Come
down before I gas you down!"

Two shots struck the couch. "Come on up!" yelled Grossi.
"And I'll give you a Purple Heart."

Flush prodded Bill with the repeating rifle. "Mr. Thurlow,"
he said frigidly. "Have you already forgotten Lesson Twelve?
Where, you dolt, are our gas masks?"

In the small, round room above, Grossi gnawed his lip. He realized immediately that if the staff intended to use tear gas, his
position would soon become untenable. There were only two
ways out of it. Up or down. Both were equally unattractive. Grossi
knew well that neither Manelli nor Flush meant him to survive
the encounter. Up, to Manelli, whose prestige would be much

enhanced by Grossi's humiliating death? Or down, to Flush, who, from sheer ill temper, would not only shoot him but gas him too?

"Be reasonable, Mr. Grossi," called Flush from below. "Come down before I forget myself."

"Come on up, Tony," shouted Manelli from above. "I'm getting kinda bored."

In the drawing room, Mr. White stirred. He groaned, his hands fumbling up towards his head. His eyelids flickered.

Mrs. Barratt laid down her knitting, leaned forward and dealt him an expert blow on the sternocleido mastoid with the heel of her shoe.

Paget, proceeding upstairs with the intention of creating a diversion in the rear, met Mrs. Carlisle lurching about on the first landing clutching at her hair.

"My *head*!" she cried. "The *noise*!"

"Quite, madam," said Paget. He was about to pass her by when she grabbed his arm and shook it.

"Where is Cyril?" she demanded. "Answer me, you old zombie."

Paget studied her. He had never liked her. She used manly language and she had nicotine stains on her fingers. He delivered his bombshell with unconcealed relish. "I understand that he has joined the staff permanently, madam." For good measure, he gave her his gayest smile and went on his way.

On top of the tower, Manelli was thinking fast. He had heard Bill's warning about gas and, for the first time in his life, was wishing that he could call a cop. He knew that Grossi would be forced upwards; he knew also that his ex-partner would not arrive unannounced. Tony had always exaggerated with firearms.

Manelli glanced over the battlements. Fifteen feet below, there was a flat roof bristling with ornamented chimneys. If he could get down there, there might be a chance. He would be able to pour a stream of lead into Grossi's slit window and later, possibly, penetrate into the house and attack the staff from the rear. His stomach turned over at the mere idea of the drop; and, even if he made it, until he could take cover he would be directly in Grossi's line of fire...

Bill, sprinting upstairs with the gas masks, found Dina at the landing window on the third floor. A Sten gun was propped against the wall and Dina was doing up a suspender. Beyond and above her, Manelli raised the Thompson on top of the tower.

Bill dived, a clumsy rugger tackle. He brought Dina to her knees. A bullet chipped a piece off the window ledge. Bill seized the Sten gun.

Dina knelt up beside him. "There he is!" she said. "Now's your chance! *Now!*"

Bill looked at her. "Dina," he said. "If I..."

"Well," she said. "Perhaps. Oh, look! A lovely shot! Now, *now*, NOW!"

Bill squeezed the trigger. There was a click, then silence. "God rot it!" he bellowed. "The bloody thing's not loaded!"

Halfway up the ladder which led to the lofts, Paget stopped and bit his lip. With each step, it seemed, his lumbago became worse. Doggedly, he forced himself onwards. An involuntary groan escaped him as he wrestled with the trapdoor. It fell back with a crash. The dust rose in a cloud and Paget was momentarily blinded. He wiped his eyes and climbed one more step. As the dust began to settle, he peered through the gloom at the broken skylight which led to the roof. In the distance, he heard the firing...

On the ground floor, Mrs. Carlisle ran into the armory. So Cyril had joined the staff, had he? So she had been jilted, had she? So she was a laughing stock, was she? She would *see* about that.

"Ha!" she said grimly.

She began to drag open the drawers, looking for the biggest and most punishing bullet available.

In the small, round room below the battlements, Grossi tied his shoelaces into double knots, reloaded the repeating shotgun and crawled forward until he could hear the voices on the landing below.

"Here they are," said Bill's voice. He was panting.

"Ah," said Flush. "The respirators. Thank you."

"One for *you* and one for *me*," said Cyril.

"Mr. Grossi," called Flush. "Do you insist upon this buffoonery?"

"Go soak your head!" shouted Grossi. He lay listening, waiting.

"*That* one is mine," Flush said. "The one in the green box."

Grossi heard somebody drop a cardboard box, then another. There was a pause.

"Roouoingerireut?" asked a muffled and indistinguishable voice.

"Currearerring," said another.

"Rot?"

"Terroucurrearerring."

"Fall in," ordered the Colonel. He then apparently slipped on his gas mask for he added, "Arretteh?"

"Roo?"

"Ree?"

There was another pause. Grossi stood up. He heard somebody moving a heavy piece of furniture.

"Rire!" roared the Colonel.

The cartridge of tear gas exploded on the spiral staircase with a dull plop. Within three seconds, Grossi's eyes had started to water.

"Joe!" he yelled. "I'm coming up!"

He began to inch up the worn stone stairs, firing as he went. The shots echoed down the tower. The noise was deafening. At the last bend, Grossi looked up. Above, he saw the blue sky, the gulls circling. With four stairs to go, he realized that there was no answering fire from above. He closed his eyes for an instant, opened them, and charged, firing from the hip. He saw at once that the top of the tower was deserted. Then a stream of bullets hit the battlements. Grossi flung himself onto his face. Four seconds later, he raised himself cautiously and peered over the parapet. Below him was the roof, a skylight, a forest of chimneys, the venomous snout of the Thompson wedged between two ornamental cowls...

"Come on down, Tony," called Manelli.

"Mr. Grossi," Flush shouted. "I'm coming up."

In the loft, Paget dragged a heavy trunk from the shadows and placed it under the skylight. The effort made him so giddy that he stood swaying for a moment. Then he dusted his lapels and clambered onto the trunk. He moaned as he raised the heavy panes. Holding his breath, he straightened up slowly until his eyes were on a level with the roof.

Twenty feet away, Manelli was crouching behind a chimney. Bullets from the tower were hammering into the roof around him.

"*Pss-sst*, sir!" hissed Paget.

Manelli's head snapped around. His mouth dropped open. "I am not armed, sir," said Paget. "Will you step this way?"

Manelli hesitated for only a moment. He fired half a clip at the tower, then began to dodge backwards from chimney to chimney. A face in a gas mask appeared briefly at the slit window. The evening sun flashed on the muzzle of the riot gun.

"This way, sir," boomed Paget encouragingly. "Two feet to the east, sir...straight back, sir...A burst at the battlements please...steady as you go, sir...Now might I suggest a running jump, sir?"

Manelli hurled himself at the skylight. He crashed through it, landed half on the trunk, rolled off, bounced off a pile of old suitcases and sprawled onto a heap of dilapidated saddles.

He lay for a full three minutes wondering whether he was dead. Then he shook his head, flexed his wrists, turned over and sat up. "Thanks, Paget," he said weakly. "Here. Have a cigar." Paget climbed painfully off the trunk. "Thank you, sir." He took the cigar and put it in his breast pocket. Then he advanced three paces, said, "Excuse me, sir," snatched up the Thompson and struck Manelli smartly on the head with the stock.

In the armory, Mrs. Carlisle found a large and likely bullet; clutched it; began to search for a gun which would suit it. Some ten minutes later, she came upon an antique, short-barreled affair which was obviously intended to discharge something of the caliber of a new potato. She tried her ammunition for size and to her delight found that it appeared to fit quite well. She crammed it into the breech, stalked into the hall and started upstairs.

In the small, round room below the battlements, Bill had witnessed Manelli's hair-raising escape and had realized that he had only one last chance of killing somebody in a good cause. He therefore snatched up the Colonel's Springfield, adjusted his gas mask and streaked up to the top of the tower after Grossi.

"Urreechrossi!" he shouted. "Rirorrourovered!"

But Grossi was not there. He was down on the roof, lying on his stomach with the repeating shotgun trained upon the slit window below Bill.

As Bill raised the Springfield, he saw Paget, apparently oblivious of danger, raise his head over the skylight and look around inquiringly. "This way, sir," he called.

Grossi looked over his shoulder. He stared. "What do you want?" he asked.

At that moment, the Colonel fired the riot gun from the slit window. The cartridge exploded dully on the roof. The tear gas rose like a ground mist.

Bill steadied himself against the battlements and took a careful bead on the center of Grossi's forehead. He drew a long breath and held it. His finger tightened slowly around the trigger. He squeezed gently; then hesitated. For nearly five seconds, he held Grossi in his sights. Then he threw the gun over the parapet and lowered his head into his hands. He could not do it; he would never be able to do it; for as long as he lived, he knew that he would never have what it took to kill somebody from whom he had accepted a cigarette. He had tried and he had failed. He was not a man, he was a mouse. Dina could never love a mouse. His life was ruined all over again.

Indifferently, he watched Grossi gather himself into a projectile and in some curious fashion project himself at the skylight. Hopelessly, he saw a sickle of bullets kick into the roof an inch from the gangster's disappearing legs. Sunk into abysmal gloom, he heard the Colonel shout an order in the room below.

"Rease Rire!"

Mrs. Carlisle, hurrying upstairs with her huge pistol, remarked the sudden silence. She stood still and listened. Except for the stair upon which she stood, which creaked with her every breath, there was not a sound.

For a wild moment, she wondered whether everybody was dead, whether she was alive alone in this monstrous house with the polter and the bolies. Fighting hysteria, she closed her eyes and laid hold of the bridge of her nose with her left hand. She heard a sound above, opened her eyes and waved the pistol.

Flush was crossing the landing above. He was frowning at a small scorch on the pocket of his velvet jacket, scratching at it with a fingernail. He moved slowly along the corridor. He paused at the far end beneath the ladder which led to the lofts. "Paget," he called. "Are you alive?"

Paget's gray face gleamed in the aperture. "Yes, sir," he said. "Thank you."

"And those...our guests?"

"They are unconscious, sir." Apparently feeling that this was not entirely satisfactory, Paget added apologetically, "Had it not been for my lumbago, sir…"

Mrs. Carlisle ran up the last flight of stairs. There was a strong smell of cordite. On the landing at the foot of the spiral staircase, she stopped abruptly.

An overturned couch lay with its legs in the air. In the center of the worn carpet lay a pile of armaments and an ashtray full of cigarette and cigar butts. The Colonel, his white hair ruffled, was sucking one corner of his mustache and looking out of the slit window. Bill, wearing a gas mask, was sunk into a dusty armchair with his chin on his breast. And Cyril, with one shirtsleeve ripped off at the shoulder, was examining a crude bandage around his upper arm with obvious pride.

Mrs. Carlisle's rage threatened to choke her. She planted her feet apart and raised the huge pistol with both hands.

Flush, steadying the ladder as Paget descended from the loft at the far end of the landing, looked over his shoulder. He realized instantly that Mrs. Carlisle presented a danger far more acute than any that the staff had faced during the past hour. He left the ladder and sprang forward.

At the top of the stairs, he collided with Dina. She was carrying a tray of coffee, sandwiches, and ammunition. She saw the horrid situation on the landing and dropped the tray. "Clifford!" she whispered frantically. "*Do* something!"

As Flush clutched at his ankle, scalded by the boiling coffee, Paget appeared at his elbow.

"Allow *me*, sir," he murmured. "I have the hang of it now." He picked up the heavy silver tray, shuffled forward and struck Mrs. Carlisle a ringing blow on the head.

As she crumpled, there was a moment of complete silence.

Paget raised his eyes and met the thoughtful stare of his master. A faint color crept into his sunken cheeks. "It was an order, sir," he said defensively. "You instructed me to create a diversion at the rear. We Pagets, sir, have obeyed orders since the time of the Stuarts."

Chapter Sixteen

An hour later, all the casualties had been attended to. The three for which Paget was responsible had had priority. Manelli and Grossi, both still unconscious, had had their heads bandaged and had been laid on their beds until such time as they should recover. Mrs. Carlisle, also bandaged about the head, had been placed in a deck chair on the terrace. Cyril, dodging about the house trying to avoid her, had his right arm in a sling. The Colonel and Paget had both been given a sedative. The Creaker and Hobson, extensively bruised, had been rubbed down with liniment. Flush, in a towering rage, had suffered his left trouser leg to be turned back to the knee and his scalded foot and ankle to be painted with gentian purple.

Matron, awash with cowslip wine, had performed these ministrations in silence. Having finished with her patients, she left the dispensary, grunting over her shoulder, "Ah well! Clickety click."

On the terrace, Mrs. Carlisle lay in her chair breathing heavily and demanding brandy. Mr. White, who was showing signs of recovery, had been arranged beside her on a bench. Bill sat at the top of the garden steps staring moodily at his feet. Dina crouched over Mr. White, watching him anxiously.

"It *may* have been an order," said Mrs. Carlisle, "but he shouldn't have *done* it. Suppose he'd killed me, where would I have been then? I *know* that he apologized, but if it hadn't been for his lumbago…"

Mr. White, his eyes still closed, groaned loudly. His eyes opened slowly. He lay for a long moment staring blankly at the sky, then sat up abruptly and coughed. "I was shot," he said. He pointed a shaking finger at Mrs. Carlisle. "*You* shot me."

"No, no," said Dina quickly. Suddenly inspired, she added, "*You* shot *her.*"

Mr. White wrenched the flask of mead from his pocket and took a long draught. "Oh," he said and drank again.

"Yes," said Dina. "You distinctly shot her. We all saw you."

Mr. White frowned. "*Why* did I shoot her?"

"It's quite all right. She doesn't mind."

"*She* shot *me,*" he said uneasily.

"Well, why aren't you dead then?"

Mr. White thought it over for some time. Then he turned to Mrs. Carlisle. "Madam," he said. "I am profoundly ashamed. Would you care for a drop of mead?"

Beyond the French windows, Paget faced the four senior members of the staff in the drawing room. "It is in our breeding, sir," he said for the third time. "Our centuries of yeoman service. Give us an order, sir, and we obey it without question."

Flush lit a cigar. "You may have prevented an ugly situation," he said coldly, "but your methods are monotonous. Moreover, you exaggerated. I am obliged to ask for your resignation. You will not, of course, expect a reference."

Paget bowed his head, unable to conceal the relief in his eyes. The Manor, with its new and unfortunate associations, no longer had its old hold upon him. Now he could take his small sepia snapshot of the earl and leave forever without the fear that the staff would track him down and put an end to him. He had been *ordered* to leave. His jubilation overcame him. His face sagged into a mask of suicidal gloom.

"You may go," snapped Flush. "Permanently."

Paget bowed and retired. He went along the passage and into his pantry. He folded up his green baize apron and stole the earl's favorite pewter tankard. He was padding happily upstairs to pack his few possessions when the bell rang. He returned to the drawing room, knocked and entered.

Flush was staring out of the window. "By the way, Paget," he said without turning, "I presume that you were also responsible for that previous piece of unmitigated cheek?"

Paget could not tell a lie. "Yes, sir." He shook his head gloomily. "There had been a lot of trouble, sir, on the far side of the baize."

Mrs. Barratt clicked her tongue reproachfully. "Your deed was premeditated?"

"No indeed, madam." Paget was shocked. "I beg your pardon, madam, but I do not approve of homicide."

"Go on," said Flush evenly.

"I assure you, sir, that the affair was entirely impromptu. Upon the night in question, I was perturbed, sir. Sleep eluded me. This fellow had been most offensive. When at dawn I observed him clearly about to utilize your swimming pool, I descended with the intention of forbidding him to do so. He refused to listen, sir. He said..." Paget stopped and closed his eyes.

"Yes?" prompted Mrs. Barratt.

"He called me 'greaseball,' madam." Paget trembled. "He spoke in a vernacular which I had difficulty in following. I understood him to say that he had been overindulging and that he believed a dip would prove beneficial. He thereupon challenged me to fisticuffs, madam. He exclaimed, 'Go on, swivel-foot, *hit* me.' So I hit him, madam."

"With the chair?"

"Yes, madam. He overbalanced and fell into the pool."

"It did not occur to you to retrieve him?" asked Flush.

"I cannot swim, sir."

"Nor to fetch help?"

"I imagined that the water would revive him, sir. Also it was time for my boiler."

"This wielding of the chair, Paget. I understood that you had lumbago."

"Yes, sir. It was most painful. I screamed, sir."

There was a slight silence.

Flush looked hard at his butler. "Are you asking us to believe that it was an *accident*, Paget?"

"I merely obeyed him, sir. Might I suggest, sir, that it was a clear case of suicide?"

"Nonsense."

"Yes, sir." Paget shifted his painful feet. "When I returned between the boiler and my teas, this beaver was still submerged. I therefore proceeded to the garages with the intention of securing a boat-hook. I could not find one, sir."

"'Obson's got 'em," said the Creaker.

Flush tapped his cigar over an ashtray. "Can you also account for the cigarette case found in the fellow's pocket? The message upon the notice board? The switching of the lantern slides? The locks of Mrs. Carlisle's hair found in the test tubes? The Disposal? The eighty-four yards of rope?"

"One hundred and twenty-four, sir. Mr. Manelli purchased a further length."

"You?"

"I, sir."

"*Why*, Paget?" asked Mrs. Barratt with interest.

Paget shuffled. "I wished to create a certain impression madam," he said reluctantly. He was unwilling to admit that he had sought to profit from the calamity. It was not to his credit that his immediate reaction upon discovering that the American was beyond aid had been one of considerable satisfaction. Now, he had thought gleefully, there would be a scandal. His employers would be exposed, humiliated, and forced to leave the Manor. When they had shown no signs of doing so, Paget had been bitterly disappointed, and had arranged various phenomena in order to depress and unnerve them further.

"Why," inquired Flush, "did you repeatedly attempt to cast suspicion upon Mrs. Carlisle?"

"I do not care for her, sir." Paget raised his long chin a fraction. "I believe, sir, that legally I am no more than an accessory before the fact."

Flush ground out his cigar. "Nevertheless," he said smoothly, "you now have the qualifications for which I had originally hoped. Upon second thoughts, Paget, I have decided to retain you in my service."

Paget's shoulders slumped. His whole body seemed to shrink. He knew that this would be a life sentence, a penal servitude of shame at, almost certainly, a reduced salary. He inclined his head. "Yes, sir," he said heavily. "I suppose that I deserve it, sir."

Half an hour later, Mrs. Carlisle had recovered sufficiently to totter upstairs and finish her packing. Some while later, she dragged her heavy suitcase downstairs and went to the telephone to summon a taxi. She lifted the receiver. "Yeah?" said a voice which she immediately recognized as Al's. "Whaddya want?"

"Al," said Mrs. Carlisle. "Can you get me Zeke White's garage? Do you know how to work that thing?"

"Sure," said Al. "Kid stuff."

The operator's voice said, "Move *over*, you big booby."

Blackie's voice said, "We can't *all* sit on this thing. It just ain't feasible."

Bill came downstairs carrying a suitcase. He set it down by the front door, went on to the lobby and emerged wearing his mackintosh.

"Can I give you a lift to the village?" asked Mrs. Carlisle. She tapped herself on the chest with the receiver. "Chloe has not only been stunned," she said with appalling gaiety, "she's also been jilted. Tossed away like a sucked glove. Her little sheep in wolf's clothing has joined the staff."

Bill sat down on her suitcase. The injustice of Dina's refusal to marry him reared up all over again. "I've been jilted too," he said. He dragged a hand over his jaw. "I even offered to join the army and volunteer for active service, but she said it didn't count."

Mrs. Carlisle looked at him sympathetically. "Not even if you wiped out a whole gun position?"

Bill shook his head. "I'd only get a V.C."

"Would it count," she asked hopefully, "if we teamed up and bumped off poor Ned? I can't possibly do it alone."

"It's too late," said Bill gloomily. He put on his hat and jerked it over his eyes. "*Every*thing's too late."

"Hey there," shouted Al from the exchange. "Old White doesn't answer. The operator here's his niece. She says some boat grounded on the Lizard and Zeke went after salvage."

Mrs. Carlisle slammed down the receiver. She tried and failed to get her hat on over her bandages. "We shall have to walk," she said. "Are you going to say goodbye?"

"No. Are you?"

"I am not. Bloody murderers. Nor," she added loudly, seeing Paget advancing along the passage, "am I going to tip that mad butler."

Dina and Cyril stood by the library window. As Bill and Mrs. Carlisle disappeared around the yew trees at the bottom of the drive, Dina turned away with a light sigh.

"He was rather sweet," she said. "In an awful sort of way."

Cyril lit a cigarette. "She tried to shoot me," he remarked. "Treacherous creature."

"I'm not being bitchy," said Dina, "but I hope he marries somebody rather unsatisfactory and always pines for me."

"I admit freely that I'm terrified that she'll write another bestseller without my help."

"They'll never qualify."

"Oh no. They were always definitely *other*."

"Yes." She looked at him sideways. "What will you do here?"

"*Well*," said Cyril. "First of all…"

"I meant work," she said softly.

"What a funny word," said Cyril. "What does it mean?" He sat down and pulled her onto his knee with his uninjured arm.

As the clock over the stables struck eight, Grossi lurched downstairs and sank onto a chair in the hall. He felt so ill that he half-wished that Paget had killed him.

Paget slid from the passage. "I have taken the liberty of placing your...er...gats in your motor, sir," he said.

Grossi raised his bandaged head with an effort. "Paget," he said thickly. "I ought to grab your head off. Where's Joe?"

Paget's gray lips twitched, "I took Mr. Manelli too, sir."

Grossi stared. "You did?"

"Yes, sir. He too is in a pitiful condition."

Grossi considered this. Then he roused himself, swung a feeble punch at Paget, overbalanced, clambered groaning to his feet and staggered out of the front door.

Two minutes later, Manelli appeared at the top of the stairs. He descended slowly, clinging to the banisters for support. In the hall he paused to devour three aspirins.

"All quiet again now, sir," remarked Paget, gliding towards him.

"Will you please drop dead?" asked Manelli. He swayed, touching his bandages delicately with the tips of his fingers. "It's not your fault I ain't got rigor mortis *all* over."

Paget straightened his aching back. For an instant, he saw himself as Paget the Desperado, black-a-vised hero of the Dankry Rising, the mystery figure who had nearly killed two notorious bandits and one bad novelist. He went into the lobby and fetched Manelli's coat. He draped it carefully around the gangster's shoulders. "Your rod is in your motor, sir," he murmured. Then filled with a sudden almost maudlin beneficence, he added warmly, "Excuse me, sir. Will you accept a cigar?"

The Creaker stood at the end of the drive waving a gray hand-kerchief. Hobson stood on the goat-track below, swinging a tin suitcase painted to look like wood.

"Mind you write, boy," shouted the Creaker.

"An' you, tosh," roared Hobson.

"Write often, boy. I like your outlook."

"Course I will!" bellowed Hobson. "I like yours."

"Don't do anythin' I wouldn't do!"

This amused Hobson so much that he collapsed onto a rock, helpless with laughter.

In the drawing room, Mr. White took his leave of the three elder members of the staff. "In view of my inexplicable behavior," he said sorrowfully, "I don't suppose that I will see you again."

Flush and the Colonel followed him onto the terrace and watched him weave unsteadily down the drive. From the garages came the roar of two powerful engines. The Studebaker and the Allard flashed past the gap in the rhododendrons.

The Colonel touched the tip of his mustache. "I wonder…" he mused. "See who was in front?"

"No," said Flush. He added thoughtfully, "Mr. Grossi, I believe, twisted a muscle in his right shoulder."

"Manelli sprained left ankle."

"Ah well." Flush gave a long sigh and turned away. "Never before have I been so relieved to see the last of a batch of students."

An hour and a half later, the staff had eaten their first civilized meal for four days. They sat in the library and took their ease with the prospect of a three-day holiday before them. The shadows lengthened on the lawns outside. The blue dusk crept into the room, but nobody bothered to turn on the lights.

Mrs. Barratt wore a pair of carpet slippers. She hummed to herself as she wound a ball of wool. The Colonel wore a shabby pair of pumps. He sat at his desk sipping a vintage brandy and counting a record yield from the Benevolent Fund boxes. The Creaker lay half asleep in an armchair. Flush sat at the open window appreciating the first cool breeze for nearly a week. Cyril and Dina sat on the sofa, exchanging notes about the evening's mail.

"I've got one signed 'Tory,'" said Dina lazily.

"Here's one from some farmer in Northern Ireland," murmured Cyril. "Something about his neighbor's cows."

Mrs. Barratt put a finished ball of wool into her knitting bag and placed a new skein around the back of a chair. "Clifford," she said pensively. "I am a mite worried about Paget. I hope that he is not going to take his new status too seriously."

"Distinctly uppish," said the Colonel. "Don't like it. Blighter told me he'd sacked Barker."

"I met him in his pantry," offered Cyril. "He was definitely power-behind-the-arras. He looked me straight in the eye and said, 'Scram.'"

The Creaker opened one eye. "'E asked me to show 'im me wire joke," he remarked. "'E never spoke to me before, but 'e was real chummy. 'E called me Birdbrain."

"I had ordered duck for dinner," said Mrs. Barratt. "Why did we have chicken?"

Flush bit his lip. "I overlooked it at the time because I thought that he was overwrought," he said slowly. "He told me that in future he would prefer me to wear tails in the evening."

"He told me," said Dina after a long pause, "that if it hadn't been for his lumbago, he would have accounted for four, the biggest bag in the house. I thought that he was joking."

"Mmm," said Flush after another heavy pause.

"Now, Clifford," chided Mrs. Barratt. "Not until we replace him."

Dina was nearest to the door. She heard the shuffling footsteps in the passage. "Cave!" she whispered. "Here he comes!"

Paget shuffled into the room and collected the coffee cups. He put them onto the tray. "Quite a day," he remarked.

"Good night, Paget," said Flush stiffly.

Paget gave each person present the full benefit of his horrific smile. He did not bother to bow. "Good night, chums," he said over his shoulder as he left the room.